Some Rights
of Memory

IAN THOMAS MALONE

Some Rights of Memory by Ian Thomas Malone

Published by Green Muffin Publishing
Riverside, CT 06878
www.greenmuffinpublishing.com
Copyright © 2017 Ian Thomas Malone

ISBN-10: 0692964886
ISBN-13: 978-0692964880

Editors: Elisha Neubauer, Beverly Ann Diliberto, Barbara Linsenmeyer Malone, and Anna Zeigler
Cover Design: Wicked by Design

Visit the author's website at IanThomasMalone.com
First Edition
Printed in the United States of America.

For Bear and Lehman

For me, with sorrow I embrace my fortune.
I have some rights of memory in this kingdom,
Which now to claim my vantage doth invite me.
    —(*Hamlet,* Act V, Scene II)

Saturday, April 3, 2010

Mary

AND A ONE, A TWO, A THREE. HAD I ALREADY TAKEN that purple one before I started counting? Then there was that one in the middle of the night. No, I took today's purple one last night after getting back from Giles' house. No fucking surprises there. Why don't we just take tomorrow's and that will be that? Oops, looks like that one's missing too. End of the week for this pillbox, guess I'll have to take from the big bottle. Separating them by the days of the week never made much sense, anyway. Today's a busy day. I'll guess I'll take two. You can never be too careful with your mental health, after all.

Now for something sweet to wash this medley down with. Where did I put that bottle? Shame my flask went missing at that CVS a few weeks ago. I should go looking for it. It's somewhere in the cosmetics aisle, I'm sure of it. Where did I put that Grey Goose bottle I'd been hiding for safekeeping from my nosy sibling? Think, think, Mary... there's a good girl. No, it's not under the bed, Giles could find it there easily. His fruit found my Bombay in the cereal box. Now there's a real treat. Pity I polished off the Captain Morgan's with the cable guy who came round. I bet old Giles would've appreciated the little pirate on the bottle. He is kind of cute.

The closet. Yes, here we are. Oh little Jack, you come in handy once again. Clever Mary picked a good hiding spot amongst the unwanted bath toys. I knew there was a reason I told Regina to give him his baths in the guest room now. Clever, clever. Ah, found it. Shame there's only a bit left. Last bottle my ass, Giles! You can't stop me. Breakfast of champions: pills and vodka. If only Aidan could see me now, wherever that fucker went. Oh, that's a bit sharp. Yum. Wakes the stomach up. And to think, it's only ten thirty. What new friends will the day bring?

Blue skirt, green shirt. No bra. Too restricting. What would Aidan think about keeping up with appearances now? You don't need to worry about that deadbeat now, Mary. Just put your clothes on like any other girl and worry not about the damned coordination. Style doesn't matter anymore.

Only a few more minutes before the happy starts to settle in. Who would've thought clouds could brighten up my day. Structure brings clarity.

I think I'll have some coffee. I haven't had any coffee in quite some time. Don't they say caffeine is addictive? Maybe that was what was responsible for Wednesday's great headache. Oh, who am I kidding—it was Giles. Always Giles. Such a fucking complainer about every goddamn thing a woman can stop to think about. There isn't enough time in the day to keep track of all his shit. Does he really think he's going to prison? They're only after him because Aidan went missing. If he'd stop and think for two goddamn seconds, he'd tell them what they wanted to hear instead of listening to that lawyer.

"Keep quiet, they've got nothing," he says. Sure they don't, that's why we're on the news. And then later he's worried. Which is it? The Davies and the Moores are the talk of Roxburgh and the New York papers because we're so interesting. The next Kardashians? Hardly. Caleb would love that. I won't entertain that notion, not for a second. He took my Bombay.

"Morning Miss Mary, would you like something to eat?" calls Regina, as if waiting until I was actually in the room would've been such precious time wasted for a woman and her help. "Regina, I know it hasn't been too long since we moved past this senorita nonsense, but I dare not think the plural form is too challenging for a woman of your disposition. It's Misses. Mr. Davies may have vanished, but I am still a married woman. Misses. Say it with me now, darling. Missseesssss." Is that really so difficult?

"Would you like something to eat, Miss Mary?" Oh well, I tried. You can't win them all. But can you win any? "No thank you, Miss Regina. I would, however, like some coffee. How about you dig the French press out from wherever it was last seen and make me a cup of some of Mr. Aidan's expensive exotic shit. Maybe your family back home grew it."

"I will get you some coffee, Miss." Ugh. I suppose life could be worse. Oh, that crying is so unnecessary! What the hell do you want, Jack? He's nearly three by now. Or is it two? I can't seem to remember Jack's last birthday party. Oh, yes I can. It was two months before the trouble started. Would've hired more than a balloon artist if I'd known people were going to stop socializing with us the second the papers turned against us. Who reads those anyway? I suppose I should say something to him.

"Jack, child, how are you?" No response. Never was much of a conversationalist, even when he exited the womb. Too busy staring at that screen with the animated critters on it. Better them than talking heads on Fox News or CNN, I guess. Who's to say we're the grownups when all we do is bicker? The people on the news don't spontaneously burst into song. Maybe they should. The kids know where the entertainment is. I'll put that on my list of things to say when someone finally stops to pay attention to me. And there goes the rumbling in my stomach. I could really use a drink.

"Regina, are you there?" I called out. Jack gives me a nod and returns to his critters. "Here you are, Miss Mary," and she hands me my coffee. Not the chemicals I was hoping for, but maybe this will suffice. She asks, "Do you want cream?" As if I'd want to taint the taste with any putrid white liquid. Funny how she can't stop to appreciate the simple things in life. Café noir.

I've got an idea. "Regina, can you do me a favor? When you go out to do the shopping, can you pick me up a couple bottles of gin, vodka, maybe a little whiskey? We seem to be a bit dry in the house and I'd hate to have nothing to offer guests should some decide to pop by." That'll do the trick. I don't even have to leave the house. What a good plan, Mary.

"No, no, Miss Mary. Mister Giles told me no alcohol in the house. I'm sorry." She doesn't look very sorry.

"Regina, you don't work for my brother. You work for me. What he tells you is inconsequential. Besides, it isn't for me. It's for the guests. When we have company, we must have something to serve them besides coffee and apple juice. Surely this is something even you can understand. We would look foolish."

"No Senorita, I'm sorry. No drink in the house," she replies with a heavy sigh. I fear she did not believe me about the guests. I can't say I blame her. They don't even come calling for Jack. The drink would be just for Mary. Maybe Caleb, if Giles wasn't around. We always had fun talking over vodkas and lime. Can't see how he shacked up with my brother.

"Miss, can I get you something to eat? Toast maybe? You should eat something, Miss Mary. You look too pale." If Regina sighs one more time, she'll be out of a job. Quit with the misery.

Of course I'm fucking pale. I can't go to the club lest I suffer the condescension of my fellow suburban housewives and anyway, the sun makes my stomach hurt when I sit out back on the patio. My last visit to the tanning salon wound up on Twitter, and besides, what's the point? If this all blows over by next month, I have plenty of time to get into shape for beach season. Time is not of the essence.

Regina isn't wrong about eating. I don't want any more hospital visits. "A yogurt would be fine, strawberry please," I say, meeting her halfway. Toast is for absorbing the drink, which I haven't had enough of to need just yet. Oh, the irony.

The house looks a little less busy since Giles and the old lawyer stashed away most of the valuable trinkets. He says he's using some to pay the legal fees and hiding the rest from any of those federal thieves looking to get some of the money back. As if the meager possessions of a Wall Street crook could begin to recoup for the damage the two of them inflicted on the world. Big surprise their little operation turned out to be a tad outside the realm of legality. One look at those two should have told anyone they were no good. I always knew it.

I'll give them credit for the twenty plus years they got away with it. Hiding in plain sight was what Giles called it. All good things must come to an end, I suppose. Which means Aidan must not be dead since he's got nothing good in him in the first place. Sweet comfort. I should use that line the next time someone asks me if I think he'll ever turn up.

It feels like the happy is starting to settle in. Cloudy with a chance of colorful critters on the TV. They should show this shit to patients in the loony bin. Then Jack could go there instead of that overpriced "children's gym," and he can sit around on the state's dime. Ideas, ideas.

Whoever discovered yogurt must have been a real sick fuck. I guess hedge funds and emerging markets must have been over his head so he fucked around with cow udders. Or hers. The cow might not have made yogurt without a woman's touch. We can't be sure of these things. Wikipedia has been known to make mistakes.

Coffee and yogurt. I should phone the paper to tell them that I am in fact, just a normal human being. Monsters don't eat yogurt and coffee before flushing the dreams of hundreds of people down the toilet, women do. Maybe monsters do, too. I guess you can never be sure.

"Do you need anything else, Miss? I must take Jack to his swimming lesson," Regina says, as she hands me the remote. I suppose I should take it as a compliment that she didn't expect me to continue watching Jack's cartoons. Then again, she might not think I'm capable of finding it on my own. Maybe if I ask again, she'll buy me a fifth of something tasty. Probably not.

"No, I'm fine. Gracias," I reply, giving her a little taste of her homeland. She always tells me I should learn Spanish, as if that'd make a fucking difference. What's the point in that now?

She should teach Jack some Spanish instead. It would be a more productive use of his time than swimming lessons for a two-year-old. I shouldn't discredit the value of exercise. Giles went through a pudgy stage when he was in middle school. Perhaps that's why he's such an asshole now.

It gets them both out of the house for a while. Regina gets to chat in her native tongue to the other ethnic help and Jack gets some human interaction that tires him out so he stops his fucking whining. A win for everyone all around. Too bad there's no champagne for me to celebrate with. Or vodka. I finished that, too.

Regina is staring at me. She wants to ask me something but she doesn't want to hear the answer, leaving a void. This little interaction between us calls for words, but there's silence. She knows I want a bottle of something I'm legally allowed to have. Whether or not she knows that she doesn't need to listen to my brother is the roadblock that we have to get through.

"What is it? Don't stare at me," I finally say. The happy cloud must have gone away for a second. How rude! Poor Regina. "Do you need me to call someone to take you somewhere?" she asks. What a silly question. Where am I to go? I can't go shopping since Giles took away my credit cards, leaving me with just one, that he gets to monitor. I don't know what I'd buy or where I would wear it, either. My friends don't want to see me. I don't know if that makes them still my friends or not.

I don't see what they're so high and mighty about. The fraud didn't fuck any of them over. They're not victims of this grandiose tragedy. And it's not like I committed the crime. Why should I burn for what they did?

Think happy thoughts, Mary. Aidan's gone. God knows where. If he'd told someone where the rest of the money was hidden, that'd be nice, but knowing him he's off with it somewhere warm and sunny. Happy. Without me. Or Jack. Fucking shit.

Jacob would know where the money is. And then I would know since twins can share thoughts. Though if that were true, I would've known when the bus was coming and I would've been able to warn him. But he didn't know when the bus was coming so I couldn't have known. Unless I was there. But I wasn't.

Happy. A word. Possibly an emotion to someone else. An illusion to dear old Mary. Maybe if I had something to wash these pills down with. That's a problem. One that needs fixing. But who's going fix it?

I know who will fix it. Me. I will go on a grand adventure to the liquor store and all will be well. Giles couldn't have been serious when he said he'd gone around and told the stores not to sell to me. He knows Regina does the shopping, anyway. Except for the wine. Aidan did that. But Giles took the wine and Aidan took himself somewhere else.

It's quiet. The TV is on mute. Regina must have left with Jack. "Hello, anyone there? Buy me vodka please." No answer. I think I'll yell, "Dingleberry," just to be safe. A funny word like that would've surely drawn some attention. There's none to be found so they must be gone. I am all alone here.

I could have a party. I used to have the ladies over from time to time. We'd sit and talk about things that we could be doing, like bridge or gin rummy. Gin, yummy. We tried to have a book club once. I didn't read the book and I suspect I wasn't alone in that. The back cover was nice. I think I would have liked it. What was it called?

What will I need for the adventure? I'll need my purse. That's a given. Sunglasses. Keys? No, not after last time. I've got the court appearance for the mailbox next week. Giles took my car away anyway and Regina has hers. I'll guess I'll need my comfy slippers for the walk. Heels won't do. It's only about twenty minutes to that liquor store on the corner near the shops. I can't be sure. I've never walked it before. Regina won't be back for a few hours. Didn't I have plans tonight? Can't remember. Doesn't seem likely.

I'll take the big purse in case I want more than one bottle. Oh, won't this be fun? If only Aidan could see me now, all self-sufficient. Maybe I should have run the company. Wouldn't have fucked things up so badly. Phone's at full battery, Regina must have thought of that. She always takes the cords away and says that they can't be around Jack. What would a toddler want with a phone anyway?

Keys? No Mary, you already thought of that. You can't drive, so you don't need your keys. If you lock the doors and you lose your keys, you might be stuck. That wouldn't be nice. Should I bring a drink? No silly, that's what you're going to get. The adventure is for the drink. If you had the drink, you wouldn't need the adventure.

All set. I call out, "I'm leaving," to no one in particular, just in case there was someone around to hear. The door opening casts a blinding light on my face. I quickly put on my sunglasses as to avoid melting in the spring heat, which can be particularly brutal in the suburbs of New York City. Our front yard has been a bit disheveled, but it isn't particularly noticeable with our long driveway. I suppose no one's called to have that taken care of. Does that fall on me now? I should be on top of these things. But how I am supposed to know what to do?

Where to now? Ah yes, the end of the property. One road leads to another and then another still. Finally, those roads lead to the drink, the reward. Which way? That way, right. Left? No, you were right the first time. Right? Right. One, two, three. Go.

Hi ho, hi ho, it's off to the drink I go. No one would help, to me it falls, hi ho, hi ho, hi ho, hi ho. Does that rhyme? Not particularly, but it sounds nice. Nice things don't always have to rhyme. I should sing it to Jack before he goes to sleep tonight. I don't think Regina would appreciate that. He's my fucking kid. She acts so motherly now that Aidan left. Or died. Or left and died. Happy, happy.

Maybe it's not so hot here. Good thing I brought a jacket. It's Jake's old football jacket from high school. Did Mother give it to me? No, Mother's gone, too. And Father. I must have found it in his stuff after the bus came and he went away.

Oh, that breeze feels pretty fucking good. Good thing I had that cup of coffee to warm me up. I wish I had another one. What do people call those cups they bring with them into the outside world? To-go cups? That sounds silly.

Wouldn't want to catch a cold out here in the wilderness of suburbia. Perhaps I'll meet a bear who will warm me up a bit and I can ride on his back to the drink.

Do people ride bears? They should. You don't get DUIs from riding a bear down the street, unless you run into a mailbox.

How long is this walk? One mile, maybe two. Maybe three for all I know. I never was a girl scout. Jacob did for a bit. Cub Scout, they called it. What a laugh that was. I could check my phone, but what would that accomplish? I'll get there when I get there. All the time in the world.

I wonder what Jack will say about his father when he's older. If he even remembers him at all. He has a good memory. He knows what shows he likes to watch and that he doesn't like to eat carrots. But, I don't think he'll remember that his father committed all those crimes and could face the rest of his life in prison, if they could find him, that is.

Or maybe Aidan will come back. Crazier things have happened. Like *The Sopranos* finale. We could all end up together around the table as the shot fades to black. He could've just gone to get the money. Wherever he put it. I don't know. I hope he does.

He should use some of that money to take us on a trip. Jack, Regina, Caleb, even Giles, and me, of course. The last survivors of the Davies/Moore clan and their Colombian companion. What a sad state of affairs. Happy, happy.

Is it football season? No, that's the fall. It's a little cold out, but the sun is out and summer is on the horizon. Except it's almost Easter and Easter comes before spring. No, that's not right, Easter changes. Jesus is always born on the same day, but he picks and chooses what day he gets to be born again. If only Jacob could've had that luxury. Wouldn't we all want that?

My friends the Rosens live in this house just up here. I think I will stop in and say hello. I haven't seen them in quite a while. I hope they're home. Stanley loves his golf and Beth has her spinning class, but I would still like to find out if my friends are here to say hello. I never did care much for those stationary bikes. Too fast and too sweaty. Yuck, yuck.

Knock, knock, knock. What a lovely rich mahogany door. The Rosens take better care of their home than the Davies. That's me. And Jack, but not Giles or Caleb. They're the Moores. Well, not Caleb since he's another man and he only lives with Giles. They're not married. They might be someday, but not now. A wedding would be nice. Happy, happy.

The door opens. "Mary, is that you?" asks my dear old friend Beth. We met at our yacht club, Seers Point, some years ago before Jack was born, but after Regina came into our service. How long ago was that?

"Ah, Beth, hello old friend," I reply, extending my arms for a hug, which she reciprocates in the form of a handshake. Perhaps she just came back from spinning and doesn't want to get her sweat all over my old jacket. How thoughtful of her.

Beth gives me a puzzled look. I can't say that I blame her. How often is it that people drop in these days with no notice at all? We've become so isolated in the age of technology. Wasn't it supposed to bring us together? "What can I do for you?" she asks. What an odd question. I wouldn't have stopped by if I wanted something. That would be a very rude thing to do.

"Oh, don't be silly, Beth. I was just going for a walk and I passed by your house and thought about how long it's been. Isn't this nice to just pop in? Were you sitting in your house expecting an old friend to come knocking at your door? Of course not and yet, here I am. Surprise, surprise."

Beth still looks bewildered by my presence. She's still got the shine in her brown hair. Mine looks all tired with all that stress and not enough drink. Forty-two years old, I think, and she doesn't look a day over thirty-six. I doubt she's had any work done, either. Beauty without deception. Isn't that lovely?

"Would you like to come in?" she asks as she motions me inside her wonderful home. Only she and Stanley live here. They never had any children. I never thought to ask why. Nosy people ask those sorts of things. Like Corrine Kalford.

Their living room has the most wonderful painting of Venice that you'll ever see outside of a museum. Whoever painted it really captured the feel of living in such a unique little town. I wish Aidan had brought home something like that once.

Beth looks at me and asks, "Would you like something to drink?" I love it when someone other than Regina asks me a question like that. I never know the answer beyond yes, which doesn't suffice. Think Mary, there's so many possibilities. Oh, I think the painting has given me a good idea.

"I'd love a Bellini, please," I reply. I stop to consider that my friend might not have peach nectar on hand and add, "Or a vodka soda will do." I don't want to be a burden in someone else's home.

My second option does not alleviate the puzzled look on her face. Perhaps I should have given a third choice.

Some people don't like to be given too many choices. How could she not have vodka and soda water lying around? It's not like she and Stanley spend all their time screwing or they'd have a bunch of little Jacks running around all over the place. Two choices were fine, but why does she look so confused? She was the one who asked the question.

Beth says, "It's eleven o'clock in the morning, Mary." I am not sure what I'm supposed to do with that information. Doesn't she know it's a Saturday? Drinks are lovely at this time of the day. I don't have anywhere to be. Oh, I get it. She thinks it's too early in the morning to be drinking vodka. Ah, yes. Giles says the same thing from time to time.

"Right," I reply, "that's why I suggested the Bellini. It's a nice breakfast drink, although I've already had breakfast. A yogurt. Did you go spinning this morning?"

Beth smiles in the same way I used to smile at the ugly rich boys at the fraternity parties back in college. Can't be rude, but what's the point in making such a big effort to be civil? I don't see it. But we're old friends so we must be polite here for the sake of those who came before us. We can't lose our manners even if we do terrible things.

"I'll be right back with your drink," she says with the same smile that appears chiseled on her face. Maybe it was by the same artist who did the Venice painting. That'd be nice, except then it would mean that she's had work done and then we'd lose a bit of charm in that department. I don't see what the problem is if she's going to get the drink. If she doesn't like it, why would she do it? It's her house, not mine.

Beth and Stanley travel quite a bit. They went to

Africa a few years ago. Aidan didn't understand why any-one would want to go to a place like that. Then again, he forced me to go to Las Vegas with him. Shows what he knows about class. Africa doesn't have any casinos. Or maybe it does. I've never been.

Here comes Beth with a tray. One vodka soda, one cup of coffee, and a tray of biscuits. Does she enjoy those biscuits on her own or are they strictly for times like this? I don't imagine people come over randomly very often. Before the trouble started, people always called before they came over. But now they don't. In that case, she'd have plenty of time to run out for some biscuits if she was out of them. I didn't give her that luxury, but she was pre-pared nonetheless. Impressive.

"Cheers," we say together and I take my first sip of the sweet stuff in over an hour. Oh, that tastes good, even though I don't think there's much vodka in this drink. Caleb makes a much better vodka soda than this one. I wish I could have one of those. It's one more drink than Regina would give me and for that I thank my dear friend Beth.

There's a void here that's usually filled with idle chit-chat. Beth wasn't expecting me to be in her house so it's not surprising that she hasn't thought of anything to say. I think it falls on me to say something. "How are things," I say. I don't really ask. These are just words that left my mouth in this particular pattern.

"Things are good," she replies, apparently appreciative of me filling the void that occupied the space between us. It does feel much nicer in the room with the addition of sounds. Just for a second as she fails to elaborate any fur-ther and the silence returns. I must give this conversation a little boost. "How is Stanley?" I ask with a little extra oomph. The vodka has sharpened my wit for these sorts of things. That was my real contribution to Aidan and Giles' little enterprise.

Beth looks a bit more relaxed. She replies, "He's doing well. We're planning a trip to Nova Scotia in August. It's nice up there at that time of the year. Have you ever been?"

Had I been to Nova Scotia? That would be in Canada, which is a few hours north of New York. The country, not the state. They call their states provinces. Or maybe we call our provinces states. Nova Scotia is north of New York, but not right on top. I've been right on top, but that's Ontario. And Quebec. Not Nova Scotia. How does that work? I think the answer is no.

"I have not. I think Giles might have gone up there once," I reply. He might have. He also might not have. It's just a thing to say that gets said and we move on.

Beth looks uncomfortable. "How is Giles doing?" she asks. I see why she's uncomfortable. With Aidan missing, Giles becomes the poster boy of Moore/Davies Capital. But the Rosens hadn't put any money with the company and they didn't get screwed over. I guess people can be uncomfortable with the mention of criminals. I can sympathize with the disposition of dearest Beth here.

What can be said about Giles? She doesn't want to hear the gloomy stuff any more than I want to say it. But I have to say something. "Giles is breathing," I start to say. I take another sip of the vodka, acknowledging the stupidity in my new sequence of words. "He's been meeting with the lawyers to try to figure out what went wrong and what to do about it. The absence of my husband complicates things. It's been hard for him, but it's hard for anyone else to care given the issue and the part he had to play." That's better. Even if he only has that one lawyer. Chomsky is his name. Creepy fellow.

Beth's left eyebrow goes up. Maybe it's the right one since she's sitting across from me. She takes a sip of her coffee and asks, "Do you talk about the case much?" Odd question. She asked about the case. No, she didn't. She asked about you. But to ask about me in the midst of his case is to ask about the case itself. I know things. Or she thinks I know things. Unless she's just making small talk. This is over my head.

"No, probably not. I don't know much about it. The two of them were so secretive about what was going on. I wouldn't be surprised if Caleb knew nothing about it since he's not protected under the same family clause or whatever it is that saves me from jail. The lawyer doesn't think the prosecution would try to touch him, though, lest the gay rights advocates storm to the defense of big business. How funny would that be? They haven't made any inclination that I'd be brought in to testify, but people don't tend to tell me much, either. Who knows? You certainly don't need to."

That made sense, I think. I've done well.

Beth looks kind of sad. I should offer her some of my happy pills and a sip of my drink. Sharing is caring. I don't think her drink has any alcohol in it. Hearing about other people's problems is sad. But she asked. She must have known the answer wasn't going to be all wine and roses. I wish it was all wine. Yum.

Who says something now? Is it my turn or hers? I don't have any more questions to ask her. I already asked if she had been spinning. I don't recall getting an answer. There's no point in asking again.

"So Mary, how are you?" Beth asks, breaking the silence. There's an extra emphasis on the word *you*. It's nice to see her make an effort to make the most of this little gathering. I hope I can give her a good answer to her question.

How am I? Shit, what a bugger of a question. I am well right now since I have a drink and I'm in the presence of company I actually enjoy. The pills are helping, too. Finally. But that question alludes to the bigger picture, when there's no company and the chemicals are out of whack. Let's not be heavy handed.

"Oh, you know," I begin, ignoring the fact that she doesn't know. Stanley isn't a criminal. Beth didn't lose her twin. "It's been hard, but people have been supportive." Lies, lies. No one has been supportive. Regina has helped, but that's her job. If the paychecks stop, she'll go somewhere else. Who calls Mary now? I have to barge in to get a piece of human companionship. "Obviously Aidan's absence creates a void that the rest of us have had to make up for, but things happen in life. I didn't do anything, but that doesn't make a difference. Who's to pity the wife/sister in all of this fucking mess?" Yikes, that came out a tad heavier than I would've liked. That was to be expected.

Even someone who's drinking before noon and all doped out on a medley of shit can see the writing on the wall in this predicament. Why did I even think to come here in the first place? Beth never called to see how I was doing. She doesn't want me in her home drinking on a Saturday morning. Who in their right mind would? The fact that she's even entertained this nonsense at all is a testament to her humanity. That should work to her benefit when the rapture comes. Blessed are they who entertain the spouses of criminals for they will receive twenty-five percent off their next order at Lululemon. Good for her.

She speaks. "I'm sorry, Mary. I know what you're going through must be very difficult. I know I haven't really been there for you." Oh jeez. This was not what I intended when I came here. I was just making a pit stop on my grand adventure. This is supposed to be happy time.

Backtrack now Mary, don't ruin your friend's day. I reply, "Nonsense. You've invited me into your home and supplied me with drinks and treats. You have nothing to be sorry about. Now, I should really be on my way." Bottoms up girl, you've done a good job with the damage control. Have one of those biscuits as well.

It's true. I really don't harbor any ill will toward Beth. How could I? When our other friends fell on hard times, we didn't send them fruitcakes and quiches. We shut the doors and locked the gates. Enjoy the real world fuckers, nice knowing you. So why should I be any different? My bed has been made. No special treatment for Mary.

Beth looks so sweet now. I should take a leaf out of Giles' book and copulate with a member of my same sex. No, I think not. With a soft voice, she says, "Mary, please stay a while longer. Let me get you another drink." Aren't those words every girl wants to hear? I certainly think so.

Beth and I talk about the good old days. I don't know whether to be sad that they're over or to be sad that this is what my life has become. The second vodka soda is a lot stronger than the first. I thank God for that. And Beth, His ambassador on this particular occasion. I don't think news of my visit will be spreading around our social community. Not that I'd be able to use her as a way back into the crowd. No, those days are over. Hey now, hey now. What was that song called?

Does a real friend stick by you at a time like this? What's forever if your family has ruined people's lives? I don't think being a true friend requires you to go down with the ship if the ship plowed right into the iceberg. When you're sunk, you're sunk and that's that. Family on the other hand…

Small talk with Beth reaches its natural conclusion as I finish my second drink. I already know that her husband is fine. They're planning a trip to India. That's in Africa? Why? Culture. Whatever that means. Rich people travel all over the world in search of something better than what they already have. Let me tell you, the grass isn't greener in some desert country filled with poverty and covered in curry. Fuck that. If she wants a vacation filled with culture, she can come over and watch Regina's Spanish soap operas. Ay, yi, yi.

I miss small talk. People can forget how easy it is to get lost in words connected with no real purpose. Sure beats sniffing out someone who's only talking because they want something. Some people just want to be heard.

Beth asks me if I need a ride somewhere. "No thank you," I reply, "I've been having such a lovely walk." And with such an energizing visit, I'll have plenty of energy to get myself there and back. Whoopdy do.

Beth tells me, "You let me know if you need anything, Mary. I know you're a strong girl, but everyone needs a little help every now and again. You don't have to face your problems alone." Oh, sweetie. How nice of you to say. What would happen if I asked you to take me out for a spot of lunch? How could you refuse after this kind offer, but we both know the terror that would fill your insides at the thought of being seen with me in public. Even I couldn't ask that of someone. Social suicide.

No, you've done your part. You entertained a leper in your home on what should've been a relaxing Saturday morning. That can be your good deed for the month. Sure as hell beats anything I've done lately. I always talked about going to volunteer at that local food pantry. Talking about it made me feel better, so that was that. Sometimes, all you need are good intentions.

I see a bit of relief trying to hide itself on Beth's face. It's less glued on than some of her other expressions that have been on display throughout the morning. Could it be possible that I've made a believer out of her? Does she see the sadness in the fall of a fellow American? I don't know. I don't know if I should care. It's only important if it helps someone else down the road.

"Goodbye, Beth. Thank you for your hospitality," I call out as I welcome the road once more. This was always about the journey and the destination, not the rest stops along the way. Though I must say this rest stop wasn't so bad. Too bad I don't have a drink for the road.

I should think of a song to hum along my walk. I don't know how to whistle, or else I'd whistle something ironic, like "Rock the Casbah" by The Clash, or "Shoplifters of the World Unite" by The Smiths. Young Mary identified with those kinds of words. Old Mary became the kind of person those bands despise. Only partially by her own volition of course. They're the ones who put their music out there for anyone to buy, who's to say that I can't hum whatever the fuck I want? The shareef can hate for all I care. Rock the casbah. Support the music industry!

Oh, look. A puddle. That presents a roadblock I wasn't expecting. What to do? I can't go around the puddle as that would bring me right into the road. A car could come and the driver wouldn't be expecting a Mary in the middle of the road. The bus driver didn't expect a Jacob in the middle of the road, after all. The puddle goes all the way to the mud and that won't do in these slippers. I must go over the puddle or under it. Under the puddle would just lead to more puddle. Flight is my only logical route.

I should toss my purse over the puddle so I'm not weighed down when I make my leap. "Wheee," says the purse as it flies across. And a safe landing for Mrs. Louis Vuitton. Excellent throw, Mary. I knew you should have played softball when you were younger. Maybe you would've met a nice butch girl to take care of you instead of that insufferable Aidan Davies. You could be the female Giles. Gross. That was then and this is now. Well, that never was then. It would've been nice if it were. Oh well.

How to get across the puddle? Hmm. I can't throw myself. I will have to jump. I'll need a running start. I can't think of the last time I ran anywhere. Maybe for the train. Or after Jack that time he took my phone.

Let's see how this is done. Move back a bit, Mary. A couple feet will do. The puddle isn't that big. Neither are you. It's wide but it isn't long. You've got this girl. Ready. Set. Go. Do I go when I say go or after? Now it's neither since I'm still here. Let's try this again.

Ready. Set. I'm off at a brisk pace. Is that fast enough?

I suppose it will have to be. Almost to the edge and jump. Heave. In the air, Mary—you've got it. What about the landing?

Ouch. I think I scraped my leg. And my right slipper is wet. It's not the left one, the left one is dry. Yikes, I see a little bit of blood. Good thing I didn't wear any stockings or they would be ruined. Always finding the silver lining. Pull yourself up. Take your slipper out of the puddle. There's a good girl. You're all right. You made it over the puddle. Victory. A wet one, but count your blessings where you can get them.

What's an adventure without a little war wound? A silly adventure, that's what I say. It stings, but it doesn't hurt. A little bit of something sweet would cure this in a second. But I don't have any sweet nectars with me. I can't go back to Beth's house. She'd see this little scrape and call Giles to come fetch me. I've asked enough of that woman already. The adventure was to get the drink and the drink will cure the fall. All will be well once I've achieved my great success. You'll see. You must carry on to victory, girl. You must.

Walking with this damp slipper isn't as comfortable as I was expecting it to be. Slippers are supposed to keep you comfy no matter what. It doesn't matter what happens. That's what they say. I should have worn my boots, but it would have been silly to wear boots on a day like today. There isn't even any snow outside. Boots would've allowed me to walk right through that puddle. If only, but not now. Now is the time of the damp slipper.

There's a fork in the road. Choices. These can be problematic to girls who don't know which way to go. I'll have to think about my options and hopefully that will lead me to the correct answer. Let's stop and assess the scene.

One way leads uphill. I see that car driving up it. Is that the right way? I don't recall town being up a hill from my house or from Beth's. Maybe it moved.

And then there's the other side of the fork. That side has a sidewalk. The path uphill doesn't. That must be so more cars can make it up the hill. People would walk on the sidewalk. Unless it's a trick. Would someone make a trick like that?

No Mary, the world isn't out to get you. Some people are, but they aren't the ones building forks in the road. A spoon in the road would be more like it. An oval. What would I do about that?

The sidewalk it is. Less chance of another puddle. My scrape looks okay. I don't think I'll be requiring medical attention. Lucky me. I'm sure they'd be thrilled to see me back at the hospital. Happy, happy.

What was that little burst of excitement I felt as my jump across the puddle started to go sour? It was as if someone was trying to alert me that a fall was in the works. Whoever sent it should've made sure I knew that before I jumped. That way, I wouldn't have a scrape. It was nice of them to send a notice at all. I could've just been out here all alone, next to a puddle by the side of the road.

Oh, this sidewalk is nice and new. How pleasant. I remember the people with the funny vests came and made this sidewalk a few years ago. A public service project was what Aidan called it. Those men didn't look like they lived anywhere in town. Where was the public in all of this? Did I miss the grand opening of the sidewalk? That must have been the night we gathered for lobsters at the club. Such messy little buggers.

It's nice to see new things spring out every now and then. Even if they're just concrete passages. Someone in some place decided that this particular street needed an improvement and then some people who don't live anywhere around here gathered around, put their orange vests on, and made it happen. Isn't that nice? Fucking progress people. Out there, someone is caring about things that people don't ever stop to think about. Thank you, kind man or woman. You're a credit to the human race.

There's a blue jay sitting up in the tree ahead of me. He's taking a rest in those branches. I think I will join him. I'm a little tired. Too tired to climb up the tree, but I'll sit at the foot of it and he can keep watch for any stray puddles that happen to come our way. The bird, the tree, and me. How nice.

I wonder if the bird knows if there's a professional sports team named after him and his kin. I didn't know until the day they came to play the Yankees and Aidan took me, and Giles, and Caleb. Regina stayed home with Jack, who was even littler than he is now. I think it was a football game. The Blue Jays were from a different country. I think it was Spain, which is famous for its blue birds. Maybe this bird flew all the way here from there to examine Roxburgh's newest sidewalk. I'd ask him but he doesn't speak English. Maybe he speaks Spanish, but mine isn't very good. Father made me take French in school. "The civilized language," so he said. Look at how far that got him.

"Bonjour, monsieur oiseau," I say to him. He flies away. I guess he doesn't speak French. Oh well, it's nice and cool under this tree. Maybe he'll come back if he has something to say.

Giles used to sit under trees and read for hours and hours. Sometimes Jake would join him. I would not. I cared little for books back then. I care little for books now. Reading is such a chore. Now I can understand why he enjoyed sitting under trees. It's peaceful and quiet. Not in my head, but out there. He'd be in better spirits if there was a tree in his backyard now like there was when we were growing up. A big great specimen with lots of leaves. I'll suggest that to Caleb if he wants to get my little shit brother a present. It's good to get people presents. It shows that at some point, other than a point in which you're in their presence, which would be the present at the point where you are, that you thought about them at some other point. Like the past, when the present was bought. Present the gift and present the time. How confusing! We need more words.

The ground is a little damp, but that's okay. Regina can wash my skirt. Or I can buy a new one. I haven't been shopping in a while. It'd be nice to go out and buy new things again, when Giles says I can spend my money, of course. He can even carry my bags for being such a stick in the mud all this while.

My stomach is trying to tell me something. Hunger? No, you had a biscuit. And a yogurt. A feast for Mary. You've lasted for days on much less than that. Another pill? No, silly you just took one. Oh. Yes. You need to go to the bathroom.

There are a couple houses around. Just a few. That's not so bad. None of them come to memory as places I've been before. I can't go knocking again. People barely like it when you knock on their door even when they know who you are. What to do about the pee-pee?

I know. I'll go around the tree. I'll squat a bit and let my stream say goodbye to the vodka and the soda. The coffee, too, if it's still up there. So resourceful Mary. It's a wonder you never enjoyed camping.

The other side of the tree has no blue jay. Not much of anyone. That's good. I don't want them to see a grown woman peeing near the road. No one can see me now.

How to do this? Hmm. Squat first. Panties down. The purple ones Aidan used to like. He'd pull them down and nibble his way up my lower area all the way to the tippy top where my mouth is and I'd be his. But he's not here now.

Push. Push. Nothing is happening. Ah, here we go. Oops, I must kick the damp slipper out of the way. Don't want puddle water and pee-pee on it. Whatever would Regina say? Not long now, squeeze the liquid out and out. That's better. Now back to the other side of the tree where the pee won't flow and get me all gross.

"Honk honk," I hear. Is it something I know? Or someone? What could be making that noise? No it isn't, they're giving me the middle finger. How rude! Why would someone think to do a thing like that? Oops, my panties are still around my ankle. How very unladylike of me. Perhaps that had something to do with their behavior.

Pull them up and all is well. At least the driver has something to talk to her friends about. If she has friends. Or if she's a she. Could've been a man. Or a transsexual. I hope none of them know who I am. Fat chance of that happening after that news article.

I always wanted to be famous. Doesn't every girl? My problem was that I didn't have any idea what that actually meant. To be famous, you have to have done something or have something done to you. An active or a passive process.

That something could be anything, which opens the playing field so much that no one actually knows what the fuck the word even means. I sure as hell didn't. Fame is supplementary. You don't acquire it until you do something that brings it to you. But I didn't do anything.

So I didn't become famous. Until something my husband and brother did. Not something I did. I got what I would've wanted back when I was fifteen and obsessed with tabloid magazines. I sure as hell don't want it now.

Or do I? I can't really say if it's been good or bad. Giles hasn't let me tell my side of the story. The lawyer agrees with him, no doubt because he pays the bills. Chomsky and Associates? Bah, I've never seen anyone with that old shady figure. I have things to say. I just don't have people to say them to. Chomsky should listen to me. He's being paid in part with money that my husband acquired. I shouldn't say earned, but rather stole, but what difference does that make? He shouldn't care where the money comes from.

I'll say some of my words to the man in the liquor store once I get there. He'll want to listen. No, he won't. Bartenders like to listen. It's their job to listen. People don't hang around liquor stores. I should go to one of those instead. I never much cared for bars. Those were Aidan's places. The club was mine and there, the bartender doesn't listen. Oh well.

How long have I been walking? The detours at the tree and the puddle complicate this estimate. So does my lack of a watch. I'll say half an hour and let that be that.

There's no historian documenting my grand adventure. It needs to be a bit grander for that to happen. I'm sure the tabloid or some rag would love to write about that. Might even make that nightly program on that stupid local station. Mary Davies jumps over a puddle, full story at eleven. That does have a nice ring to it.

I see the liquor store up on the corner. How on earth did I manage to make it here? God must be on my side or I'd be sitting in a McDonald's drinking one of those milkshakes that doesn't have any real ice cream in it. Someone decided to throw Mary a bone today. But not now.

It's open, too. Two great miracles in a row. After the disapproving glance I got from Beth at the notion of drinking so early, I probably should've considered this problem. Well, it's not a problem. It's something that I do not have to worry about on this lovely Saturday morning. Afternoon? Happy, happy. That's better.

I forgot how marvelous liquor stores look on the inside. Imagine that. You can walk into a store and it's only filled with things you actually want. I could never understand what all the fuss was about when it came to department stores. They have everything, but only a little bit of what you really want. Guess what? That isn't everything. Maybe that's why they've fallen on hard times. Having a specialty is a rare trait in this world. Liquor stores know that and that's why they're doing so well. People should care more about being great instead of simply being good.

The vodka section is filled with choices. Whoever said that vodka all tastes the same is sorely mistaken. I can tell Skyy from Smirnoff in a heartbeat and that shit that comes in the plastic bottle reeks before you even take the cap off. Differences.

Flavored alcohol. I hear that's all the rave in college these days. No wonder the country's gone to fucking shit. Blame my husband all you want. He's not sipping cupcake vodka while he moves money to places it doesn't belong.

The flavored shit takes the character out of the whole process. If you make something that tastes so good that everyone will guzzle it down, you'll wind up with a bunch of sixteen-year-olds puking in the gutter. No, no, no. You give someone a drink with character. Something that has a bite to it. You know what that bite does? It saves you. It weeds out all the fucking pussies. Those who can't handle the bite don't take another sip. They gag and move on to white wine or light beer. Or water. Good. They've discovered something isn't for them. Alcohol doesn't need to conform to lightweights.

Well, now, let's not be hypocritical. What about mixers, Mary? A gentleman can enjoy a martini or a bourbon old fashioned after a long day. Isn't a mixed drink the same as flavored alcohol, you might ask?

No. It isn't.

That flavored shit can be drunk straight from the bottle just like you'd guzzle a gas station slushie. And that is a crime against the human race designed to knock us all on our asses before the real fun can begin. Oh, the horror.

I might not have much as I've entered a period of disgrace, but I have my character. I have all the characteristics that got me to this point in my life. My character doesn't drink flavored shit. I drink the way it's meant to be done. Like a man. Or a woman. Or a drunk. I'm one of those, right? They can't take everything away from you if you never had anything at all.

I'll get a smaller bottle of Grey Goose and another

Bombay gin to make up for the one Caleb found in the cereal box. I won't be able to fit much more than that in my purse and still manage to get it back home without an accident. That'll tide me over to at least the middle of the week. Maybe by then Giles will lift his embargo on what can and can't enter my body.

Suppose I told him I wanted to be with a woman. Would he let me drink for that? Or would he let me drink to stop it from happening? Probably not. You can't seduce anyone without alcohol. Or money. I haven't got much of either. Giles should tell the prosecution to give me my money back.

Wouldn't it be nice to just lie on the floor here for a while? Be around the things that make people happy when they're feeling sad. Stores like these are good for the country. If you had a bad day at work, you can come here and get something to make you feel better. I didn't have a bad day and I already feel better. It works at any time of day. I suspect that's why people don't want you to drink in the morning. If you did, nothing would get done for the rest of the day since you'd be too happy to care about anything important. But people forget that being happy is important.

My thoughts are interrupted with a "Can I help you find anything Miss?" from the store employee. He might be the manager. He might be the owner. I don't care to find out. It's important to know what is and isn't important.

"Oh no, thank you. I'm doing quite well. I've got what I came for and I'm just looking around for a bit until it's time to go back home. There's so many different choices, you never know what you'll find. Isn't that nice?" He gives me a weird look. That makes sense. He must be used to sad people coming in here to get better. Someone who's already happy must be a novelty. I hope I can brighten his day with my cheerfulness. Just being in here has made me feel so much better.

Tequila never sat well with me. That's a common ailment, but I never saw the point in consuming something that I knew would put me square on my ass after only one or two. We'd be sitting on the beach in Cancun and Aidan would tell me to try a margarita. Why? I don't want one. I wouldn't sit at the club in New York and think to have one. We're somewhere else, which is one change already. I don't need another. There isn't any point to it. Maybe in the summer, I'll get Regina a bottle just to show Aidan I can be flexible. Fuck him, wherever he is.

Money. Do I have any of it with me? I must make sure or else this will all be for naught. My bag doesn't have much in it. Here's my wallet. Oh dear, there's only that credit card and some assorted receipts. Maybe fifty bucks. I might need the money for a cab if I get lost. Always have an escape plan. Not that I'd be able to find a cab out here in the suburbs. What a mess.

I think I will pay with the card. Wouldn't want to be stranded out here with no hope for rescue. Giles can see what I've done and know that I'm not going to sit around at home all day waiting for him to bring me more bad news or shout at me if he needs a scapegoat. That reminds me, I think I am supposed to dine with Caleb and him tonight. So he says. He can fetch me if he cares. Wherever I am.

Giles *should* see that I'm buying alcohol. I'm a grown fucking woman. He can't take away my ability to spend what little money the two of them didn't piss away. God damn, why didn't they do a better job of not getting caught? Booze is cheaper than therapy, anyway. That's better. Happy, happy.

The employee is back behind the counter. I don't see any other customers in here and I didn't need any help. I guess the checkout protocol should be fairly standard, like it used to be. I don't need to show my driver's license since he couldn't possibly think I am under twenty-one. That'd be a compliment, but an unnecessary one. Even I know that I don't look like that anymore.

"Just these two," I say as I put my miniature treats on the counter. Are there any drinks that combine gin and vodka? I can't seem to remember. I'll do some experimenting when all of this is over and I won't need to worry about rationing. That'll be nice. When this is all said and done, I'll have a taste testing party with Beth and Regina. Jack can watch while he plays with his trains.

The man stares at me for a second. I know what he's doing. He's thinking to see if he recognizes me. That tends to happen every now and then. Every housewife's fantasy. That's me. I don't know him, but he might have seen my picture in the paper. He doesn't look like the sort who would read the paper, but I shouldn't be judgmental.

"Cash or credit?" he asks. If he knew who I was, he'd demand cash. My family doesn't have much credit anymore. Nobody trusts us. Thankfully, he seems to be the trusting sort.

I reach into my pocket to take out my credit card. Well, Giles' credit card with my name on it. He gets to see what I bought and then he has to pay the bill. Fair trade I suppose.

The man takes a long look at my card. Then he looks

at me again. His eyebrows rise. Oh dear. Inquisition. This man knows who I am. Let's see if that's a good thing or a bad thing.

The man asks, "Do you have a brother named Giles Moore? The one who's been on the news?" Bingo. He's won. The prize is he gets to sell alcohol to Giles' sister paid for by none other than Giles himself. What a lucky man.

How to answer? "Yes," I reply. That's the only answer that makes sense. He knows who I am. The question was merely a nice formality on his part.

His inquisition turns to disappointment. "I see," he says. "I'm sorry Mrs. Davies, but I cannot sell to you. Your brother came in a few days ago and asked me not to sell to you."

That fucking piece of shit. I cannot believe he actually did that. To think the bastard went around to local boozeries and told them not to sell to his own flesh and blood after what he did. That fuck! The nerve! The insanity! Giles, Giles, why have you forsaken me?

Keep it together, Mary. This man is expecting you to be unreasonable. The only way to get your treasure is to prove him wrong. You must show this man that you are someone who deserves the treats he's withholding from you. The truth will set you free.

I say, "Oh, there must be some mistake." What mistake might that be? "You see, Giles is going through a bit of a midlife crisis brought on by his career misfortunes. You may have read about it. I don't know if you've faced something similar in the past. That's none of my business. You see, he wasn't in the best state last week and he decided to take it out on his poor sister. That's me. Now, I'm sure he didn't mean what he said to you and I don't think anyone would mind if you sold me those bottles and I went on my way."

Good going, Mary. You've made your case. This man seems like a reasonable fellow. He'll see the error in Giles' way. It's ridiculous. Plain and simple. You've done a good job.

The man sighs. Is that good or bad? "Look, Mrs. Davies. The last thing I want is to be involved in someone else's family drama. I can't say I approve of what your brother did and that goes for more ways than one. But that doesn't change the fact that he came in here expressing concerns about your drinking that appear to be legitimate. I look at you and I see blood and mud all over your leg. You appear to be wearing bedroom slippers. I can smell the booze on your breath from all the way behind the counter. It would be gravely irresponsible of me to sell to you. I could lose my license. I'm sorry, I really am. I wish the red flags weren't so obvious. But they are. I'm sorry."

Who does this miserable twat think he is? I reek of booze? False, I reek of the sweat of my victory getting to this grimy shithole. I toiled on the long, unforgiving road to get here. Who is this petty liquor salesman to tell me otherwise? He is not the keeper of who gets to drink and who doesn't! Fuck this man.

"Mister, this is all a terrible misunderstanding. You see, my brother is a criminal aboard a sinking ship. The only way for him to feel better about himself is to take me down with him. I am no alcoholic. I am merely trying to support the local economy by making a purchase at your establishment. Does it really make sense in times like these to turn business away?" I think not. I've got him right in my grasp. Good work.

Apparently not. He replies, "Look, I really don't want to get involved in your family mess. I'm not looking to find right and wrong here. It's just that I won't be selling you any alcoholic products today. You would've probably been turned away even if your brother hadn't come in. You smell terrible. I'm sorry if that's rude, but you must understand where I'm coming from."

Must I understand? Of course not. My moves are limited. I could cause a scene and hurl bottles around so that the place smells as bad as I supposedly do. That would mask the scent, but then I'd have to leave. Mary might have done that in her youth. Now I fail to see what that would accomplish. Justice? Yes, but what's that even worth? Justice is so overrated.

Is the battle lost? You can't reason with a man whose mind is already made up. I have been tried and I have been found guilty. The sentence is sobriety, in a few hours that is, once my morning cocktails escape down my urinary tract.

I fail to understand why people always tell you to take the high road. The low road would feel so good. Bottles flying everywhere, Mary screaming at the top of her lungs at a world that's written her off. Yes, yes. Take a sip of the bottle before you hurl it at this fuck. Won't that feel nice? Yes, yes. No.

"I see," I say. "And there's positively nothing I could do to change your mind?" That sounded oddly sexual. I don't really mean that. I won't be blowing this man for two fifths of not top shelf booze. I might let him feel my breasts, but those would only be appealing to someone who hadn't gotten any in while. Which certainly could be this man. Don't whore yourself out to the likes of this scum. It simply isn't worth it. Not even for a sip of the good stuff.

The man looks sad, as Beth did when pity started to take hold. He replies, "I'm really sorry. Believe me, I am. But there's a right and wrong way to run a store like this. Selling to you is the wrong way." He hands me my card back. Ugh. There's that right and wrong again. What does that have to do with this situation? Nothing. I'm not crazy. He is.

"Have a good day," I say as I turn away. Fuck him. I hope he has a shitty day. I hope a vagrant shits on his floor and pukes all over it so the smell loses him business. He doesn't know jack shit about running a business anyway!

What to do now? Could the adventure have come to an end? No. Failure is not an option. I came for the drink and I shall leave with the drink. Anything less is unacceptable.

First, I must put my card back in my purse. Lest I be left with no funds besides the cash, which I might need. There's a bottle in my purse. Could it be that I have forgotten that I had drink right from the start? Sadly, no. A girl can dream. It's a bottle of eau du toilette. Fucking perfume. The man did say I was sporting a foul odor, though. Perhaps this is fate. I think I should spray some of this on me to mask the booze and puddle.

There's a tavern across the street. Dreadful place. Aidan loved it there when he'd had a bad day at work. I shouldn't have taken pity on him knowing what he was up to. That cheating fuck probably took a mistress there, too. She's probably sitting in there right now wearing Daisy Dukes and drinking a tall glass of some cheap light beer.

Must watch the figure. Piece of shit.

I hear an "Excuse me, Mrs. Davies. Excuse me," coming from behind. Has the cavalry come to rescue me? It appears it might have.

"Yes," I reply, as I turn around. It's a woman in a pantsuit. Probably one of Giles' cronies camping outside the liquor store. Horrible fashion taste. That must mean she's in league with my brother. At least her hair isn't in one of those haircuts that makes her reek of lesbianism. Fucking Giles.

She smiles. "Hi, my name is Natalie Franklin. I am a reporter for the *New York Tribune*. I was wondering if I could have a few minutes of your time?" She is cordial yet affirmative. At least she's upfront with her desire to have something of mine.

What's my time worth? Not much. Though to her, the price is whatever I choose to say. Value lies only in what people are willing to pay. Which gives me the power to pick something nice. Let's see what she has to offer.

I answer her with a "Sure, why not," eager to see what her next step is. If she wants to sit on a park bench, I'll just be on my way. Makes sense, doesn't it?

She smiles some more and replies, "Great, do you want to go across the street?" pointing at the tavern. Oh yes, she speaks my language.

To be sure, I reply, "Only if you're buying." Déclassé yet affirmative. My time is worth a few drinks. That is the price tag I have placed on myself. A fair one given my current disposition. "Of course," she replies. She gives me a mischievous grin, like one college Mary might have used. "Follow me."

We cross the street without incident. One can never

be too careful when crossing an area populated by cars. My twin brother found that out the hard way.

I haven't been inside this tavern in quite some time. The last time I came in here was for some baseball event hosted by the McCarthys a few years back. That was before that wife had the affair with the high school kid and took off somewhere. People say my life is fucked up but at least I never cheated on Aidan. I should have. Then I'd have something over that miserable fuck.

The lighting is perfect. It's dim. Anyone who is inside a bar on a Saturday afternoon can appreciate the ambiance that this place creates. Perfect for the cast-offs of the world to enjoy a little relaxation from their sorrow. This reporter wants me to relive mine. Quite the contradiction.

She asks me what I'll have to drink. "Vodka cranberry," I say to switch things up. She doesn't question me like Beth did. I sit with my back to the bar in case Giles has been in here, too. To be denied service on account of my brother in front of a reporter would be very bad indeed. For him.

"Thou shalt not talk to reporters," is actually Giles' firmest commandment. He cares about that more than the drinking. Even Aidan told me that before he went missing. "Reporters are worse than lawyers," he said one night in bed. He neglected to mention where criminals fit in on that chain. Below the two in his book. I'm not sure where they fit in mine. Reporters didn't do shit to us until he gave them a reason to. This is all their fault.

I know what she wants. She wants answers. They all want answers or they don't want anything to do with you at all. Beth didn't but she was probably afraid she could be called into court if she knew anything. They can't make me testify. They can make Beth if they thought she knew anything. Good thing I was smart in her house. Clever girl.

Natalie gives me my drink. She has a cola of some sort. I doubt there's any spirits in her beverage. I drink alone once again. Such is life. I say thank you before realizing that I, myself, have a question for this so-called reporter. "If I might ask, how did you come to find me?" Roxburgh is some ways away from the city. We must be sure she's not stalking me.

Natalie laughs. It's an odd laugh. Fake. Laughs can be defensive. Or she's trying to diffuse an awkward situation. "No, Mrs. Davies, I am not stalking you. A girl from Roxburgh is going to some science competition in California. I did a profile on her and her family. Fluff stuff that makes the world feel safer having a young bright mind in their midst. I thought I recognized you."

She came to me from behind though, didn't she? I could ask her more about this science girl. That would tip her off that I think she's up to something. She doesn't need to know that.

I say, "I see. That must have been interesting." Yawn. What a shitty job. Worse than daytime television.

Natalie looks like she's waiting for more out of me. She must yearn for conversation. She's not getting any. I don't care about that stupid science girl. "So Mrs. Davies, or can I call you Mary? How are you?"

Can she call me Mary? I don't think I'll answer that. It would be rude to say no, but I don't want to say yes, either. I won't answer the question.

"I am fine, thank you for asking," is my answer. It's short and to the point. Swallow your pride, Mary. She can call me what she will, but not because I said she could. I see why Giles hates reporters.

Natalie pauses for a second, undoubtedly trying to figure out what her next question will be. Will it be a softball or a real hard one? I'd rather she waited until I've finished my drink and then she can go and get me another one.

Her smile returns as she says, "Tell me how you met your husband." The smile is undoubtedly an effort to mask the awkwardness of such a question. It's not even really a question. She must know Aidan has been missing for over a month. The police say that missing persons gone for more than 48 hours are usually dead. Aidan isn't some normal person, though. He could come back.

She can have her answer. "He was my brother's roommate for a few years in college. They were in the same fraternity." Oh, how life would be different if only Jake hadn't pledged. All that silly nonsense. He joined Father's old one, but that didn't stop Giles from saying no. Why did Jacob need to be special?

I see that smile on her face. Natalie knows how this can transition into some meatier questions. "Oh, that's nice, is that where they got the idea to start the company?" Yuck. Wrong brother. She thinks I'm talking about Giles.

I take a sip of my vodka cranberry. Maybe I should just go along with that. No, she's probably tricking you. She has to know about your other brother or else she wouldn't be following you. You've entertained your paranoia, now stick with it.

"No, not Giles. Jacob. He was my twin brother. He died during our senior year in a terrible bus accident."

The thought of Jacob's death often brings me to tears, but I won't waste them for this horrid reporter. One wrong move and she awakens the monster inside of me. I won't have people criticizing my good family.

Dearest Natalie's smile gets turned upside down. It appears as though I've killed the mood once again. "Oh! I'm so sorry, Mary. That must have been horrible." Not as horrible as hearing my first name without my permission, you stupid twat.

I reply with a simple, "Life goes on." It did and it does. I miss my brother, but that was a long time ago and now I have my own life perils to face. What if they take everything? Grief can't fix that.

There's a pause. Natalie must be deciding if she wants to follow the dead brother route or the missing and possibly dead husband path. I think she'll go with the living brother who's soon to be condemned.

"Have you grown closer to your brother in the wake of your husband's disappearance?" This time, she definitely means Giles. Unless I'm meant to be a practitioner of Santeria. Or voodoo. I don't talk to dead people. Only to myself.

"We do what we can." Nice and cryptic. Doesn't mean anything by design. Just what a reporter like her deserves.

Natalie doesn't look too amused. She isn't getting a very good return on her investment of one alcoholic beverage. That's the risk she took. I bet this is house vodka. Serves her right.

"Does that mean you're helping him cover up the trail?" Really? This woman thinks I'm involved in this mess. Oh, please. Me and my fucking communications degree played a big part in the largest hedge fund fraud scandal since Bernie Madoff. Which makes it seem more impressive than what it is. Especially since we're in a near-by town. Aidan would be sad about that. He would've liked all the attention.

"What is there to cover up?" I reply. Play dumb Mary, you're good at that. Let her think you're drunk. Oh, Giles would be proud if he saw what I was doing. I should record this conversation on my phone. If I knew how to do that. Fucking touch screens.

Natalie is now most certainly not amused. "I'm not sure if you understand the gravity of the situation, Mrs. Davies. Your husband and your brother stole millions of dollars from hard working people. Lives are ruined. All because of the greed of your family." Ouch, she called me Mrs. Davies again. Is that supposed to sting? I'd like her to elaborate.

Don't fight tit for tat, Mary. This woman isn't worth it. "That's for the courts to decide, Natalie. Not for fluff reporters taking a stab at investigative journalism. I merely wish the best for my brother."

The fire rises. "Where is your husband? What happened to him? Is your brother involved in something bigger than a Ponzi scheme? Where is the money hidden? Your husband stashed away millions of dollars. You know, Mrs. Davies. Tell me. The people have a right to know. The people you stole from." Yikes, someone hasn't had enough to drink today. Glug, glug, glug, this drink tastes delicious.

Smile at the poor woman, she's not right in the head. Count your blessings, Mary. At least you have your mental health.

"I think that's enough, Miss. I'm going to have to ask

you to leave," says an unfamiliar voice. He isn't looking at me. He's looking at Natalie. Someone has come to my rescue. It's a deep voice. Almost angelic. Like Morgan Freeman's. I'm confused, but I can't be annoyed with this nosey savior.

Natalie replies, "You've got to be kidding me. Do you know who this woman is? What her family has done? And you want to ask me to leave?"

The man motions toward her. "No, I've already asked you to leave. What you're doing right now is harassment. Isn't that right, Mrs. Davies?" Ooh, he wants me to participate. "Here, here," I reply and I raise my glass to this savior.

"This woman is a drunk and a criminal and you should be ashamed of yourself," Natalie says, as she stands up to take her leave. That was interesting. I thought I would have to fight my own battles. Who would have thought someone would come to my aid? And yet the kindness of a stranger rescued me from that horrible wench.

The man looks at me. He doesn't look like he works here. I hope my husband didn't screw him over. I should say something to this hero. "Thank you" is all I come up with.

The man smiles. "Is there someone I can call to pick you up? Family maybe?"

Oh, Giles would freak if he saw me here. The reporter would love that. Why was she so mean? Some might say she did it for justice. I can see why some might look to altruism in her case. We only need to look at the facts. She had something to gain, so it can't be altruism.

There are facts of which I cannot be sure. Motives are not really facts, I suppose. Like the motives of this man.

"Why?" is all I ask in my effort to seek clarity on the subject. Is one word enough for him to understand what I'm trying to say? It was all I could muster in my flustered state. I like to think I'm a woman who can take some punches, but *my God* was that a lot to handle. Stronger women than I would feel the burn.

The man licks his lips. He's not hungry. He's confused. He's thinking to himself, why does this woman care why I shooed the reporter away?

I did. That's all that matters. Does she think I'm some big supporter looking for a way into the good graces of the Davies? No. Who knows what he's thinking.

"I'm no fan of what your family has done," he says, "but you've suffered enough for the crimes of your kin. What that woman was doing wasn't right."

"Fair enough," continues my streak of wonderfully elaborate responses. Get yourself together woman. This man must be wondering how someone like me could even fall into the arms of a criminal mastermind in the first place. If only he knew where Aidan came from.

Truth be told, Aidan was always a bit melodramatic about his origins. Could never fathom why no one gave a rat's ass that he grew up in a swamp. He was also a bit too preoccupied with my family's social standing. What he saw was a way up the ladder. It didn't matter that we weren't on the top rung. The Moores were a step up and Aidan knew how to work with uncompleted projects. The declining health of Father, Jake's death, and Giles' sexual preferences all gave him the positioning he needed to become the new patriarch of an old family.

Did any of that really matter? Was I some grand prize

for him? No and no, but stupid is as stupid does. Aidan wanted his dream to be a reality so he made it that way. Even if it continued to be a dream after it had seeped into all of our realities.

It's too bad Caleb and Jack had to get sucked into this. Caleb had a choice I suppose. I didn't think I'd be able to conceive and then when the timing couldn't have been much worse, I got preggers and little Jack came into the world. Too bad he won't get to remember the times when his family meant something.

The man is still standing there. I'd be talking if I were him. Just so people could hear my majestic voice. What does he want? He's not getting sex for what he did. I could've just thrown my drink at that fucking reporter. What he did was noble to a point. A point, which has now passed, and that's it. There is no reward for doing the right thing. Not here anyway.

I slurp down the rest of my drink. It's time to go. This creep must return to the other barflies with his story of how he saved the damsel in distress. Am I still a damsel? I hope so.

I say "cheers," to him as I walk toward the door. Clever choice of words. Saying that opens up the possibility that I could be persuaded to stay. He could say, "No Mary, let me get you another drink. You must be so shaken." No. I'm fine. I'm always fine.

The patrons of this bar all look up as I take my leave. I don't imagine I'll be welcome back here any time soon. My kind is welcome as long as we don't make the news. Causing a scene tends to make that problematic. Too many people were screwed over and this is a place frequented by drunks looking for something to get all fired up about. Rape and violence runs rampant when it's socially acceptable. Look at the Middle East.

Where to now? It must be midafternoon. Time flies when you're having fun. The sun appears to have faded a bit. I could be wrong. I'm often wrong.

There was an adventure to be had. I was supposed to get more alcohol. I did get more alcohol twice. Alas, it was only temporary alcohol, which has gone away. Three times if you count the two drinks at Beth's, though the first was rather weak. Success?

No, not success. This is a poor man's victory. The drink with the reporter doesn't fucking count, nor does the drink you practically cried over at Beth's. Drinks are for celebratory purposes and you haven't achieved that yet. Finish what you started and do it right.

But how? The man at the liquor store turned me away. No chance he'll sell to me, not even with a bribe. The man inside the tavern will help if I suck his dick or something foul like that. No, you need to enlist the help of someone who doesn't know who you are. But where to find one of those people?

Look, a vagrant. On the corner. Perfect! He's sitting there begging for change with his big gray hooded sweatshirt. Little does he know that there's honest work to be had.

How to approach a vagrant? Their kind is not well versed in the art of negotiation. Your kind isn't really either, Mary. Perhaps dropping the elitist attitude could work in your favor.

But what to say? Hello? No, people don't say hello to vagrants. They either give them loose change or they walk by them as quickly as possible while avoiding eye contact. These are two things that you do not intend to do. You must reinvent the wheel on bourgeoisie-bum relations. No. Stop it with the snobbery! Don't forget the eye contact.

Walk toward him. Yes, that's right. Don't be afraid. This man will help you if you give him enough incentive. Give him a reason to want to invest in your cause.

I'm standing right before him. He looks like he could use a shave and a trim, but otherwise he could pass for an upstanding citizen. If he got a nicer sweatshirt. Or a sweater. I hadn't thought about who should make the first contact. I guess I thought he would, but he's not saying anything.

He says something. "If you're going to stare, you've got to give me some paper." Paper? Is that supposed to be sexual? No, paper money. More valuable than coins. Less valuable than sex. Not everything is sexual. I see. He's developed his own little lingo. How industrious.

Go on, tell him what you want. "How about something better?" No, no, no. Do not say sexual things to this man. "I have a proposition." No! Fucking stop. You are not a prostitute and if you were, you'd be the worst of them all. Prostitutes do not solicit homeless men.

He laughs. "I'm listening." He speaks in a sly manner, letting the words slowly roll off his tongue. Typical vagrant ambiguity. Maybe that's just his accent. He's not getting any sexual favors. Not even for a big bottle of Grey Goose. I'd probably drop it anyway. Or Giles would try to take it away again.

He's listening, so tell him what you want. "I want you to go to that liquor store over there and make a purchase for me. For that, I will give you twenty dollars plus the change left over." Seems like a fair deal. Excellent.

The vagrant looks confused. He asks, "Why don't you go over there yourself?" Fair question. One that he's not going to get an answer for.

"Don't ask questions you don't need the answers to." Good answer, albeit a slightly rude one. This bum is probably used to having his stupid questions rebuffed like, "Can you spare any change?" Everyone could, but not everyone would. Silly man.

He doesn't bat an eye. Maybe he should play some poker to win some money. Or maybe that's why he's in this mess. Overextension is a curse of man. "How do you know I won't run off with the bottle?"

Why is he testing my patience? I've asked him to do a simple task. That's all. Yes or no would suffice. He wants answers to questions he doesn't need to ask. Aidan always said not to ask questions I didn't need to know the answers to. So did Jacob. Maybe it runs in the family. That's why he and Giles got away with things for so long.

This man wants to be entertained, so I'll entertain him with his little question. "It's simple really. The bottle I want costs less than the money I'll give you to go in there. Now once you've made the purchase, you can certainly choose to run off with the bottle and the change. Or you can honor the arrangement and give me the bottle at which point I'll give you twenty dollars. The difference is a few dollars, though given your current modus operandi, that isn't a negligible difference. I trust you can see that your maximum profit comes from completing the full task?" I hope that wasn't too much for him to comprehend.

The vagrant thinks for a second before replying, "I

do." We appear to have some sort of understanding. This looks like it could work.

He picks up a cup next to him filled with change and stands up. He empties the cup into the pocket of his trousers. I wonder if he thinks I'm going to steal from him. I'd laugh, but he probably stopped trusting people a long time ago. Smart guy.

"What kind of grog do you want?" he asks me once he's got his treasures together. Grog? Oh yes, that's a slang term for alcohol. Good thing I didn't ask him or he might think I'm not used to these kinds of situations. I wouldn't want to be taken advantage of.

What kind of booze do I want? I should only get one bottle. If I got two, it'd be gin and vodka like I tried before. That guy behind the counter would undoubtedly wonder why a vagrant was purchasing identical bottles as the woman he turned away before. Or is that paranoia? Perhaps both. Best not to risk it.

I answer with, "Gin. A fifth. Bombay. No. Something cheaper. But not much cheaper. Use your best judgment."

He looks at me like he's checking me out. "Will do," he replies as I give him the twenty dollars. This could end poorly, but I don't see any other options for me to fulfill the main objective of my grand adventure.

I wonder what this guy did to get into this mess. Drugs or alcohol seem to be the most likely bet. That isn't particularly fair as I too enjoy drugs and alcohol and I don't live on the streets. At least, not yet.

The reporter asked me a common question. One that I ponder every single day. Giles asked me just yesterday. Fucking bum. That old lawyer asked me. Everyone has asked me except for Regina. And Caleb, but that's not his business. And Jack, but he's too little to ask questions like that.

Where is the money? I know there's money. The FBI or IRS or whoever was responsible for discovering their little charade didn't find everything. The whereabouts of the missing funds are a subject of great concern to many. Even me. If I knew where the money was, I could run off to somewhere warm and drink margaritas by the beach. Tequila—yuck. Perhaps Aidan is doing that right now. Fuck him.

It must be a large amount of money or else they wouldn't care so much. Maybe they think there's more than there actually is. Much ado about something I do say. No one knows except for Aidan. And no one knows where Aidan is except for Aidan. It's convenient how he can just run off like that, taking all the answers with him.

I don't know much about our finances. Giles tells me not to worry and that he'll take care of things. I don't want to believe that. He got us into this mess. Common sense tells us that it's up to him to get us out, but that doesn't change the fact that he fucked everything up in the first place. He was dishonest. Maybe he's dishonest now. Who can I trust?

They can't kick me out on the streets with just Regina and Jack. No silly, Regina won't come. She'll be fine because you took care of her while she took care of you. They won't take the salary of an immigrant who actually came to America the legal way. That would be a bigger media nightmare than our scandal. MSNBC to the rescue! No, Regina will come out of this unscathed.

Giles best be sitting out here next to me. Caleb can leave him. That's the one advantage of this gay marriage debate. We can sit next to each other and drink cheap booze and beg for money. The vagrant can teach us. That's about the only way he'll stop hounding me about money. Having a child to help will make things easier.

Where is this bum? What's taking him so long? He's probably run off with my money. I guess that's karma. My family steals millions of dollars and a hobo gets twenty from me.

Or perhaps it really hasn't been that long. Time hasn't been your strongest attribute lately. You don't wear a watch and that stupid phone is always in your bag. If there were any people who actually wanted to get in touch with you, they'd be screwed. Luckily, there aren't.

I wonder if the bum gets much traffic here. It doesn't look like he does. Did he move here from some other spot? Why did he move? Was there a big turf war with the other vagrants? Is he merely keeping this spot safe for someone else? Does he go to Florida for the winter? Being out here in the cold doesn't sound like much fun.

I should ask him these questions. People always want to know what other people's lives are like. But does anyone ever ask him what his life is like? The reporter should've interviewed him instead of me. What was her name? Nadine? No, Natalie. I don't think she gave me her card. I don't have any way to contact her to tell her about this great human-interest piece. The bum at the side of the corner. Better than the California girl. I should learn his name.

Ah, there he is across the street. He has a brown bag with him. Success. I knew I could trust that friendly man.

He's even walking towards me. I knew this would work. If Giles were here, he'd criticize this entire plan just because I was the one who came up with it. But it worked. Maybe I should be in charge of his defense. I'd say, "Your Honor, look at this man. Does he look like someone who could pull off a scheme like this? Of course not. The defense rests." Good girl, Mary.

I reach into my purse for the twenty dollars I owe the vagrant for his service. He hands me the brown bag with the bottle and I give him the money he's owed. He doesn't try to give me the change. I guess he didn't get to where he is by being a gentleman.

Finally, success. No more drinks that have to come with the baggage of company. Just Mary and her drink. Best of friends. Mary can sit and be merry. Finally, happy. I'll wash down my afternoon pills will this bottle.

What kind did he get? Let's see. "Gordon's! No!" I shout a little louder than I should have, but that's okay. The situation calls for that.

The homeless man is alarmed. "What's wrong?" he asks. "You told me to get you gin and that's gin isn't it?"

Correct. In theory. "Yes, but Gordon's is harsh. A woman with a stomach like mine can't drink it straight. That's what Bombay and Beefeater are for." Drunks know these things.

Apparently, I was wrong about this man. "Look lady, I know this might come as a big surprise to you, but I don't drink. You told me to get you gin, I got you gin. If you didn't want that kind, you should have said something before I went in there. I can in fact, read. My end of the bargain has been met."

It has. He did his job. He can go back to begging with a clean conscience. I should say something nice to him.

"You did. Thank you." It's not his fault I didn't give

him a list. Though people get blamed for things that aren't their fault all the time. Why should this be any different? Because it can be different. Injustice doesn't need to exist here.

I ask him, "Do you know where I can get a mixer? A soda of some sort?" He can feel useful by supplying this information and I can show him that I value his input. Value is a funny concept.

The vagrant shakes his head in bewilderment at my sudden change in tone. "Yeah, there's a Taco Bell just up the road. I assume you don't need to pay someone to help you out with that?" A joke?

He would assume incorrectly. Well, sort of. "A Taco Bell? What does that mean?" I ask. Probably a stupid question, but my mind is starting to fade and I don't want to have to look for taco bells, whatever the fuck that means.

Boy, this bum must think I'm something else. "Jesus lady, what's your deal? How do you not know what Taco Bell is?" Because I'm a drunk and I've lived a sheltered life. Ah yes, Taco Bell is the Mexican McDonald's. They serve fast food. Good for clearing out your system if you're not a fan of enemas.

"Rough day," I reply. That's a stupid thing to say to a homeless man. His day is undoubtedly worse. I shouldn't end things on this sour note.

"Thank you for your help." Didn't you want to ask him something? Ah yes, the reporter. "What's your name?" I add.

The man must think I'm crazy. I am crazy. He replies, "Don't ask questions you don't need the answers to. Good luck." He walks away.

Smart bum. He remembered my sarcastic comment. I didn't mean to be rude. There are just things you don't need to know. That man didn't need to know my life story. I didn't need to know his name. It's as simple as that.

In that sense, I didn't need to know his name either. What would I have done with that name? Remember it fondly as I look back on this part of my life? Please. I'll be lucky if I remember this shit next week. Well, no. I'd be lucky if I could forget it by next week. Some memories are best forgotten. But then are they even memories at all?

Where is this Taco Bell? That way, if the vagrant is to be trusted. He's proven that he could be trusted. But he didn't walk that way. He also didn't say he was going to Taco Bell. It's smart to remember these key differences, Mary. Not everyone is out to get you. It only seems that way.

The reporter. Is she somewhere nearby? Probably. That matters less and less right now. What I need is a drink.

I'll just take a tiny sip of the gin to see if it goes down smooth. It's been some time since I've had Gordon's. Maybe they've changed the recipe.

I should smell it first. It smells strong. That's because it's gin. Just a tiny sip to inspect what you're dealing with. Down the hatch it goes.

Yuck. Too strong. Fucking vagrant. No, it's not his fault. He doesn't drink. You didn't tell him what to get. Your fault. A bum buying Bombay would be a tad suspicious as well. This is the way things needed to be. Beggars can't be choosers, especially when dealing with other beggars.

I must go to Taco Bell to find a mixer. They must have

fountain sodas. All the better. I haven't had one of those in quite some time. All that sugar is bad for the complexion, but a little splurge every now and then is fine.

Down the block. The adventure continues. We are one step closer to the desired outcome. Mary, her drink, and peace and quiet. Serenity in a fast food restaurant. Oh, how the mighty have fallen. Ease up on your pity, girl. You've had a long day.

One step forward. No steps back. Father would be proud looking down on me with Mother and Jake. Not Aidan. He's somewhere else whether it's on this earth or below it. I hope he never found the money. Giles will take care of it.

My slippers look a tad worn. Especially the one that took a dip in the puddle. That's to be expected. I'll have Regina take me to Lord & Taylor's one of these days. There isn't a specialty shop for slippers. Not one that I can think of. Think, think. No.

I'm past due for more of my happy pills. Won't be long now. Just a few more steps. Or a few more than that. Mathematics was never my strong suit. I was always more of a sit there, be quiet, and look pretty kind of girl. Did that fade as I got older? You're barely past forty. Quite the pity.

I see the sign for Taco Bell. What sort of restaurant needs to advertise with a big sign that shoots up into the sky? It says, "Low class here." Can you imagine a French restaurant with a big sign that said "Escargot Cloche" for all to see? My French hasn't faded as much as the rest of my skills. C'est une bonne fille Mary. Is that right? Who cares? N'est pas.

I wonder what kind of undesirables hang out in a

place like this in the middle of the day. The tavern was bad enough. The juvenile delinquents should be in school. Well, no, it's a weekend. I should know these things.

It's empty. No one to be found. Just me. On the plus side, the place doesn't smell like diarrhea. One must learn to be an optimist at a time like this.

This place is gray and grungy. There are advertisements on the wall for food they sell. There's something wrong with that. You shouldn't need to have huge posters of the shit you sell in the actual restaurant—using the term *restaurant* in the most liberal way possible—when you have a big fucking sign outside it. What the hell is wrong with these people?

A woman comes up to the cash register. I forget that fast food places have you pay when you order. Undoubtedly in an effort to stop the riffraff from ditching out on the bill. To be in a place where the patron/establishment relationship is this sour right off the bat. Oh, the horror.

"Welcome to Taco Bell, can I take your order?" she asks. Fool. As if I would order anything. Now, now Mary, that is hardly a ridiculous question. You are in the restaurant. You must come down from your high horse if you want to complete your objective.

Order, order. Never. I could be starving in a gutter with the vagrant and I wouldn't eat this crap if it were served on my finest china. No, not I. Not Mary. Say no to the food.

"Uh, yes," I reply. "Just a soft drink." There's a good girl.

The waitress looks just a teensy bit puzzled. It's certainly been a recurring theme throughout this day. She says, "I see. What size would you like?"

Size? What is this, a coffee shop? I say I want a drink and that should be the end of it. No size nonsense, come on now. Get your shit together Taco Bell.

She holds up a big cup. She's trying to rip me off by selling me the largest size possible. I see through her tricks.

Civility will prevail. Can't be rude at a time like this. "How much does that one cost?" I ask without giving away that I'm on to her bullshit.

Looks like it worked. She has no idea what I'm really thinking. "$1.99. Plus tax, which wouldn't be much. Is that a problem?"

Two dollars for that huge cup? What kind of madness is this? How does a business expect to make money if they give out large quantities of their product for practically nothing? Fools. Well, at least we know if Giles needs work, he can come in here to fix up the management and explain to them the simple concept of economics.

Don't laugh at these prices. This waitress isn't upper management. She is only doing her job.

"No. No problem. Sorry, it's been a while since I was in here and I forget how cheap soft drinks are." Good recovery. "Here you go, keep the change," I say as I hand her a five-dollar bill that had been loose in my bag. I should keep better track of my money.

My behavior continues to baffle another fine citizen of the USA. Well, she could be an illegal alien for all we know. A place like this wouldn't be above employing their kind. "Thanks," she says. She points to the side of the room where the soda fountain is.

My brain doesn't care to choose. There's Coke, Diet

Coke. Sometimes Pepsi instead. Tonic water, the lemon one. "Something sweet please," I mutter to myself, feeling a bit confused. I hope she didn't hear me.

She disappears for a second. Maybe there are more drinks hidden in the back. I bet that makes her feel powerful. People have let smaller things go to their heads. Aidan certainly did. Giles tried his best to keep him in line, but he failed. It's hard to blame him. No one could keep Aidan in line.

She returns with a bag. I didn't order any food. "Here you go," she says. "I put an order of cinnamon twists in there in case you get hungry. Refill the soda as many times as you like."

That was nice of her. Was it out of pity or kindness? Or because I gave her a tip at a fast food restaurant? She could probably get in trouble for taking tips. Somebody would think she stole it out of the register. No good deed goes unpunished. We all learn that the hard way.

I reply, "Thank you very much," as I take her offerings. I can't think of the last time someone thought to give me a present without wanting something in return. Calling these crunchy looking things cinnamon twists is a bit of a stretch but I'll take what I can get. They might even be good! Giles would cringe if he saw me eating this crap.

The waitress disappears to the back of the restaurant. Where to next? I suppose I should sit down and have a rest. It's been quite a long day. I'll need to take my happy pills and put some of that horrid gin in my sweet drink. Busy, busy. A rest will do me wonders before I need to figure out how to get home.

That shouldn't be too hard, right? I'll just go back the way I came. No, that is hard. But I'll make do. I always do.

I take a seat. These seats aren't very comfortable. The surface is hard. I don't assume the people who frequent these sorts of places come here for the ambiance. They come for the soft drinks that barely cost any money. That's why the vagrant recommended it. He must come here all the time. His expenses ought to be low if he doesn't have a house and he eats here a couple times a week.

Let me look in the purse for my pills. Good thing I didn't forget them. That could lead to a nasty accident later. Let's see. Two of the purples since I've had such a taxing day. These white ones are small. I'll take three just to be on the safe side. And to balance it out, one of these pink ones. Pink looks like red, which looks like red velvet cake. Red velvet cake is tasty so this pill must do something good.

But first, let me pour a little of the gin into this big drink. Was she joking about the refill? This thing costs a little more than two dollars and you get more if you finish. Who could finish a drink like this? Aidan couldn't even after he smoked a little grass. He didn't do that much after college. Preferred the white powdery stuff instead when he needed a little extra oomph that alcohol couldn't provide.

Me? No, I was never into drugs. Father said that was the quickest way to throw your life away. But he died anyway. He must not have given that advice to Mother, who was no stranger to Quaaludes. They got her, too.

Thank God I don't do drugs. Just a little alcohol here and there plus these little happy candies that make the day feel so much shinier. A day without sweetness isn't much of a day at all.

Oh, this drink sure is sweet. I taste sugar and liquid

and nothing else. This concoction is perfect for the foul gin. I'll pour a little in at first and see how that goes. Stir it around a bit with the straw, what a treat. Oh yum, that tastes simply delicious. I should bring this concoction to the tavern and show them what they're missing. What a charming mixed drink this will make. Or better yet, Giles could open up a gay bar that serves nothing but this drink. We'd be saved!

Open sesame, down go the pills. All seven of them. Was I supposed to take seven? Ah well, it's not too long now.

Now I'll sit and enjoy the rest of my day until it's time to start making my way home. What's left of it that is. I wonder how Regina made out with Jack at his little exercise group with the snickering mothers who think that I'm some horrible wench who committed a travesty against the human race.

I don't care that Aidan did what he did. I really don't. I doubt the lowlifes who would do business with those two weren't in some sort of mess themselves. Who's innocent when everyone is guilty? It wasn't fraud. The government didn't give them enough time to fix the problem. Accountability. What bothers me is that he skipped town leaving his family to endure the fallout of his actions. We were supposed to be in this together.

Someone is coming inside. It looks like Caleb. That perfect hairline that any man would kill for at his age. Wait a second. It is Caleb. No, Mary, you're only imagining him. Caleb doesn't eat at places like this nor would he pop up at a moment of your convenience. Well, no, it's not convenient at all. He'll want to take your drink away from you. And then this whole day would be for nothing. We can't have that, can we?

Don't worry. He isn't real. There's no way he'd be able to find you. Well, he could've asked the bum. But Caleb wouldn't ask a bum where I was. Giles might, but Caleb wouldn't.

Maybe Caleb is cheating on Giles and this is the rendezvous point. A handsome yoga instructor is bound to walk in at any moment. Giles deserves it. He's been so bitter lately.

"Mary," calls the spirit of Caleb. It's walking toward me. Oh dear. I don't want to have to entertain this stupidity. "Go away," I say. Now I'll be quiet. That won't work but it is worth a try.

"What are you doing here?" it asks as it sits down across from me. This thing smells like Caleb. That perfume or cologne or whatever it's called. It does look like him. The waitress has reappeared. She's looking at him. Unless I truly am going crazy, there's a slight chance that this thing might actually be my brother's partner.

"I could ask the same thing of you. Are you stalking me, Caleb? A reporter was already after me today. This might have made sense fifteen years ago, but I'm not the catch I once was." Funny. Self-deprecating humor to an audience of one.

Caleb smiles. "No. Giles had an app installed on your phone that allows him to track where you are. Before you get all mad about privacy and all that, just know that Regina called and we were worried. But here you are, safe and sound."

An app installed on my phone? What the fuck does that mean? My criminal brother can track my every move. "Does Giles understand that this disregard for the rights of others is precisely the kind of nonsense that got him into the mess he's in? When will he learn that he can't do whatever he wants? The nerve that man's got, Caleb." I can't believe him. Take a sip of your drink and then you'll be happy again. Nice and easy.

Caleb looks down. He's thinking about what to say. I've got him. He says, "Look Mary. You have a right to be annoyed. But you stink of booze and some other things I can't describe and don't want to. There's probably alcohol in your drink right now. You can be mad, but that doesn't mean that Giles didn't do the right thing. God knows where you'd end up. Just relax."

Relax? He knows about your drink. Hold it tight Mary and he won't be able to take it away. There's a good girl. This drink is yours, it's not his. Kick your purse behind your seat, too. Protect what's yours. Do what Aidan couldn't.

Caleb laughs. "Mary, I honestly don't care if you drink. That's Giles' beef, not mine. You don't have to be so defensive. Everything is going to be okay."

No. It won't. He's lying. He wants you to put your guard down so that he can take your drink without causing a scene. Clever Caleb, but he can't fool me. He won't be taking anything away from me.

"It's mine," I say. "I went through a lot of effort to get this and you're not taking it away from me. It's mine. You can have what's in the bag." A peace offering will do the trick.

Caleb takes a peculiar look inside the bag. "Ooh, cinnamon twists. I haven't had these in years." He pops one in his mouth and adds, "delicious."

He's up to something. No—stop being paranoid.

There aren't many people on this earth who care about you and he's one of them. For whatever reason.

But why? Why doesn't he leave? He isn't married to Giles. He has a perfect out. He can escape this fucking mess. Just walk out and live your life away from this garbage. Better yet, he could write a book about it and he could make some money for himself. That idea has to have crossed his mind at some point. Ask him.

"Why are you still here?" I ask. "What do you mean?" he quickly replies, defensively. I can see how my question was vague. Best to keep it that way. You can take your out now and avoid alienating one of your few remaining allies. I feel the pills starting to take a greater hold. Let it go, Mary.

I sense Caleb got the idea anyway. "Look Mary, Giles and I are both aware of the shit storm that you've been sucked into. It's fucking awful. Believe me, I feel it, too. But this is a mess that we need to face together. The three of us are it. Giles is working on solutions with the lawyer, but we're all we really have in this life. We're family and you need to know how much that matters. Giles has a lot on his plate and that's led him to treat you in a way that's hardly indicative of how he really feels. It's not your fault, but I hope you can understand where he's coming from."

Oh sure. He blames me for Aidan. I see it. Bullshit. We never would have had to deal with that fool if it hadn't been for Jake, but Giles certainly didn't dump him when we had the chance. Mary has to take the fall.

He's hiding something. He has to be. No sane person would stay once the reporters started digging into all of our lives. Why didn't he leave?

Enough of this. A cloud blocks the bad thoughts.

Caleb didn't do anything wrong. Don't be so hard on people trying to help you.

"Giles needs to stop with the drinking mandates," I say. I must have some sort of victory in this. "Life sucks and I prefer to drink when things are shitty. You don't need my wit to get out of this. I just need to stay quiet. I did that today. A reporter bought me a drink and tried to ask me questions and I played it just like a politician. You would have been proud."

I reach for a cinnamon twist. Caleb touches my hand before reaching into the bag as well. I taste the crunchy concoction for the first time. It tastes good. I can see why people come here.

"Mary, let me say this again. I really don't care if you drink." Oh please. I think he heard that. "No really, it's fine with me," he adds. "It's a little dangerous with your medication, but you're doing what you need to do right now. It's probably for the best that this is all a blur. What's important is that you're staying strong for Jack. He needs you."

Jack. My son. He has Regina. I'm merely a prop in the room for the people to acknowledge every once in a while when they come make a visit. A slightly more attractive cigar store Indian. This place could use one of those. Indians like Mexican food, right? They'd like these cinnamon twists.

"What are we going to do?" I ask. I haven't asked a ton of questions about what comes next. No one really knows since Aidan's been missing. That makes sense. That is the question on all of our minds. Certainly Giles'. With Aidan gone, he's going to have to burn for this. But if he could be found.

Caleb is definitely hiding something. Or maybe he's just reluctant to discuss the writing on the wall. He says, "Tomorrow is Easter. Nothing is going to be solved until after that. If next week doesn't bear fruit, then we'll adjust. Giles is not without friends or options. He's not going to prison. It's going to be okay."

Adjust? What, are we going to run? Boy, that's a great idea. Why don't we go on a Thelma and Louise style heist while we're at it? Jesus. They say I'm the crazy one and this is the alternative? Giles would probably like prison.

Let them play with their delusion. You've got no choice, anyway. You can't exactly offer yourself to the police without anything to offer. You don't know where the money is and you don't know where Aidan is. If Giles and Caleb run, you run with them. That's the move to make. Family first!

Think about what an adventure that'll be. Jack will love it. So will Regina, if she chooses to come. Maybe we'll wind up on some Caribbean island where I can drink rum all day in one of those glasses with the tacky little umbrella. Won't that be fun?

"Sure, Caleb. I trust you," I say as I take a long swig of my drink. I do, sort of. Whatever happens will happen and that'll be that.

He smiles the way people smile at funerals. He knows it's all a big dream but he asks, "Do you want to come over for dinner? We can pick up Thai on the way." I do enjoy Thai. Weren't we supposed to have dinner tonight, anyway? Who can keep track of all this shit?

I've had enough adventure for today. "No thanks, I'm beat. Can you drive me home?" I'd hate to have to figure out how I'm going to get home from here. That doesn't appear to be a problem.

"Of course, do you want to bring your gin and Mountain Dew in the car?" he asks, briefly prying it from my hands to take a sip. "Oh, that is good," he says, puckering his lips.

Caleb drives a Porsche. He got some flack for that in the local paper, but I don't see the problem. The government hasn't seized it and it is worth more to him than some used car salesman. Let him enjoy his pleasure. You can get criticized for just about anything, though. Caleb was guilty in the court of public opinion before he even had a chance even though he didn't do anything. Guilt by association. Fucking bullshit.

We drive with the windows down. It's a nice drive in a nice part of the country. I thought I'd miss the South when we came up here but Aidan was right. This was a good place to lay some roots down. Until things went to shit.

Caleb probably agrees. He's from Michigan, though. Too cold for my taste. Giles hates it up there. It'd be a good place to hide from the Feds. Who would think to look for him there?

I think we passed the puddle. Caleb never asked about the dried blood on my leg. He knows not to ask questions he doesn't need the answers to. Good Caleb. Good Mary. Happy, happy.

Don't worry. Everything is going to be okay. Even if it isn't. One way or another, this is all going to be over someday. And when it is, things will be better. Giles will pull through with the money. Caleb said so.

I just wish he wouldn't yell, like he did yesterday. Have I yelled at him for all of this shit? No. But that doesn't matter. It's his fault.

"You okay?" asks a voice that isn't mine. Caleb. "Yes," I reply. "It's been a long adventure." It has.

Caleb feels my forehead. He says, "You should probably lie down. I don't know what you've been up to, but you sure do look tired." I am sleepy. Too sleepy to deal with Giles right now, but that's okay. We're going home. To my house. Not his.

We pull into the driveway. I take a few more sips of my drink and leave it in the cup holder. If he takes the cup back to Taco Bell, I'm sure they'll give him a free refill. He also probably thinks I'm giving up my booze. Little does he know the gin is still in my purse. Silly Caleb.

"Goodnight and thank you," I call as I run up the stairs to my house. It feels weird being dropped off at home by a boy. It's like I'm on a date except for the fact that my date is in a relationship with my brother. Weird, right?

I walk in the door. I'm tempted to yell, "I'm home," but Jack is probably asleep. I don't really remember what time he goes to bed. Early, probably.

Regina comes running up to me. She says, "Miss Mary, where have you been? Are you okay?"

Silly Regina. "I'm lovely darling, I had a wonderful adventure."

Thursday, February 12, 1985

Jacob

L OOK AT THAT BIRD ON THE TREE. IF MY BOY SCOUT training still serves me well, that would be a Northern mockingbird sitting up there. Always liked bird watching. Not as smelly as fishing, but you get the same experience. Minus the food, of course. Elegant bird. Gray body with those wings. Black and white undertones. Or is it overtones? Anyway, it's a damn fine looking bird.

Puff, puff, puff goes the cigarette. Aidan likes the pre-rolled ones you buy at the drugstore. Fucking hick comes round to the big city and wants to live the high life. Makes sense, right? You get your tobacco at a real tobacconist. None of this factory-made bullshit. A man and his cigarette form a bond when you've created it with your own two hands. You know every fiber of its existence because that's something you created.

If you get real good, you know the points where you should take that extra puff. Nature rewards hard work. Buying some cheap pack of menthols only says at one point in your life, you had yourself a little luxury. Money ain't meant for shit like that.

"Phone call, Mr. Moore," calls a voice. That voice

belongs to Jeremiah, the caretaker of our fraternity house. "Who is it?" I call back. Who else could it be? "Your mother, Mrs. Moore, sir," returns our trusted companion. Ah. Mother. What could she want?

What else? Oh goody, that senator from Oregon is speaking at a party tonight. And the Moores were invited. Well, four of us at least. Mother, Father, Giles, Jacob. Mary said she didn't want to go and Father didn't put up much of a fuss. You could tell he was pissed off about it, but he said, "Don't worry about it, four is a better number than five." What does that even mean? It's a fucking cocktail party.

It means that Father is losing his touch. The man is barely past fifty and yet he looks like he's on the verge of death. His hair is almost all gone. Not gracefully either. It's old, white, and scraggly like a man pushing eighty. His daughter does jack shit to attempt prosperity at this university and he does nothing about it. What the hell, Pops?

I guess it's hard to blame him. He's got two sons at the same university doing all right. That's what happens when you have three kids all within a year and a half of each other. Irish triplets? Is that what they would call it?

My cigarette is almost done. It's not worth bringing into the house. It'd be out before I could find an ashtray. Fuck. I didn't bring any matches outside so I guess I'll have to do this phone call without one lest I leave Jeremiah on the phone with Mother. The horror, the travesty!

"I'm coming, I'm coming," I call to Jeremiah as I run up the porch stairs as if it's a long distance phone call. My folks are barely two hours away and yet Mother calls and calls. Thankfully, I'm not home most of the time - but then that just means someone else picks up the phone and then

I have to hear about it, which can sometimes be worse.

Too often, that person is Aidan. Yack, yack, yack to Momma Moore about *Cheers*, and *Dallas*, and *Knot's Landing*. Is the man without shame? No, he doesn't care that we rib him for, watching his soaps on the sofa with a big cigarette filled with grass in his hand and a bottle of that cheap fortified wine. What a life.

If you have to talk about how cheap a bottle of booze is, you know it ain't worth drinking. All Aidan says is "Do you know how much I paid for this?" like it's some fucking mystery. Yea, we know you have cheap booze that you can buy in a store just like the rest of us. If you don't have anything interesting to say, don't say it at all. Or go home and ramble in your swamp to whoever will listen. I'm not interested.

The phone is on the table. I could just walk away and no one would know. Jeremiah would. But then she'd call back. Fuck. I guess I should pick it up lest I put Jeremiah in the position of having to explain to my mother that I was here but now am not. That'd be awkward.

"Hello," I say. Standard greeting. None of this "Hi mom, how are you?" crap. Strictly business. I would probably kill myself if I had to get all excited every goddamned time she called. She could get some genuine affection if she could leave me the hell alone for more than three seconds.

"Jacob, is that you?" says the phone. Oh boy. "Yes Mother, it is I, Captain Vegetable." I saw him on *Sesame Street* one morning. They need puppets to get kids to eat shit that isn't loaded with sugar. What is this world coming to?

"Captain who?" Mother replies. "Never mind," I say,

"what can I do for you?" She always wants something. She fails to understand that I'm not supposed to be doing things for her anymore now that I'm in college. Let Giles do it. He lives for that shit.

"I'm calling to tell you that your father and I will not be coming to the party tonight. Your father is sick and I don't think a car ride is a very good idea right now." Great. Does this mean I don't have to go?

"I'm sorry to hear that. What's wrong?" I'm not sure I want to hear the answer. She replies, "He's coughing up blood." Nope, didn't want to hear that. Fuckity, fuck, fuck.

"That's not good. How does one cure the coughing up of blood?" Maybe Captain Vegetable can help.

I hear a sigh on the phone. Oh boy. Where are my cigarettes? Upstairs, with the matches. Oh joy. Did Aidan leave any bottles lying around? No. Scowl, scowl.

"I brought you some tea, sir," Jeremiah says. Something harder would've been nicer, but God bless this kind man. That's why they pay him the big bucks. I actually don't know how much they pay him. The fraternity alumni board or whatever it's called pays him to make sure we don't break everything in the house. As if there's anything of value in this fucking shithole. The tea is an added bonus. Father is on that board, which is probably why Jeremiah likes me more than any of my so-called "brothers."

"Thank you," I whisper, lest Mother start to think I'm giving her anything other than my complete undivided attention. Heads would most certainly roll if she thought I was talking to the help. The water is a tad lukewarm. When did Jeremiah make this?

"There's not going to be a cure. Your father has cancer.

He's dying." Out goes the water. Now there's a puddle of slightly warmer water on the floor mixed in with my saliva.

"What are you talking about? Dying? Where did this come from? What are you talking about?" This is a phone call about a missed social obligation. There's no dying here.

Mother laughs. "Oh you're so naïve, Jacob. We've known for weeks. Just couldn't think of a good time to tell you, that's all." Yea, that's all. Real fucking simple.

"Is this such a great time? Wouldn't it have been better to tell someone this kind of news in person? I think that's the normal thing to do." Jesus Christ.

She laughs again. Apparently this is some big joke. It might be for all I know. Mother has been known to be melodramatic. That must be where Mary and Giles get it from. "You're probably right. Well no, I would argue that there's no good time. Remember honey, you are the one who asked."

This woman is crazy. I didn't ask shit about death. I asked what the cure for blood spit was. Big difference. One that I probably shouldn't bring up. Mother doesn't need me arguing over verbiage at a time like this.

"So, what happens next?" I ask. I don't really want the answer, but that's the sort of thing that gets asked. I need to know. Need is a strong word, but it's the logical next step in this unfortunate conversation.

"Next? He dies. That's what comes next. What do you think, he's going to become an angel who flies around singing songs by The Beatles?" Mother says, laughing her ass off. What the fuck is she talking about? I'm surprised she knows who The Beatles are.

I'm getting tired of this. "Mother, why have you called? Say your bit and let me get on with my day." Rude? Maybe, but this conversation is bound to drone on and on until she forgets who she's even talking to. If Jeremiah was in the room, he could just take over. But he's gone. Plotted his escape to greener pastures.

"The guest list. God, don't you listen. Our absence creates two vacancies at the party that must be filled. Empty seats will not look good if people see that we aren't there. We must keep up with appearances, Jacob."

I'm glad she has her priorities straight. Father is dying and all she cares about is that people don't blame her if some West Coast senator is pissed off about a couple of empty seats. I'm at a loss for words.

"Who am I supposed to find? The thing starts in a few hours. Am I supposed to go door to door asking if people want to hear some congressional hack spout out some nonsense about redistribution of wealth or some other fragrance of manure? Jesus. Why didn't you call Giles?" Good question.

"I don't have your brother's number. You are going to be the man of the family Jacob. You best fucking get somebody. This is simple. Imagine how difficult life will be when your father is a fucking corpse. Take your sister and that boy Aidan you're so fond of. Problem solved, you jackass. If I were there I'd give your behind such a smack, you insolent twat." Ouch. That was uncalled for. How rude.

Or maybe not. She's got a lot on her plate. Aidan has been asking to go to this since he found out it was happening. I was hoping not to have to invite him, but it looks like these are the cards I've been dealt. At least he's reliable and it saves me the trouble of having to ask anyone else. Then there's Mary. Two birds with one stone. Two annoying birds that didn't die, that is.

"I'm sorry. I'll take care of it. Is there anything else you need?" Why would you ask that? Do you want to know the answer?

She sighs again. Oh dear. "Just keep things together, Jacob." What does that mean? You know what, don't ask. You don't need to know what that means.

"Will do. I love you," and I hang up the phone before she can say anything else. Shit. What a mess.

"Is everything okay, sir?" Jeremiah sees the spitty liquid all over the floor. That was rude of me, even if it was understandable.

"Oh Jeremiah, I'm so sorry about that. I'll get a rag and clean it up. My mother got the best of me on the phone." Jeremiah shouldn't have to clean up my crap.

"Not to worry, sir. I've got one, already." He cleans the mess up. I'd tip him if I had any money on me. He might not appreciate that. "Thanks," I say as I head to the couch to have a nice sit down.

Dad is dying. Let that soak in for a bit. Do I think Mother is being melodramatic? Probably, but she wouldn't make the whole thing up. He's not dying this second, but shit is hitting the fan and I don't care for it one bit.

I should probably tell Giles at some point. Not now. Before the party or after? Before. He'll want to know why they aren't at the party and he always knows when you're lying. It's best to be truthful.

Don't tell Mary the truth. She doesn't need to know shit. So much for twin instinct. I could tell her I was taking a plane to Mars and she'd want to know if there's going to be an in-flight movie.

What did Mother mean when she told me to keep things together? Fucking cryptic. It's the mindless nonsense of a crazy old woman. She isn't that old, but she's definitely nuts.

Aidan walks through the door. Oh joy. Four other people live in this house, not counting Jeremiah, and he's the one who walks in.

"Jakey boy, how is my main squeeze doing on this lovely afternoon? To think February could be this nice this far north." What a jackass. We're in Georgia, not Maine. What the fuck is a squeeze in this context?

He ignores my lack of response. He pulls out a bottle and asks, "Want a swig of Canadian Club?" Vile rye shit. Why can't he drink something else?

"Sure, why not," I say and he hands me the bottle. A vile drink for a vile disposition. Aidan isn't good for much, but he's always had good timing.

Yum. In an ironic sense. What a bad taste. "You got any matches?" I ask. Time for another cigarette. He hands me the box. Fuck, my cigarettes are upstairs. "Can I bum a butt too?" I add. Jesus Jacob, get your shit together.

"Someone's needy," he replies as he tosses me his pack. He turns on the TV. "What have you been up to all day?" he asks. I suppose the TV is just meant for background noise.

"An eventful phone call with Mother. She's in a rare mood." A *Dallas* rerun is on the TV. Aidan's favorite. Maybe he'll focus on that instead of me. Thank you, J.R.

Aidan looks at the TV for a second and then back at me. "Isn't she coming up tonight with your pa for that lecture?" He knows it's not a lecture just as much as he knows I don't call Father "Pa." Calling it a lecture forces me to clarify that it is in fact, a party. He's just fishing for an invite.

Which he's unfortunately going to get. Look at him sitting there with his whiskey and his rerun, getting everything he wants while my world crashes down all around me. I should tell him to fuck off.

"Yea, about that. It turns out that they can't make it. Pa is a little under the weather. I was wondering if you wanted to go?" Ugh. He'd asked already. I had said there wasn't room. I never checked. I didn't want to entertain his nonsense at the party. I don't wish to be responsible for anyone other than myself.

It looks like I'll be responsible for two fools. "I should have added that I need the second seat filled as well. What would you say if I invited my sister to join us?" Excellent.

Aidan thinks Mary is in love with him. They have been on a few dates. But Mary has also been on a few dates with some other people. That's the way she operates. Truth is, Mary doesn't know what she wants. Who does? She wants someone to tell her. I don't know who that's going to be.

She must be one of the last girls in the United States who genuinely wants an arranged marriage in this age of women's suffrage. She wants Father to set her up with some rich man so she doesn't need to worry about anything. Mary doesn't like to worry. Who does? But people worry because that's what people do. That doesn't concern my sister.

"Yeah, I can do that," he replies. "What will be the dress code for this occasion?" Why does he care? He thinks everything is black tie. If it were, I would tell him because he'd need to borrow clothes from Giles or me. God forbid he makes an effort to ask someone else for a favor. Nope. Just members of the Moore family.

Giles didn't pledge our fraternity. There wasn't any pressure to. I think Mother wanted him to more than anyone else. Because it's a manly thing to do. I did it because Father did it. That appeased him well enough.

I never really talked about it with him. I suppose I probably should have with the way Mother gets all excited by the yearly picture. I asked him if he was interested and he said he had enough on his plate between class, art club, and whatever else he gets himself into. Mary thought that was a fruity answer, but then again Giles can be a fruity guy sometimes.

Aidan tried to set him up on a date earlier this year. Giles took her to a school production of *She Stoops to Conquer*. The girl fell asleep, Giles changed seats at intermission, and that was that. I don't see the point in pushing the issue.

"I just thought of something," Aidan says, smoking a cigarette of his own. He's staring at me, waiting for the inevitable, "what," that I am obliged to utter. I must entertain the fool.

"So, you know how the *Star Wars* movies are episodes four through six?" he asks. I want to roll my eyes but instead I reply, "Of course." Naturally, that's the logical answer. Everyone knows that.

Aidan takes a puff and continues. "So they've got three more to make. Episodes one through three. Now Lucas didn't direct the last two, so I think he's not going to want to do these, either. So, what if they bring in Stanley Kubrick to blow everyone's mind with his style? You know, the guy who made *2001: A Space Odyssey*."

How am I supposed to respond to that? I have no idea. "I don't know. Is that something that's being discussed anywhere but here?" I take another drag. I wish I had the bottle of whiskey, but Aidan is holding it while he talks about his stupid bullshit.

"I don't know," he replies. "Kubrick hasn't done a sequel before. Maybe he'd like to try one, especially one like that. I bet they would pay him a lot of money."

Aidan likes money. His parents don't have a lot of money. He's here on scholarship. He has a part time job doing accounting for some of the professors, but he makes a killing on the poker table. He's better with numbers than anyone I've ever seen.

We met in class freshman year. We're both economics majors. Aidan is a better student than I am, but he does less work. Most of the time he sits around and drinks and smokes and watches TV. Or he's pining after some girl. Well, not so much anymore now that he's got his mind set on Mary, but I've seen his eyes wander a few times. That's okay as long as he doesn't expect me to help him win over my sister.

He says, "After we hit it big in the city, we can just finance the movies and pay Kubrick whatever the fuck he wants." Right. "You think there will be potential investors at the party tonight?"

Aidan has a big plan for next year after graduation. He wants Mary and me to move with him to New York City, where we're going to open up our own investment business. I suppose Mary is expected to marry him in this fantasy. It's not a terrible idea as a long-term goal, but it is problematic right now. You don't exactly get a scholarship to open up your own business. We'll need money and kids just getting out of college don't have that. He can talk Ronald Reagan all he wants, but Mr. President isn't going to give us a loan.

What do I want? I guess the answer is simple. A job. Somewhere. As long as it pays for me to live, I can handle the uphill climb. Father can help me get some interviews. It's not something that should be terribly hard unlike shouldering a company right out of college.

Of course I'm nervous. A lot of people in my grade are married or engaged or probably about to be. I broke up with a girl named Amy before Christmas break. It wasn't too serious. She was sort of fun but she kind of annoyed me and we're seniors and that didn't bode well for the future. Now it's too late to develop anything meaningful enough to last, before graduation sends us all out into the real world. Or back home. And that's okay.

"You didn't answer my question. Stop daydreaming man," yells Aidan. I dripped some ash on myself. Shit. I brush it off as quickly as possible.

"Investors," I reply. "This isn't really that kind of thing. I mean, I guess you can try to get some information if you prod around properly. But be smart. Don't go asking people for money like you're on a cold call. Father would hate that."

That does it. Aidan isn't going to do anything that might potentially jeopardize his reputation in my father's eyes. He craves that shit. His parents are still hanging around the swamp doing diddily squat. They are happy though, which counts for something. But Aidan has his eyes set on bigger prizes.

"Prod around," he responds. "I can do that. There will

be those kinds of people there, right?" It's shit like that that makes you feel bad about being a dick to Aidan. He's not using me so much as he is trying to figure out how to make it in a world he doesn't quite understand yet. He's got the brains. He's just not as savvy as he needs to be. It will come in time. I think.

These things can be learned. I can see how he values me despite my inferior grades. I'm not just his friend and a way in. I'm his resource for these sorts of opportunities. He can't afford to go wasting them. That's where I come in.

I should give him some reassurance. "Just don't drink too much and you'll be fine. These old fucks like to talk to young people and hear about what we're trying to do. Use that as your way to get them to notice you and ask them some questions. They'll love you. Show some initiative, you've got plenty of that. Go for the business cards."

He tosses the Canadian Club into my lap. I guess that's his way of saying thanks. The cigarette is almost out. I put it in the ashtray.

"You're coming around to the store-bought ones. Those filters are great." He takes a final drag of his and leans over to put it out.

"Aidan buddy, let me tell you something. Those filters don't do shit. All they do is remind you what the filth you're inhaling looks like. I don't need to see that shit." I take a small swig of the Canadian Club.

I check my watch. It's a little after three. I haven't done much schoolwork in the past month, though that's not uncommon for a senior. Giles is a junior. He's a man of routine, which means he'll be studying in the back corner of the cafeteria on the south side of campus.

I get off the couch. My jacket is on the chair near the phone. That should be all I need. Aidan is fixated on the TV. He's undoubtedly seen this episode of *Dallas,* but that shouldn't stop him.

"I'm going to see my brother," I say. Aidan looks over and replies, "Do you need me to do the same with your sister? Maybe I'll do a little more." Gross. I don't dignify that with a response.

My cigarettes are upstairs in my room. I run up to grab them in case I need a smoke later on. I've only got a few left, but at least there's plenty of matches. I'll roll some more later if I have the time.

Campus is about a ten-minute walk from the house. We're on the outskirts of where the frat houses are located. Some of my other "brothers" complain about the walk, but I like it. It's also better for social functions. I can always have a cigarette on the way to class, but I don't have to worry about stomping it out in front of the building. That avoids labels like "the kid who is always smoking." I might smell like smoke all the time, but so do most students. Appearances, appearances.

The trees are in their weird wintery state. Students from up north talk about how warm it is for February. I suppose that's true, but I don't know. I went to Washington D.C. once with Father and Giles, but that's as far north as I've made it.

I don't know how I feel about the idea of moving to New York City with Aidan. I have a hard time believing Mary would. Eh, that's not true. Aidan could convince her in about two seconds if he gave her a copy of *The Beautiful and Damned.* She wouldn't even need to be told that the Fitzgerald autobiographical stuff toward the end wouldn't happen to her. She wouldn't care if it did.

My own company. Well, half of one. Though if Aidan married Mary, it'd basically be like the whole thing. A Moore/Davies united front. Now that'd be something.

He could pull it off too with his numbers and I'd make up for his social deficiencies. We could even cut Giles in when he finishes law school. *If he* goes, but I suppose he will. What else would he do with a political science degree?

It'd be nice to work together as a family. Trusting someone can be so difficult. With Aidan and Giles by my side, that wouldn't be an issue. It'd be nice to have something I built that I could pass on to my kids. Someday.

Ah, the cafeteria. Big building, shitty food. Eh, it's not that bad. You just need to know who's cooking.

Aidan told me that trick. Know the chef. Say hello. Ask them about their children or their siblings. Or their favorite television program. Treat people like people, especially those in service jobs, and they'll remember. Too few people do. It's fucked up, but that just works to our advantage. I couldn't imagine someone talking smack to Jeremiah. Good Christian man.

Giles is in the back as usual. He wears his tie loose even though he doesn't need one at all. Fucking hipster. Always had a weird sense of fashion. He's got a cup of coffee with him. Typical. The man loves his coffee like I love my cigarettes. We've all got our vices.

"Hello brother," I call out to him. He looks up from his books. He's surrounded by them with only a briefcase to carry all his shit in. Half that crap is probably just there for theatrics. Giles likes to look more important than he actually is. Don't we all?

"Hello Jacob, how are you?" he replies. He never calls me Jake. That's what Mary calls me. And because she does, so does Aidan, and now the rest of the house. I like "sir" the best. Jeremiah has it right.

"I am well," I say. I see a book he has open on the table. "Why are you reading a history of the United States? Shouldn't you know all that crap by now?" Giles is the smart one in the family. It would be a shame to be proved wrong about that.

He laughs. "It's a book by Howard Zinn. *A People's History of the United States.* He basically argues that pretty much everything that happened in the United States was done at the expense of the poor or through some other form of oppression. It's a fun read." It doesn't sound like one.

I grow concerned. "You're not turning into some liberal Marxist, are you Giles? What would Father say?" He wouldn't be happy.

Giles takes out a cigarette of his own. "Father could use a couple hours with this book. It's good to read shit you don't agree with. Helps you understand why you think the way you do. Me? I'm a man unto myself. This guy's not an idiot, that's for sure." I can see that. Confusing.

I came here for a reason. To tell him some unfortunate news. Unfortunately, I don't feel like delivering bad news. Let's see how this goes.

"Are you excited for the party tonight?" I ask. Fuck. Why lead off with that? Get him excited before you drop a bomb? How fucking thoughtful. Where does that go from here? Nowhere. Shit. You'll need to backtrack.

"Yes, I suppose. I'm excited to see what this fancy West Coast politician has to say to a bunch of cultured

Georgians. Is he going to talk down to us or try to educate us about the future? Or is he going to pull that Southern gentleman nonsense that all politicians love? In any event, it's an open bar right? Should be a good time."

Yeah. A good time. Which means that now is probably not a good time to tell him about the deteriorating state of our father, who art to be in heaven soon. Fuckity, fuck, fuck.

"When do Mother and Father get in? Are you cleaning up that dump of a house before their arrival? Father does enjoy reminiscing about that place. Or you could just set Aidan loose on them and then you wouldn't have to worry. Oh Aidan, you are a darling. Mother sure does enjoy that hick." Giles rolls his eyes.

I pull out a cigarette and hold it between my fingers, deciding whether or not to light it. "About that," I start to say. Bombshell or no bombshell? That is the question. Who wrote that original line? Faulkner? No earlier. Shakespeare, you fucking fool. "Mother and Father won't be joining us. Aidan and Mary are coming instead."

Giles starts laughing in a manner which sounds a lot like cackling. "Oh, that is rich, Jacob." I don't follow. "What do you mean?" I ask.

"Aidan came up to me in the quadrangle the other day begging for an invite. Wanted me to get him on the guest list. He wanted Mary there, too. A full portrait of the Moore family if I remember his words correctly. What a load of shit. Is he our biographer now?" Giles laughs into his book.

Giles has always had an interesting relationship with Aidan. Aidan and I are friends, but much of our companionship has to do with proximity. I don't always want him around, but a lot of the time that's just kind of tough shit. He is around.

He's not around Giles by chance a lot. That doesn't stop him from trying to be all buddy-buddy with my younger brother. It doesn't take a rocket scientist to see what he's up to with that.

Aidan sees Giles as a potential key to Mary and me. He's known the two of us for the better part of four years, though Mary has been more of an off and on acquaintance. By her choice. Certainly not his.

It's clear Aidan wants to marry into the family. It's also clear that he's hit a wall with how far he can go to make his case to my twin and to a lesser extent, me. Barring some bank loan or embezzlement scheme, reality is a long way's away from this proposition. So he's cozying up to Giles. Not the worst move, nor is it particularly dishonest. He's just doing what he thinks will get him to where he needs to go. Giles has always been the voice of reason, even if Mary never cared to admit it.

"Do you think he's going to make a fool out of us tonight?" I ask. Giles isn't one to keep his opinions to himself but he's not unfair with his commentary regarding the people who attend our university. He might be the only fair gossip around.

"Us," he replies. "Eh, I don't think so. He might say something that the highbrow people might not like, but then again, so could we. You never know what might draw the ire of those sorts of people."

I hear a girl's voice that breaks my train of thought. "Oh Giles, you must hear the good news." The girl practically leans over me to grab my brother's hand.

"Hello Charlotte. I take it your test went well," my

brother replies. Giles works as a tutor for some rich students. He seems pleased with himself. He likes ego boosts. That's probably the only reason he does it. He certainly doesn't need the money.

"Oh yes, Giles! I got a B+. Father was so pleased. He said to me, you get that tutor of yours something he likes as a thank you. I didn't know what you liked so I got you a bottle of wine." She pulls out a bottle from her purse. White. Giles does like white.

Giles's skin starts to turn a shade of red. Rose might be the more appropriate color for this instance. "Oh, you didn't have to do that," he says. Lies. Giles loves presents and praise.

He turns his glance to me. "Charlotte, have you met my brother Jacob? He's a senior and lives in the Psi Kappa Zeta house. Jacob, this is Charlotte, a sophomore from Kentucky. Her father did business with ours a couple decades back if one can believe the coincidence. Time does fly."

Charlotte extends her hand. Her hand is limp, suggesting I'm basically just supposed to touch it and not shake it. What else can you do? Mary has always had a firm handshake. Charming. I wave the limp hand up and down. Giles looks away, trying not to laugh at his pupil.

Giles asks, "So Charlotte, did you hear there's a senator all the way from Oregon here tonight? Jacob and I are going to hear him speak. Isn't that nice that a university like this can get people all the way from across the country?"

Charlotte looks puzzled. "Where's Oregon?" she asks.

I hold my breath so as not to laugh. Giles bites his lip a bit. "It's next to Washington, sweetie." Jesus Christ.

"I thought Washington was the one a few hours north? Are you sure about that, Giles?" Now I'm really trying hard not to crack up. Mostly because Giles looks terrified to be in this position. He must hate the notion that I know he spends his time with people who don't even know basic geography. Even if she pays for his company.

Giles keeps a straight face. He'd be a good actor. "No, no, that's Washington D.C. George Washington was a very important man, as we've learned in our studies together. There are many places named after him."

"And currency, too," I say, chiming in. "And the football team with the Indians on the helmets. A most exciting man." Boy, this conversation is really invigorating. All it needs is for Aidan and Mary to add to the intellectual depth we've been fortunate enough to explore.

Charlotte looks confused. She looks into her purse for a second. "That reminds me," she says, "I must get going to the bank before it closes. I'll see you on Monday, Giles. A pleasure to meet you Giles' brother. Jacob, right?"

That's a first. A girl who thinks the world of Giles forgets my name. We can't write off the fact that she knew him already given her quite questionable intelligence. I merely wave as Giles says goodbye. What an idiot.

Giles is looking at his new bottle. "Is that a good one?" I ask. I don't know what makes a bottle of wine good. Giles might.

"Yes, probably cost her about twenty bucks, which is ten more than she should've spent for the occasion. I hope to get twenty dollars of enjoyment out of it. Funny that she picked a white. This is a Californian bottle. I wouldn't be surprised if she didn't know where that was." Oh, jeez.

"How did you find her? Did Father put you in touch

with her?" I wouldn't have expected him to get so involved in Giles' extracurricular activities.

"No, I found that out on the phone with him one evening. She needed help with the American Revolution. She came up to me in the library one day and asked. That's the problem with the library. People are so flustered they'll do anything even though the reason people go to the library is to avoid that kind of crap in the first place. Though in my case, it led to a nice little job and a bottle of wine."

Giles' story is odd, though so is he. "What do you know about the American Revolution?" I ask. Giles doesn't study history. What's he doing teaching it?

He laughs. "I didn't know much at first. Only the basics. Lexington, Concord. The middle school shit you don't need Zinn to learn about. And then I did something that she didn't seem capable of doing." He pauses, waiting for me to ask the obvious.

"And what might that be?" He smiles and continues. "I read her books. You might think that was a drastic waste of time, but it wasn't. You see, it was all part of a test I was conducting, one that appears to have been a great success. I wanted to see if a theory I'd developed had merit." Giles stops again. I don't want to entertain his ego, but his story is rather interesting.

"Go on," I say. He sips his coffee, which must be cold by now. "Breadth vs. depth, brother. I was no Revolutionary War expert and there were plenty of people available to coach young Charlotte who were much more qualified in the subject than yours truly. And yet, Charlotte gets a B+. Now, it's perfectly reasonable to wonder whether or not she might have received an A- or even an A had she actually had a history scholar at her disposal. But you heard her speak a few minutes ago. Did that look like an A student to you?"

"No. Certainly not," I reply. "I'd say you've done the Lord's work with that girl. Are you into her at all?" I ask, even though I know the answer.

Giles chuckles some more. He's certainly in a good mood. "Heavens, no. Don't get me wrong. She's a sweet girl, but not my type. I need someone much smarter."

Do you? Smart girls have come and gone in the past. What is Giles' type? What's my type for that matter? I can't fault him for not going after someone who doesn't know where Washington state is while I remain an eligible bachelor.

"You should go after her," he adds, smiling. "No, thanks," I reply. There's something I find quite alluring about this little test of his. What could his motives be? Why teach yourself history just to tutor a girl you're not even interested in? I must hear more.

"I'm still confused as to why you chose to carry out this elaborate plan," I say. He's clearly thinking of the bigger picture. "Isn't money enough?" he replies. His tone is different. Giles is holding out on me.

"I know you too well, brother. You wouldn't do something like this just for the money." It's true. Father gives us all generous allowances. He threatened to take Giles' away when he wouldn't join the fraternity, but he eased up on that.

"Perhaps you're correct, but there are larger issues at hand," he replies. "Let me ask you a question. What do you want to do next year after graduation?" What does that have to do with anything? Is he trying to dodge the question?

"I don't know," I reply, honestly. "Some sort of business job. Maybe something Father can wrangle up? Is that an adequate answer?" It better be.

"Oh yes, that works quite well. So, just to clarify, there isn't something you desperately want to do above anything else? A passion project? It isn't Wall Street or bust?" He's isn't taking me on a merry go round. But where is this going? "I suppose not. It's good to be flexible, right? One should be open to whatever comes his way."

He slams his hand on the table. "Exactly brother," he exclaims. "We must not limit ourselves. And yet, that's exactly what our majors do. You're economics. I'm political science. But is that who we are? Let's say I want to work in business. Can you think of a good reason why I couldn't do that?"

I'm feeling a little lost. "No," is all I say. Feeling stupid, I add, "Is that what you want to do?"

He smiles again. "Maybe," he replies. "But that's not the point. What I learned from this little experiment was that I could effectively carry out a job involving explaining something to someone that I knew very little about. Most of what I taught her was regurgitated from shit I'd read in her books an hour before our sessions. I may not have been an expert, but I did my homework. I showed up to tutoring prepared to tell Charlotte what she needed to hear. Now, that might be unethical from the standpoint that I chose not to disclose that I wasn't really an expert on the subject, but who's to argue with my results?"

I think Giles has a few screws loose himself. "Fascinating," I say. "How do you expect to apply this to the real world?"

Giles waves at a girl with a pot of coffee to come over

and refill his cup. It's nice to see that some cafeterias haven't abandoned this completely. Serving yourself can be quite an effort.

"There's plenty of real world applications. Knowledge of the great unknown isn't important, Jacob. It's the perception of knowledge. You don't need to be an expert, provided those you deal with think you're capable of doing what they need you to do." He's on to something, but he's oversimplifying. Giles has a tendency to do that.

"Fair enough, but what happens when the jig is up and you find someone who's not a complete fool like Charlotte? Certainly then, you're going to be in trouble," I say. The girl with the coffee pot has brought me a cup. How sweet. I reach in my pocket for a coin to give her. Perhaps Giles should teach her American History, too. He might have better luck courting this lass.

Giles shakes his head at me. "You're looking for the worst in me when you fail to see what the whole point of this was. I wasn't trying to manufacture success. I was trying to see if I could create an opportunity. It's not about bullshitting people throughout the entire process, it's about bullshitting them long enough to get them to give you a chance. If I had told Charlotte I was studying political science, she would've just walked away. Well, in her particular case, maybe not, but again this was just a test. I got her to look at me and when I got the opportunity, I went and put some work into acquiring enough knowledge to keep the charade up. The illusion is for the opportunity. You still need to work for the payoff."

I've got to hand it to Giles. He won me over. His plan is more simplistic and less evil than I would've hoped, but it's a smart plan. He's right. Getting yourself in a position where people will even listen to you at all is hard enough.

"Well, your plan seems strong. Are you planning on putting it to use tonight?" I ask. "Perhaps you could teach Mary some tricks of the trade and she can find a husband there."

Giles flicks his nose a few times. A tell sign that he's backtracking in his thoughts. He says, "I think Mary has a date tonight with Thomas Jones. That lanky kid from South Carolina who runs cross country. That's what I heard this morning at breakfast."

What the fuck? "Why didn't you mention that when I said she and Aidan were coming tonight?" I say, louder than I would have liked. The coffee pot girl looks at me from a distance, possibly afraid that she's somehow to blame for this unpleasantness.

Giles bites his lip. I've got him here. "Slipped my mind. Who's informing her of the change of plans? You best do it. She wouldn't take kindly to my intrusion on her social calendar. This is all on you, anyway. Unless you want to invite Charlotte instead?"

No. Mary must come. Mother has asked for that and the Moores must stand together. Giles is also right in saying that I should be the one who goes to do the convincing. Fuck. What if Aidan wants to go over there? Maybe he thinks I'm there already.

I check my watch. *Dallas* must be almost over. Shit. If Aidan is going to make a move, it's going to be soon. But *Knot's Landing* comes on next. A rerun, but he'll undoubtedly stay for at least the first few minutes. Maybe he's finishing a cigarette. There's still a chance he's just lounging around like an idiot. He's probably not even thinking about going over there. Why would he? Because he's Aidan, that's why.

"Say Giles, would you mind doing me a favor?" I ask. Giles sighs. He doesn't want to be involved with this crap. "Would you mind popping over to my place to distract Aidan for a bit? I don't want him thinking he can swing by Mary's house to meddle around. Tell him you thought you'd pop in and help him pick something out for tonight. My closet if you must. That should be fun." It might actually be fun for Giles. He never misses an opportunity to instill culture upon Aidan, or anyone else for that matter.

Giles gives me a smirk that shows he doesn't completely hate what's being asked of him. "Fine Jacob. I can swing by your place and see what ol' Aidan is up to. I might even take him to my apartment and show him a few outfits for tonight's soiree. Your style can be so boring, brother." Giles sounds weird when he says outfits. He sounds a little too much like Mary.

We both stand up. Giles puts his stuff into his briefcase and drops some coins on the table. "I'll see you tonight," I say as I exit the cafeteria.

I forgot to tell Giles something important. About Father. Shit. It can wait. It must wait. Can it? Let's say he died tomorrow and Giles has a little conversation with Mother. She would definitely tell him that I knew. He would be most cross with me.

Or would he? Especially given the circumstances. It's not like I've made my peace with the man just yet. Mother didn't tell me to come home immediately. She told me to give their tickets to Mary and Aidan. Or was that code for come home? Women can be so deceptive. Another thing Giles could have helped with. He doesn't need to know just yet.

Stop it, Jacob. This can wait. This will wait. You've missed your opportunity to reveal the big news and now you have to take care of preparations for this evening. Figuring out what to do about Father can wait until tomorrow.

Off to Mary's. Oh, joy. Mary lives in a sorority house a few minutes away from here. The sorority houses are placed intentionally far away from the fraternity houses in a fairly futile effort to curtail intermingling. Like that would ever work. Many of my "brothers" spend a fair amount of time there. I only go when it's desperately asked of me. People tend to take advantage of the fact that a member of my kin lives with a big group of girls.

Mary is not a big fan of living there. She joined because Father recommended it and also because I joined a frat. Otherwise, she'd be perfectly happy living alone like Giles does. She's not much of a community dweller and takes no interest in the cleanliness of her surroundings. That's something that will have to change when she gets married. She'll make a fairly decent trophy wife for someone and not much else.

I should be more excited to enter a house filled with girls than I am. Aidan would be pissed if he knew I was going over here without him. That's what Giles is for. Hopefully he didn't decide to take matters into his own hands.

It's a larger house than mine. I think all the members live inside it, but I'm not entirely sure. Only a few of us live in mine. We had the option of expanding or moving into a new house, but that was voted down. Change can be such a burden to the people it affects.

I knock on the door. I know most of the girls, but I

don't feel comfortable entering without an invitation. Who knows what could be going on inside? Probably a pillow fight.

Annabelle St. James opens the door. A cute little blonde who's in a few of Mary's classes. At one point, I think she had a thing for me, but I was dating Beatrice Cooper at the time. That was then and this is now. But now is February of senior year, so where does that leave us? She's awfully cute.

"Hello Jacob Moore," she says with a sly tone. "What brings you here? Come to see Tyler?"

Tyler? "Who?" I ask. She laughs in a condescending manner as if I'm supposed to know who she's talking about. "Mary, you fool. As in Mary Tyler Moore. What were your parents thinking when they gave her that name?"

Good question. They probably didn't give a shit about popular culture. Probably still don't, except for soaps. Mary is an old family name on my mother's side. And *The Mary Tyler Moore Show* came on well after we were born. "I don't know. Why don't you ask my father what his thought process was?" You won't have much time to do that if what Mother says is true.

Annabelle rolls her eyes. "You're so serious all the time, Jacob. No wonder you can't get a date. Come on in." She acts as though the insults should be ignored. She's probably right about that. I shouldn't engage this nonsense.

Janice, Sophie, and another girl whose name I forget are sitting in the living room. "Girls, you remember Mary's brother, Jacob," Annabelle says, seemingly forgetting that my sister is supposed to have some sort of stupid nickname.

They say hello, almost in unison. I'm not sure what to think of their collective consciousness. "Care for a drink?" asks the one whose name escapes me. "We're drinking wine spritzers. They're all the rage in California."

What? "Uh, what's a wine spritzer?" I ask. Laughter ensues. Too bad Giles didn't come. He'd know what it was and he's got wine with him already.

"Silly Jacob," Annabelle says. "It's only white wine and club soda. Very refreshing," she says as she picks up her drink off a copy of *Cosmopolitan* on the table. Aside from the lowbrow magazines, the room is immaculately decorated with paintings that look like they belong in a museum but were painted by student artists. Not bad for a college dwelling.

There is something I don't quite understand. "Why would you mix white wine and club soda?" I ask. White wine is barely alcoholic as it is and diluting the taste doesn't really make much sense. Who wants watered-down wine?

More laughter from the peanut gallery. "It tastes good. That's why," Janice says. "Try it," she adds as she hands me her glass. I take a sip. It tastes like watered down wine. Big fucking surprise there.

"So?" I hear from one of the fools. I assume I'm supposed to give some sort of feedback on the beverage. "It's lovely," I say, hoping to avoid more laughter. It comes anyway. Louder this time.

"It's no different than putting water in whiskey, Jacob," Annabelle says. Jesus. Of course it is. Water opens up a whiskey. Just a little bit. None of this bullshit with soda water. How much did they put? Too much.

Don't engage. You won't win. The mob is against you. It's four against one and you didn't come here to argue the merits of not putting carbonated water into wine. You'd need Jesus' help to rectify that sludge. What would he have done at the Wedding at Cana if there were bubbles? He might be shit out of luck.

"Where's my sister?" I ask. I sound less polite than I'd hoped. I hand Janice back her watery wine. I know the answer, but asking gives me permission to seek her out and to ditch this conversation. It wouldn't look good for a boy to travel up the stairs of a sorority house without permission.

"Where do you think?" Sophie replies. "Up in her room. She's a bit moody. It might be the time of her moon blood." I hear a unanimous gross from the other girls. No spritzers were harmed in the making of that vile comment.

I bid adieu and make my way upstairs. Moon blood. Disgusting. No wonder Mary hates living with these wretched creatures.

I knock on her bedroom door. No answer. Typical. I knock again. "Go away, I'm busy," replies my sister. Bullshit. She never does anything. I go inside.

"I told you not to come… oh, hello Jacob," Mary says. She's lying on her bed. She doesn't appear to be napping. Who was she expecting? A record is on her turntable.

"What are you doing, sister?" I ask, unsure that I want to hear the answer to that. Well, I guess it couldn't be that bad. Unless she was masturbating.

She scowls. Typical. "I was listening to *With Sympathy* by Ministry, but side A is over. Be a dear and flip it over on your way out. Ta-ta brother." She barely moves on her bed.

I ignore her request. I don't care to listen to Mary's music. That's not why I came. I came to convince her to come to the party tonight. Mother's wishes.

"We need you to come to the party for the Senator tonight. Giles and Aidan will be there too. Our parents cannot come." I neglect to tell her why.

"I cannot come tonight, Jacob. I have plans," she replies without lifting her head off her bed. She's staring at the ceiling. Doesn't ask why they can't come. Also neglects to elaborate.

Which forces me to. "And what might those be?" I ask. She sits up on her bed and stares at me. She says, "A date if that's believable enough for you." She doesn't mention the name of the lucky man. Mary loves to brag about the boys who took her out, at least she used to. Not so much lately. The fact that she didn't mention him by name shows that she's not proud of what she's doing. This is good.

"A date," I reply. "With whom? How long has this been on your social calendar? I saw you the day before yesterday and you neglected to say anything." She should take the hint. I'm onto her.

She scoffs at me. How rude. "Must I tell you everything? It's Thomas Jones. There. Now are you happy that you know bloody everything going on in my life?"

Thomas Jones is a lanky boy who wears a dinner jacket to class sometimes. Bizarre fellow. Definitely not Mary's type. I don't like this. Mary can do better.

"Thomas Jones," I reply, taking careful consideration to say the name as slowly as possible to maximize my blatant disapproval. Truth be told, I have nothing against the man. I hardly know him. But tonight, I must ruin his evening. My sister must come with me.

"Yes Jacob, Thomas Jones. We're going to some bar-beque place he recommended. Classy, I know, but do you really think we're going to find some upscale Italian restaurant around here?" Of course I do. Sister is trying to justify her actions. This will end well for me.

I don't want to be rude, but I fear I must walk that line a bit. "Don't sell yourself short, Mary. This guy comes out of the blue to ask you to eat at some ribs place as a first date. And you say yes. What is wrong with you? That's certainly not the Mary that I know." Bam. That'll do it. Excellent. There's no way she'll want to come across as easy.

Mary is getting a little red in the face. This must be hard for her. "Oh stop it, Jacob. As if you've never gone on a date with someone below you. Who was that bimbo last year?" She's talking about Valerie. She's not entirely wrong. Valerie was a sweet girl, but she wouldn't do. Giles and Mary laughed and laughed. Aidan didn't mind, prob-ably because he would have wanted to make moves in the event that she and I didn't work out. I can't remember if he tried. No. It doesn't make sense to deny it. It doesn't matter.

"I didn't waste my time on people beneath me when I had family obligations. And I was not the one who was asked on short notice. Being the one who does the asking is much different. Don't try to defend your poor decision. Give his place a ring, pick out a dress, and be done with this nonsense." There's a good man.

What's that? It better not be a tear in Mary's eye. She tilts her head so her long brown hair covers her face a bit. She squirms around in a defensive manner, grabbing the covers. Just cancel the date and be done with this already.

"Jake you don't know what it's like. You can't," she whines. Melodrama. Mary's specialty. And Mother's. And Giles'.

I don't want to entertain this nonsense, but I don't have much of a choice if I want to have my way. If I'm too hard on her, she'll pull back and I won't get anything at all. "Tell me what's the matter, sister. I'm sure it's not so bad." That depends on the problem.

She glares at me, clearly angry at the notion that I might know how to fix her problems without knowing what they are. "Oh really? Do you know how many girls in my grade are engaged? It's ridiculous. How am I supposed to feel? Am I supposed to put on some fake smile and pretend like I'm happy for those bitches? No, it's bullshit, Jacob. Where is *my* ring?"

The true bullshit is what Mary's really all pissed off about. She doesn't care if she finds a husband this year. In fact, she'd probably prefer if she didn't. She doesn't want to get pregnant and start a family anytime soon. That's not what's at stake.

Pride. Which is stupid since the value of said pride is less than the marriage that would come with it as a prerequisite. Mary could get married to Thomas Jones tomorrow if she wanted to. Engaged at least. That would certainly solve her predicament. But she's not going to do that. She values her position. She just doesn't like it.

"Mary, it's 1985. The notion that you should be married in college, or immediately after, is absurd. You don't need to worry about that. You shouldn't worry about that."

True. We live in an area that one might consider behind the times in some regards. But we don't have to let that control us. It's controlling her now because she's letting it. I need to put an end to that. I must be in control.

She gives me a blank expression like I'm stating the obvious or something. "Oh really? I wasn't aware. Since you're so full of answers, why don't you tell me this, what am I going to do next year?" She looks helpless.

We've found the root of the problem. Mary doesn't want to get married. She doesn't want to work. Ah. She's jealous because she knows there are people who don't have to do shit next year except sit around and watch *Dallas* and the daytime soaps. Bingo.

I know what to do. I must make sure she understands the value of coming tonight. That will do the trick.

"What's the real reason you're hesitant to cancel on this guy?" I ask. "You've never been one to care about reneging on plans with men. Unless of course you really want to go. Maybe you've got a little crush on dear Thomas." Excellent work Jacob.

Mary moves closer to me. "No Jacob, don't be stupid. It's out of principle. I'm not going to cancel with him just because you tell me to. You're not my father."

A crossroads. Now could be the perfect time to tell her about Father's condition. Well, the perfect time would be never as I could have just told Giles and his gossipy nature would have taken care of the rest. But that ship has sailed. For today. That's something to consider.

Is that the only way? No, of course not. You don't have to lay down the law as the patriarch. You need to lay down the law for the patriarch.

"I'm not telling you to - Father is," Yes. "He told me to make sure that you and Aidan take his and Mother's place. I am relaying his orders. If you choose to go on your date, just know that you're disobeying him, not me."

Lies. They're Mother's orders. That doesn't matter to me. Mary is more likely to do something if she thinks it's what Father wants.

But why do I care really? I could just as easily find someone else to go. One of my housemates or a girl downstairs. There are many choices.

Yet, I'm pushing hard for Mary to come to this. It's not about the event, it's about the power I need to have as the head of this family. Mother won't do anything when Father goes. She'll nag me to do everything and that means I need to be the one who can make shit happen. Like this.

"Ugh. This is stupid. Can't you just tell him that I went? I don't even want to go." The cracks start to surface. I'm making progress, but I'm not home free yet.

"You know I can't do that," I say, trying to sound sympathetic to her cause. It is somewhat unfortunate that she has to miss her date for this. "But what would Father's friends say if they only saw his sons in his stead? We need to look united if he's unwell. We are the next generation, Mary. Besides, why wouldn't you want to meet a senator? There might even be eligible bachelors there. Ones that are much more appealing than Thomas Jones. It's good for appearances, Mary. I know you care about that."

Bullshit. There is no real reason we have to look united. In public, I mean. This is all bullshit. It would be nice to be united for my sake.

The important thing is that Mary feels like she's part of something. Her being there needs to matter, even if it only matters to me. And Aidan.

"Besides," I add, "Aidan will be there. Surely he's a

better match for you than Thomas Jones." Mary is bound to get sick of him if I keep saying his name.

She laughs. "Of course you would think that. He's your best friend. That swamp rat has made progress over the years, but he's hardly husband material. Maybe once he has his fancy company."

I feel defensive hearing the swamp rat comment. Mary is hardly in a position to judge someone like Aidan. "Oh, don't be a snob, Mary. You could do far worse than Aidan. He's determined to make something of himself in this world and you'd be wise not to bet against him."

Hang on a second. Was that acting or do I actually believe what I'm saying? Am I defending Aidan as a legitimate match for my sister? It looks like it. Perhaps I'm talking him up because I want to join him in his little postgraduate business endeavor. Fucking subconscious.

"He's a work in progress, I'll give you that." Mary seems to have formulated an opinion on my dear friend's prospects. I never said he was a work in progress, but it doesn't behoove me to correct her. "Perhaps he's worth another chance. Fine," she adds.

What have I done? I don't want Aidan and Mary sweet-talking each other at the party. That's one of the last things I want. I don't want it. Well, maybe I do. Maybe that's exactly what Mother wants. She did request Aidan's presence in her absence.

My work here is done for now. Mary is coming and all is right with the world, until the next catastrophe strikes. Who knows what her behavior will be like at the party? It'll probably leave much to be desired. That's not my problem. Her sobriety isn't a problem either unless it becomes a problem.

I should go and get ready. "Be outside the Grant building at a quarter after six. We'll go in and have a drink before the speech starts and all that shit. Don't drink too much beforehand." She'll probably be late and drunk, but the prospect of having catered cocktails before the festivities start might compel her to make an effort. That isn't my problem. Sort of.

She looks confused. "What, no one is coming to pick me up?" she asks. Fair question, especially from a self-proclaimed Southern Belle. But no. No time to waste with the Aidan/Mary games that would follow from an invitation inside the house for a couple glasses of watered down wine. Maybe there is. It's best to keep the two of them separated until we get there and it doesn't matter. Besides, bringing Aidan around here is the quickest way to ensure that he would find out that Mary had a date and then he'd be grumpy all night. That wouldn't do.

"What sister? Do you want me to bring Giles and the swamp dweller over? Too much snobbery for one and too little for the other. What an interesting combination." Playing the game of logic with Mary simply requires you to be one step ahead of her thought process at all times. Not a tall order.

Mary isn't actually a bad student, though her studies are a joke. I shouldn't say she *isn't* a bad student, as I don't know what sort of work she actually does. I imagine very little. But her grades aren't completely crap and that's enough to keep our parents at bay. That's enough for me.

She pauses, adjusting her spot on the bed. "I suppose you're right. Aidan would make a fool of himself in front of these creatures and Giles would just make fools of them. Well, actually, Giles might like a spritzer or two. Is he bringing anyone tonight? How long has it been since our brother had a date? Longer than you, I'd say. Did the two of you take a vow of chastity? How cute."

Mary and Giles have an interesting relationship. They're more similar than either would ever care to admit, but that only works to their benefit a small portion of the time. Giles is the smartest out of the three of us and doesn't care to hide that from anyone. Which leads Mary to grow frustrated as she often does for whatever reason. And then she can get a little nasty.

Which is what she's doing here. She's hinting at the potential problems with Giles' love life. It's no secret Giles could very well be a homosexual. He also just might not be attracted to women at this university. They tend to fit a sort of mold, which he just might not be into, being a man with worldly ambitions. Either way, it's not for us to care unless he makes decisions which impact the rest of us. I suppose I might be expected to care when I'm patriarch, but that time hasn't come yet. It's on its merry fucking way.

"Actually sister, I just came from the cafeteria where I saw him chatting it up with a cute little blonde girl." Not lies, though not the full story, either. Giles would never go for Charlotte but she was cute and he was chatting with her. Mary looks unconvinced.

"Well, how about that? Father will be so pleased. Maybe he'll turn his focus to Giles instead of you if he can manage to get his act together. What will you do then, brother?"

If only you knew. A battle for a different day. I really should go. Mary must get ready and so must I. "I'll cross that road when I come to it. See you in two hours. Don't be late or you'll miss the free cocktails." That'll get her there. I give her a hug before I go. She smells of perfume meant to mask alcohol. Vodka probably. She's coherent so it's not my problem. But I will need to keep an eye on her.

I exit through the back door in the kitchen. I discovered this escape in October when I bedded Mary's "sister" Katherine. A fool who wanted no-strings-attached coitus that day. That's precisely what she got. Katherine took the semester off. Must not have been enough strings attached. How tragic. Not for me anyway.

The girls' voices carry into the kitchen. Filled with wonderful things to say. No, not really. Fools with their wine drinks. Wine goes with wine. To think some of these types of girls might actually be at the same parties as me someday. The ones I'm supposed to be interested in. The horror. I hope none of them are present tonight. I'm not ready for that crap.

I should be thinking about marriage more than I have been. If I'm to run the family, I need to carry on the family line. Mother will undoubtedly hound me about it. Of all the things I could blame her for caring too much about, I'm not sure that would be one of them.

Survival. Not just in this life, but after it. It's primitive, but it's not wrong. Of course she cares about her family's future. I don't. Not yet. Why should I? Would that solve all my problems? Indecisive about your future, here's a fucking kid. Now stop your pondering and clean up its shit. That'll fix everything. Jesus.

I'm hungry. It's not time for a meal. Time for a cigarette. Puff, puff, puff. A walk through a campus is never complete without a cigarette. A flask could help, but it's not mandatory. Not like a cigarette. They say smoking kills, but smoking relieves stress. Stress kills, too. Always a bigger fish out there ready to gobble you up. You just need to be able to pick your poison properly.

Chew and dip never interested me. You lose the urgency when you're not holding something burning, and then you forget it's there. Which can be rather off-putting if you decide you want to clear your throat and find all that juice down where it doesn't belong. Aidan chews from time to time. He makes spittoons out of our cups when he does. Jeremiah doesn't like that. Who would?

I hope Aidan is ready by the time I get back. I don't worry about Giles, but Aidan often needs a push in the right direction. After dealing with my sister, I'm not particularly in the mood to be a babysitter for a bunch of should-be adults. It shouldn't be my burden and yet it is. Such is life.

Is this what it's going to be like when Father is gone? Well, possibly. It would be worse if Mary or Giles were younger, but we're not dealing with a bunch of children in that sense. That might be too much to handle. Could you imagine having to raise your siblings? Mary is bad enough as a twin.

How does that affect the New York City plans? Why had I not thought of that before? Because it's a dream. Not a reality. If your reality is staying in Georgia to manage Father's estate for a few years, so be it. Do your duty to your family. There's no point in taking Aidan's shit seriously until he can piece together some capital, anyway. Who knows when that will be?

And then what? Does plausibility affect actuality? One would think. But how much? If I'm entrenched where I am and I have a woman, why change that? For

Aidan's dream? No. Send Giles instead. He wants to branch out, he can become Aidan's partner in financial glory. Take your fortune where you can find it.

My path is clear. No, it isn't. It's clear to a point. A point that isn't necessarily clear itself. There's no timeline on Father. Hence, there's no reason to think my next move is set in stone. I don't need to move back home to take care of him. That would be Mary's job if they couldn't afford to hire help, which they could. She'll just be there, anyway. Mary's best bet for next year is to sit around while Father finds a match for her.

But where does that leave me? Work. Somewhere. Obviously, I'm not going to sit around in the prime of my life. Mary will. But where? And what?

Therein lies the appeal of the plan of my good friend Aidan. Fuck. I don't want to flip-flop on key issues. Yes, the little plan of owning my own business is lovely. It is a wonderful dream. That goes for everyone else in this goddamned world. Opportunity. That's what he needs. If he can find that, I'll be on board.

Puff, puff. That's better. The stress of finding things to be stressed about is stressful. Mother prefers for me to feel this way. Misery loves company. She can sit back in her chair tonight and think about her son Jacob and how he's struggling to make sense of the world around him. All thanks to her. I love you Mother. Sometimes.

There is another alternative, of course. Well, one that leads to many other possibilities. What the hell is keeping me here? Or anywhere, for that matter? This is America. I can go wherever I please. And if nothing pleases me, I can just go somewhere else. Why do they say the world is my oyster? Oysters are slimy. Now if Aidan had said that,

I would've criticized him for being a redneck. So why can I say it? Double standards.

It's stupid, but that's the way life is. Well, no. It isn't entirely stupid. Or unjust. Aidan is a swamp dweller who put in the time to disguise that fact from most people. He can go to parties and talk and people will listen to what he has to say. Or would they? A rich slob who wanted to talk about nothing but cheap beer and heavy metal wouldn't last long at a party no matter who his family was. Is that messed up? I don't know.

We see the world in large generalizations and that puts us down. What is down can come up and what is up can fall. The difference, of course, is that one requires you to exert more effort than the other. People don't like effort. It tires you out.

The lazy people will get their due, just slower than the rest of us. Isn't that just a little ironic? No, it's just hard to fathom if you look at the world from a black and white perspective. If you're lazy, it takes longer for you just to experience the joys of an unfulfilled life. Or maybe money is the real concern and those people already have money. Why chase what you already have? We can never be sure.

Aidan doesn't put down the rich. Giles and Mary do, but that's because we're rich, too. Not as rich as everyone thinks, but my family is doing more than all right. It wasn't always that way, but those days were before I was born, so it might as well be.

Which puts Aidan above many of the other people at our university, especially the ones we have class with. He works hard. You can basically divide our class into two groups - the boys at least. You've got the ones who hope to follow in their father's footsteps, or their father's friends' footsteps. In that way, class is almost just a formality. A way to get the opportunities that they would get anyway, by birthright.

Giles isn't too far off in his theory that most of this shit can be picked up on the quick, provided no one around is staring right through your bullshit at precisely the time you choose to deliver it. The factor Giles left out is that with this particular group of people, you almost don't even need to put up a front with the bullshit. The minimal amount of effort will suffice. Depending on who you know.

Which of course incurs the wrath of the second group, the dreamers. Those who think the world rewards hard work on a linear scale. *X* amount of work *equals Y* amount of reward. Makes sense, right? Wrong. The work is only done to put you in sight of the reward. It doesn't need to happen at all depending on where you started. And where you started could determine if you see the reward at all. But for this group, they're bitter that they didn't get to start somewhere pretty. Like me. Or countless other members of my class. Now that does suck, but what can you do? Our country has already had its revolution.

Resentment makes perfect sense. I don't resent the resentful. It's no different from a poker game where one person is dealt pocket aces while the other gets a two-seven offsuit. Sucks doesn't it? For one of them at least. Doesn't change the way the cards were dealt. That's just how it goes.

Which makes Aidan a special case. Born out of nothing and yet, you wouldn't be able to tell it on his face like you would many other people. You wouldn't hear it come out of his mouth, either. Unless he was talking about his mother's crawfish. Pride exists where it is cultivated. That's how Jeremiah can take pride in his work, just the same as Father could. One makes more than the other, but both excel at the tasks put before them. What we see is excellence in various shades.

But what does Aidan see? A way up? I hope so. I wish him well. I wish to join him, though I don't know how. Father's health makes the concept of borrowing money difficult. Especially at stage one in the game. If we can figure out a way to show that we're serious, we can get somewhere.

And that's the problem. Aidan is serious. I am not. Not yet. I want to be, but snapping your finger and clicking your ruby slippers together doesn't quite solve everything. Does it solve anything? Wouldn't that be nice? I am serious. Badda-bing, badda-boom. Hardly. A man can dream, but he can also do a lot of things.

Like figure shit out. Blah. No. Yes. Maybe. Not now. Right. You can't just call Father up on the phone and demand money. There must be a plan. Responsibility.

Or maybe he should just trust you. Maybe he does already. You're supposed to be the new patriarch, right? Isn't that word marvelous? That comes with an added bonus of being expected to achieve greatness. Preferably you get some fucking help along the way. Only preferably, though. You're capable of that because someone said you were. That alone puts you in the position.

No, it doesn't. That's what entitlement tries to do. You fail to understand that because your eye is set on the prize and not the journey it takes to achieve greatness.

But what is the prize? Money? You've got that. Women? You can get one of those when you want to.

Simply say, "I'm Jacob Moore. My father was something, so that makes me something." A wonderful pickup line.

Pride? Yes. Now we're onto something. We must seek a justification for our emotions. Without just cause, the principle of it all feels so droll. But it isn't droll if it makes sense. We have figured it all out.

I wonder if Giles thinks about this sort of stuff. I would imagine so since he's in pursuit of something greater than his studies. If he was content, he'd do far less than what he does now. Limitations. Giles doesn't see them in places where they're quite common. In places I see them. He does what he sees himself capable of doing and lets the world be damned. Yes, that's what living must feel like.

And now what? I see those houses right before my eyes. Who cares? Another day, another dollar. Well, no dollars. Not yet, at least. Eventually.

I walk inside. That's the beauty of belonging somewhere. You don't need to be invited in. Like the *Cheers* bar that Aidan loves so much. That isn't real. This is. Similar?

"Hello," calls a chorus of my friends and family. Here's Sam, David, and Charlie along with Giles and Aidan. Everyone has a beer. Except for Giles. He appears to have a glass of whiskey. Or Aidan's Canadian Club. Which is rye, not whiskey. Although rye is whiskey so maybe it is. It's fine, as long as I don't have to drink any more of it.

David hands me a beer. Pabst Blue Ribbon. Wonderful. "Cheers," I say, to the room. My good wishes are reciprocated. Isn't that nice? They like me. They really like me.

I turn my attention to my brother and my closest friend. Giles is wearing a gray suit with a pink tie. His signature look that blends his taste for Southern charm with modern fashion. His words, not mine. Typical style and yet he looks classy with his matching pink pocket square and his slightly pomaded short hair.

And look at Aidan. Sports coat with slacks, a checkered tie with a matching pocket square. No pomade in that scraggly blond mess of his. Giles' work no doubt. The square is unusual, but it looks good. One might think that Giles did that to make a fool out of Aidan. And that would be an unfair assumption.

Giles is merely working with what he's got. Aidan's broad shoulders and limited budget restrict the wardrobe possibilities. He can fit into his pants though and they've done well coordinating the outfit with Aidan's sports jacket, a well-worn but classy piece. Aidan looks good.

"You're looking sharp my friend," I say to Aidan as I sit down next to him. He is the kind of person who needs reassuring praise. My world is, after all, far different from his. Thankfully, he knows how to take advice from a person like Giles. Giles never needs praise from anyone but himself. Mary would never let him mess with her style, even though she could use it. Especially if she wants to find a husband.

"I'm glad to have the best to work with a scallywag like me," he replies as he hands me the bottle of whiskey. I take a sip and wash it down with my beer. Yuck. There's been considerable damage done to this bottle. I hope Aidan and Giles aren't too drunk for tonight. That would be most embarrassing.

Should I light another cigarette? Yes. The answer to that should always be yes. Shit, don't I need to get ready? Of course. Fuck.

"Gentlemen, I must get ready," I say as I stand up like

it's some matter of importance. Don't let this patriarch stuff go to your fucking head. I take my beer with me to my room. I can drink and dress. Isn't it nice that humanity has reached such a high level?

My room is fairly plain. I used to have posters up, but that hasn't been a top priority now that I'm a senior. Aidan still has a Lynyrd Skynyrd poster up in his room. He shares with David, but I get my own room since my father was an important figure in our little fraternity of men.

Suit or sports coat? Doesn't matter really. A suit might make me look more presentable in Mother's eyes, but Mother won't be there to see. Jacket and slacks it is. No pocket square. Not my style.

I unbutton my shirt to replace it with a fresh one. I'd shower, but I took one this morning and chances are that Aidan's been in there using up all the hot water. As I start to take my belt off to change my pants, I hear a knock on my door.

"Go away unless you want to see me naked," I call out. I hear a, "Wouldn't be the first time," and Giles opens the door. So much for courtesy. The world lacks a proper understanding of courtesy.

I should be bothered by this intrusion of privacy, but I'm not. Giles is family. He doesn't care how I look. I hope not.

"I came in to see if you needed any wardrobe advice seeing as I did such a good job with Aidan. I didn't think much of the pocket square at first, but it's been growing on me. Which is probably for the best since it's my pocket square." He sips his whiskey. He appears to be a bit intoxicated.

I don't really need help, but I indulge him anyway. "What color tie?" I ask, holding up my rack. He spots the one on the end and replies, "Peach. Represent the home state for that West Coast hooligan." He laughs.

"Hooligan," I reply. "Don't care much for politicians? Seems a bit strange given your area of study." This could open up a train of thought I'll probably regret in a matter of minutes.

He takes another sip and clears his throat. "Well, we don't want to lump them all into one category brother. That wouldn't be nice. I don't hate all politicians. Just the ones who genuinely think it's their duty to try to convince people that they're going to save the world. All of them think that they're fucking geniuses, but it's how they project themselves that really interests me." I'm not really sure what that means.

Do I care to ask more about this theory? No, but I'm getting dressed and it's something to pass the time. "So I guess you'll hear what he has to say with an open mind then? Going to give him a fair shake?" I ask. Was that a backhanded compliment? I didn't intend it to be, but I fear that's how it sounded. Oh well.

He laughs. "I suppose. I'm not even sure what the point of this thing is. He comes, says a few words, has some drinks, and then leaves to go to a different school to say the exact same thing. Which is what they all do, so I can't hate him for that. But what's the point? Why is he here unless it's all for some preliminary presidential mumbo jumbo? Probably wants money. I'm not going to hate him at all unless he wants to preach about the similarities between the Northwest and the Southern mentalities that they all seem to think exist. Blah, blah - who gives a fuck? Say something original or shut the fuck up." He laughs again.

Oh, Giles. "Well, in any event, it's a party with free drinks and those little whore's ovaries. Or, hors d'oeuvres, as the civilized folk say. I don't give a shit about the speaker. Senator. Really, it's all about the free booze."

Giles sits down in my chair. "Who's the one who isn't being open-minded now, brother? You don't give a shit what he has to say? How rude. What if he wants to give you free candy?" He laughs some more. Giles should watch the whiskey.

"It's not that," I reply. "I just don't care about politics. People talk and then sometimes, some small thing gets done. Occasionally, it's a big thing. But it's usually just nothing. Does it affect me? Yes, I guess, but how? I don't know and I don't care to. Why bother when there are better things going on to care about? There isn't going to be another war. Aidan feels the same way."

Giles starts to play with one of my pencils. He's twirling it around in his hand. "Oh, I wouldn't write Aidan off. He was trying to tell me about some plan for a loan to start a business. He says that if all goes well you'll join him and he'll take Mary as his wife. What a catch! He can have her without the loan. Free to a good home." He chuckles some more.

Here's an opportunity for some revelations. My brother's commentary could come in handy.

"What did you think?" I ask as I put my tie around my neck. Perhaps Giles' opinion could shed some light on whether or not Aidan's master plan has a realistic shot at becoming a reality. Our reality. My reality.

Giles smiles and puts his feet up on my desk. He's

getting comfortable. Signature Giles. He loves it when people ask for his opinion on other people. It validates his gossipy behavior.

"There's no denying your friend talks a big game. He's sort of sweet under all the insecurity. He's desperate to be a part of something great and he only tries a little to hide that. He's not unique in that aspect, but he's smart. In his own way."

He didn't answer my question. Probably on purpose knowing him. I take a sip of my beer and bite the bullet. "You didn't say what you thought of his plan." Giles smiles. Fuck. I knew it. He was jerking me around.

"Ah, now I see. You do want to go into business with him. How romantic. A unification of Houses Moore and Davies. I fail to see what Aidan gets out of this? Who wants to have Mary as his wife? Yuck. The plan? Obviously it needs work. That goes for any scheme hatched by a college kid. The question that must be asked is whether or not you think he's capable of following through on his lofty intentions. That's all that matters. Talk is cheap."

He's right. That is all that matters. I face the question of whether or not this is a reality or a senior year pipeline dream. Should I have faith in Aidan or not? Furthermore, is that a question that needs to be answered now? It'd be nice.

"Well," Giles says. "Now it's your turn to answer the question. Is your buddy legit or not?" He drops the pencil onto the desk.

"Yes," I answer. Words. Well, word, in this case. It doesn't really change anything. Life will continue regardless of the answer. Giles might stop heckling me, which makes it all worth it for the here and now.

I finish dressing and we head downstairs. My hair is just a bit messy, but I keep it that way. A little chaos is always nice. Thank you pomade.

"We should go," I say to Aidan as we reach the living room. He gleefully stands up and leans over to put the Canadian Club bottle behind the sofa. He slips a flask into his back pocket. I hope he hasn't forgotten about the open bar.

That leaves Sam as the only person still in the room. He's a man of few words. He might be bummed that he's not going to this little party, but he wouldn't make a show of it. Good man. The world needs people like him.

"A bunch of us are going to The Old Barn for dinner and drinks afterwards if you guys finish at a reasonable hour," he says. "I think some of the sororities should be there." How thoughtful. We go to an exclusive party with a member of the United States Senate and my "brother" still thinks to invite us to an old romp around with some of the ladies.

"We'll see you there, Sam," I say and we take our leave. Jeremiah is smoking his pipe on the front porch. I probably should have rolled more cigarettes. Fuck. "Have a good time, gentlemen," he says and we give him a wave.

And we're off. The gathering will take place outside the Grant Building in a small secluded area. I don't imagine there will be much more than a hundred people there. A decent sized crowd.

"Are we picking up Mary?" Aidan asks. Of course he would ask that. "No. She's meeting us there," I reply. Precisely for this reason you shit. "Oh," Aidan says. He doesn't like that. He wants it to be more of a date. "Is she going to the Barn afterwards?" he asks.

This is where Aidan could really use some work in the social grace department. Here he is with Mary's two brothers, and yet he insists upon blatantly pining after her. Now, one might be tempted to excuse him given his relationship with said brothers, but it's still something that should be addressed. He cannot go unchecked. That would be the cause of all of our undoing.

"I don't know, Aidan," I start to say, "you should probably ask her yourself. In a way that doesn't cause some big scene." Yikes. There was definitely no mincing of words there. My brotherly/apprentice patriarchal instincts kicked in.

"What Jacob means to say is that many of our parents' friends will be there tonight." Giles to the rescue. "Given Mary's often-temperamental disposition, it wouldn't be wise to go hard with the public courting. You understand of course?"

Aidan nods his head and pulls out a cigarette. He offers one to Giles and me. I accept. Giles declines. "Yes. Good call. Thank you. I meant no disrespect, of course. I can get wrapped a bit with things like that. You know, ideas that seem better in your mind than they are when you say them out loud?"

Giles shoots me an amused look, making me think back to our previous conversation. "Now, now dear friend. There was nothing wrong with your plan. Mary is quite fond of you. We must be sure that your execution is top notch. Mary is not one to let go of mistakes easily."

He's right of course, but his motives aren't for the sake of truth. Well, I can't be sure of his motives. He could just be doing it to fuck around with Mary. That would hardly be surprising. But is that all he's up to?

Is it possible that brother considers Aidan to be a friend? What an odd thought. Giles is a peculiar man when it comes to friends. He goes out and charms people at parties and functions. But then that's it. He doesn't turn it into anything more. He doesn't care for friends even though he possesses the means to acquire them. It drives Mary nuts because she can't figure out what the hell is wrong with him. Maybe nothing? Who am I to judge?

"You're probably right, Giles," Aidan says. "You'd know her better than most." Yes, but is that a good thing? It could be.

What effect would Giles' stamp of approval have on Aidan's chances with Mary? The simple answer would be very little. It might even have a negative effect if she thought there was something queer about it. It would be out of character for Giles to interject in such a manner. He meddles, but not with Mary's love life.

Which is why his opinion could be important. Giles dislikes most people. If he were to approve of one of Mary's suitors, she might take him seriously, especially given my own friendship with the man. These are deep waters.

"Don't waste your cigarette good friend," Aidan says. He gives me a pat on the back. He pulls out his flask and takes a swig. He offers it to Giles, who readily accepts. I decline. I should have my bearings straight for tonight, or at least until the older folks have had a chance to catch up, what with their diminished capacities.

We approach the building. Mary is standing outside in a blue dress with stockings and heels. Very ladylike. I guess I shouldn't be surprised. Moody as she might be, Mary would never show up to a party looking like a ragamuffin.

She pretends not to notice us as we make our approach. Giles snickers but Aidan pays it little attention. "My dearest Miss Moore," Aidan says as he breaks away from us to kiss her hand. Good grief. She rolls her eyes. So much for casual.

"Ah Aidan. Whatever brings you to this congregation? A guest of my brother, I presume?" She's fucking with him. I can't tell what to make of that given her solemn attitude earlier coupled with her general demeanor.

"Mary," Giles says, in a sarcastic attempt at formality. Both can appreciate the gesture. She nods at Giles and then at me. I feel an obligation to say something. It always falls on me to squash awkward silences.

"Isn't this nice? The three Moore siblings and our cherished friend Aidan," I say. My tone drops off around the point I say cherished, as I realize how stupid that sounds. Some head of the family you'll make. Giles laughs. Mary simply looks confused. "Isn't that sap supposed to be saved for toasts?" she asks. "Or perhaps not at all. I'm fine with whichever." I suppose she makes a fair point.

"Shall we go in?" Giles asks. He can often be more difficult than he needs to be, but he appears to be in my corner for tonight at least carrying some of the burden of shepherding this crew around. We approach the check-in desk, which is manned by an elderly lady and a girl who appears to be a fellow student. I see a security guard a few feet away.

"Hello, I'm Jacob Moore. My brother Giles and I are on the guest list. My father came down with an illness so he and my mother will not be able to attend. In their place

I've brought my sister Mary and my friend Aidan Davies. I hope that's all right."

What if it isn't? Would they really tell us to get lost? Tough fucking shit. I take a drag of what's left of my cigarette.

The woman looks more saddened by this news than she should be. "Oh, I know your mother Meredith quite well," she says. Doubtful, I don't know who you are woman and I go to this school. You can't be very important.

She adds, "That's quite all right, I'll make an adjustment to the list for security purposes. There's a coat check in the corner over there. Have a lovely evening." Good. I'm spared the small talk with this woman who probably *doesn't* know my mother "quite well."

None of us have bags so we proceed into the outdoor-gated area. There's a bar set up in the corner and a bunch of chairs stationed in front of a podium. You would never guess a senator was to speak here in just a little while. It doesn't have the extravagance that we've come to expect from Washington.

"You didn't put us on the guest list?" Aidan asks, once we're out of earshot of the table and anyone else who might hear. He's embarrassed. Seriously? Fuck that.

"No. There was no time for that and it doesn't matter," I reply. "I found out just a few hours ago." He looks angry. Why? What a jackass. I take back all the nice things I've said about him.

"I agree with Aidan. This is most unacceptable. You force us to come to this function and you don't even bother to make sure we're properly addressed. Ridiculous brother." Great. Mary had to jump on the bandwagon.

I glance at Giles with a pleading look in my eyes. I

don't want this to get out of hand. Not this early in the evening. "Come Aidan, let's get drinks. Mary, do you want a white wine?" he asks as he grabs Aidan away. Divide and conquer. Excellent. I wonder if he learned that in his tutoring reading.

"Yes, with nothing in it—no club soda," Mary replies. Giles looks confused, but he leaves without further questioning.

It's just Mary and me again. Charming. The area is starting to fill up, but I don't see anyone I know and I don't care to engage strangers in casual conversation until I've had a proper drink in me. No cheap beer or shitty rye.

"Do you have to pile on at an event like this?" I ask my sister. She starts to laugh but stops as I glare, trying to convey my frustration through the telepathic twin connection. I doubt that's even a real thing.

"Come now, brother. I thought you'd be pleased that I took your little friend's side. If you're going to limit what I can say amongst our own company, you should've let me go on my date. Thomas Jones doesn't care if I make fun of you."

Some of what she's said is fair, but she doesn't need to know that. "It's not that. It's your filter. Or lack of one. You can't undermine me in places like this. It makes our family look bad. What would Mother say?"

Mary licks her lips. She's thinking. "Undermine you? When have you ever cared about that?" She pauses and then adds, "you're hiding something."

Yes. Does she know that? Or is she just saying it to gauge my reaction? I don't think so. I hope not. "I'm not hiding anything," I reply. "I merely don't want to be made to look like a fool by my sister at an important event. Is that too much to ask?" I hope that did the trick.

"You forget we shared a womb. I know how you are, Jacob. You know something you're not telling me. Your hand is twitching and you're practically tearing apart that cigarette filter with your teeth. Tell me why our parents aren't here. Is something wrong with Father?"

Fuck. She's onto me. How? That womb shit is pure nonsense. But no one else knows. I doubt she talked to Mother or she would have said something already. But something is fishy.

Or maybe you're reading too much into it. Don't be paranoid. That's what gave you away in the first place. I toss the cigarette onto the floor. It was done anyway. How do I get out of this one?

I know. I don't have to get out of it completely. "Father is sick. I told you that earlier. As the oldest, I'm the one representing the family. Friends of our parents are here. That is why you are not to make a mockery of me. Understand?" There we go. I've made my point without telling her that our Father will be dead soon.

She flips her hand at me. She probably doesn't believe me. Of course she doesn't. That's Mary for you. Giles and Aidan return with the drinks. "I got you a bourbon old fashioned, old chap," Aidan says. He's in better spirits. Perhaps Giles said something nice to him.

"Cheers to Father's health," I say when we all have our glasses. It might seem weird that I would bring him up once I dodged the issue already, but I think it reinforces the notion that I have nothing to hide to my sister, who is undoubtedly sporting a bit of the old Doubting Thomas under that façade of hers.

"Did I hear a voice belonging to a Moore?" asks an

unfamiliar voice. I turn around to see an old gentleman with a thick moustache. He looks familiar, but I can't seem to put a name to the face, even though he could put a face to my voice. Odd. Maybe he just saw us.

"Mr. Frankel, how lovely to see you sir," Giles says. He's always had a better memory for faces. Ah, now I remember. The lawyer from Charleston who's been to stay with us a few times. He and Father would drink scotch and talk business while Giles and I played catch in the yard. How long ago was that?

Mr. Frankel joins our little circle. Mary looks uncomfortable by the presence of an old friend of Father's. She hates hearing how grown-up she looks. Apparently, even at twenty-one, any reminder that you've aged is considered a grave offense so dire that she can begin to grow angry before the words have even been spoken. Perhaps I'm too hard on her.

I introduce our entourage and explain our parents' absence. Aidan looks eager to jump into the conversation. I should figure out a way to include him. Mr. Frankel says, "So, three seniors in our midst. I guess it's safe to ask the obvious question. What's next?" Looks like he took care of that for me.

Jesus. I hate that question. Does this old fart know that I've been asking myself that very thing all day? Blah. I need another cigarette. It might be a little hard to manage standing up with a drink. I don't want to look like a glutton.

Aidan is eyeing me, seeing an opportunity to jump in. "I've been trying to get some feelers out for any good business opportunities. Economics gives you a wide spread of possibilities and I'm trying to approach the next stage with an open mind. I tend not to be too phased by culture shock, as that's something that tends to happen to many people from my part of Alabama. Hopefully that expands my range of opportunities. In the future, I'd like to open up my own company, focusing mainly on investments, but securing the capital for that is a little out of reach for someone of my age. For now, I'm mostly trying to learn all I can, and hopefully down the road I can put some of that to good use." Aidan takes a sip of his drink. It wasn't as eloquent as it could be, but Aidan did good.

Mr. Frankel's well-defined brows arch a bit. He has a wonderful beard. He looks like an old Confederate general. "Most impressive," he says. "You don't find many students your age with as good a grasp on how the world works."

Giles takes advantage of the pause in conversation. "I'm curious, Mr. Frankel, on your views of this little world of ours, seeing as you've opened that door. Not to be obnoxious, but rather to have some more perspective on what somebody our age needs to do to make it in the age of Reagan." If this old lawyer wasn't a family friend and Giles wasn't my brother, I might be a little annoyed with Giles' pompousness. But he's asked a good question. Funny how that works.

Mr. Frankel smiles and takes a sip of his wine. Red wine, with no club soda. "You certainly are Robert's son. I don't want to give a lecture. We're all here for that anyway. I'm sure you've all heard about opportunity to the point where even the word itself can inspire some bland soliloquy from an old geezer like me. My advice is to take opportunities when you see them. There's plenty of information to absorb from the people at this little get together.

You won't even get to crack the tip of the iceberg if you can learn. But you don't need to. You'll see a common strand through most of the successful ones. An opportunity that stands right in front of you is lovely. I think we can all agree on that." Giles, Aidan, and I all nod. Mary looks bored. I'm not sure how much of that made sense and I'm not even drunk. Mr. Frankel takes a deep breath.

"The problem I have is that opportunities don't just sit there in plain sight for you to trip over. Often times, they don't even exist at all. It's great to tell somebody to wait for the moment, but what if the moment doesn't come? You follow the careers of the people who gave that advice and you'll see that they didn't sit there with their thumbs up their asses waiting for some dipshit to give them a break in life. They worked for it. And sometimes you've got to just create your own opportunity."

This old man is giving us a lot to consider. It's my turn to play devil's advocate for conversation's sake. "How do you know when to create the opportunity as opposed to just waiting for some other one to come? They do come sometimes, don't they, Mr. Frankel? Surely rash behavior isn't rewarded in the workforce?" Is it?

Giles watches me while Aidan remains fixated on the old man. These sorts of chats are exactly why he wanted to come. They're also exactly why Mary didn't.

The gentleman smiles. "Rash behavior is rewarded, Jacob. Sometimes, of course. They say good things come to those who wait. Well, sometimes they come to those who strike first and seize what they want. I'm not telling you to be rash and go guns blazing into the world like Butch Cassidy. Just that you can't apply a singular mode of thinking to something and expect that things will always work out the way you want them to. There's more than one way to succeed. That's one downside to the generalizations you'll hear from so-called 'motivational speakers.' Far from the only one. Don't be afraid to get out in front of something and take what you want." He basically disagreed with me completely without making a mockery of me like Giles might. He made his point well.

The waiters are ushering people to their seats. We sit in the third row. Close enough that Mary can't try to nod off without being afraid of being seen, but far away enough that Giles' inevitable snipes stand a chance at not being heard. Aidan slips the waiter a bank note to get us all refills. The drink line is a bit crowded.

"Wasn't that man fascinating?" asks Aidan, as he takes a sip of his flask. He's not in conservation mode. We're seated so it's less of an issue. "Certainly had more interesting things to say now than back when we were kids," I reply. I turn to Giles and ask, "Do you remember that guy from when we were growing up?"

Giles looks back at the gentleman for a second and says, "I know he did some work for Father up in Charleston. I guess they made some deal that worked out well because he would stay with us sometimes on his way to Savannah. I take it he liked old fashioned cities. I won't hold it against him for living in South Carolina." Mary laughs. Aidan says nothing. Figures.

The waiter brings us another round. Mary receives what looks like a gin and tonic or a vodka soda. I pause briefly, worried that she might be upset with the change in order, but she has a smile on her face as she takes a sip. "Good choice," she whispers to Aidan. At least something is going well.

The Dean of Students introduces the Senator. His name is Paul McIntyre. We learn he was originally from Montana. Politicians are often from places other than where they represent. Giles chuckles. Snobbery goes well with alcohol as he drinks his old fashioned. Hopefully this isn't a sign of poor behavior for the speech.

The Senator is wearing a suit like Giles'. I wonder how he feels about that. I dare not ask for fear of encouraging chatter amongst my companions during the speech. That could get real tiresome, real fast. The Senator shakes the Dean's hand and waits for applause. He gets it, though I can't understand why. He hasn't done anything yet. I can see why people like him are disliked.

"Thank you," he says. He has a bit of gray in his black hair, but he looks to be in remarkable shape for a man who must be over fifty. He wears the fake sly grin that you often see on politicians. "I must say, I owe a debt of gratitude to the South for my scandal-free term in Congress. It was your great general Robert E. Lee who once said, 'Never do a wrong thing to make a friend or to keep one.'" Giles elbows me and starts to make throw up gestures toward the ground. He doesn't appreciate this reference to a beloved Confederate leader. It's a bit clichéd to mention him in this kind of setting. Well, Giles doesn't particularly care for the Civil War anyway. I'm sure others don't either. We lost. Well, the state lost. I wasn't alive.

The Senator continues. "I'm constantly amazed by how much Oregon shares in common with your region. I see the great tender care your people have for your community. To look out at how many of you showed up to this function on a February evening to welcome me to your fine state - I am truly touched. The Southern hospitality has been in full effect since I crossed the Mason-Dixon Line just a few days ago." It's as if he stopped at a rest stop and picked up a pamphlet on how to impress a Southern crowd.

Giles continues to gulp down his drink at a somewhat concerning rate. "Aidan," he calls over my lap. "Toss over your flask. I want to top my drink off." He pours more whiskey into his cocktail. This is not a great idea.

"Why don't you slow down a bit, brother?" I suggest. He sticks out his tongue and replies, "Blame our Congress. This Southern hospitality bullshit is driving me to alcoholism. Could he be any more fake if he tried?" He's right, but no one else needs to hear it.

"Just be quiet about your criticisms. It's not polite. Sip your drink and shut the fuck up," I say. Harsh? No, he needs to realize that some things don't need to be shouted for everyone to hear. I can't blame him.

I struggle to pay attention. His speech is boring and I lose track of time. Aidan seems to be the only one of the four of us who actually cares about this senator. I light another cigarette to see if that will help me pay attention to this nonsense.

The Senator does catch my attention as he addresses the students in attendance. There aren't too many of us. "I was asked to give some advice to the students who graced all of us with their presence. We must never forget that academic institutions are the true heart and soul of this nation." Oh please. We're all here for the free booze and you're here to get money from our parents. Let's call it what it is.

"People are always asking me how they can succeed in today's America," he says. "I tell them it's no different than when I was a kid, there's just more opportunities. Work hard and pay your dues and you'll be rewarded when the time is right."

Giles and Mary are both laughing. I elbow Giles and notion for Aidan to do the same to my sister. He grabs her hand instead. Oh dear, this could turn out poorly. I'm starting to not care as much about that.

Mary doesn't react to Aidan's hand. She looks over at me. I pretend not to notice. She turns to face the Senator, still holding on to Aidan's hand. Well, this is interesting. I motion for Giles to take a look. This might create some gossip further down the road, but it's worth the risk if it distracts him from making more jeers at our honored guest.

I hear the Senator once again. "We're a nation that often divides itself for trivial reasons. It's the year 1985, distance is no longer a problem and yet we find ourselves struggling to relate to each other. Have we forgotten The Youngbloods' call to smile on your brother and to try to love one another? That is often the case in Congress and it's a problem we work tirelessly to try to rectify."

I hope Giles didn't hear that. The reaction on his face of shock and awe suggests otherwise. Instead of laughing, he says, "Wow. Wouldn't have taken this guy for a 60s rock fan. Maybe he's not so bad." What's this? A statement of approval? This is an interesting turn of events. Giles suddenly approves of this man. Or maybe the liquor is softening him up. Either way is fine as long as I don't look bad.

No one has really looked in our direction. Perhaps I've been overreacting. Well, specifically in our direction that is. Plenty of people are looking past us to see the podium. Father says that people aren't going to care about your business unless you give them a reason to. I haven't heard any shushes yet so I suppose we're doing something right.

How different would it be if Father were here? A lot different I suspect. The conversation with Mr. Frankel wouldn't have happened. We'd talk about some project they worked on with only a small bit of time devoted to the youth of America. Aidan and Mary wouldn't be there so the whole emphasis on life lessons for undergraduates probably wouldn't happen. Though I wouldn't have had this kind of day either, so I wouldn't need to hear what he had to say as much.

Or would I? Father's illness doesn't really change all that much. It means I have to make arrangements for Mother, but it's not like life is suddenly different. The only real impact it's had so far is on this event. It's the uncertainty of it all. Change is coming. Big fucking deal.

Mr. Frankel's words had value regardless of timing. Opportunities. I'm better equipped to make them than Aidan. Perhaps I should start looking for some of my own. He could use some help on that front.

The Senator's speech reminds me of all the things I won't miss when I graduate. Having this sludge shoved down my throat gets tiresome after a while. If I work hard, I'll succeed? Tell that to all the plantation workers who were promised a fair deal.

It makes perfect sense that most of these old farts wouldn't want to spew out any meaningful advice. Many of them aren't even retired yet. Why encourage competition when you don't have to? That's a key to success right there. Just tell them to work hard and wait and it'll come.

Fuck all of you.

"And finally," the Senator says. Shit. I've been day-dreaming throughout all this crap. That's probably for the best. "I'd like to remind the students once again of something that I've always tried to keep with me as I've navigated through this grand adventure called life. It seems clichéd to talk about dreams. You find that stuff in kids' movies. But there comes a point in people's lives where they forget the dream.

Some call that reality setting in, but I don't believe that. We forget because it's easy to forget. My advice to you all is to never give up on your dreams. It isn't worth it, even if it feels like all is hopeless. When you get to be my age, you reflect on this crap more than you'd like. The conclusion I've gathered is that I'm satisfied with my life because I achieved the goals I set out to achieve. I chased those goals. I didn't chase money or cars or attractive women. I went after my dreams. There will come a time where you stop to evaluate the measure of your life's work. I pray to God that when that day comes, you'll find satisfaction. Thank you."

A wild round of applause follows for this crock of possum diarrhea. Follow your dreams. Ha, ha, ha. Let's make this shithead the star of the next Disney movie. The altruistic senator from Oregon. That'd certainly make a million. Or would it be reduced to afternoon television? I don't think this guy would care as long as he got to hear himself speak.

"Wasn't that lovely?" asks Aidan, whose wide eyes show that he's actually serious. Good Lord. I guess this shows that the Senator is good at what he does. He can have skeptics like Giles and me, but that spiel of his translates well to his core audience… idiots.

"And now for a few questions," says the Dean, who reappears behind the podium for a second as the applause starts to die down. Great. Questions. Now the Senator can really dive into his narcissism, as softball questions are lobbed in his direction. This is why I hate these sorts of things. These aren't questions. People are just stroking this guy's ego.

"What is your favorite part about being a United States senator?" asks a man a few rows behind me. Boy, that's a tough one. Better bring David Frost in to take over for this amateur. This guy is definitely out of his league. I hope the rest of the world isn't as cynical as my family.

The Senator smiles as he answers, "The ability to be a force for good in our country." More applause. I want to stand up to see if he's bothered by the smell of his own manure. I'd bet the answer to that is no. It must be a pleasant fragrance.

Giles snickers. I'm glad someone is enjoying this half as much as I am. Another voice asks, "Is college football as big in Oregon as it is in Georgia?" That'll really get him sweating. "Go Ducks," replies the Senator and the crowd goes wild. What the fuck?

"What do you think of President Reagan?" asks a female student. Finally, someone asks a question that takes more than a second to answer. Giles whispers in my ear, "That girl is a member of the College Democrats." Interesting. I wonder how she finagled her way into an event like this.

"I think the President is doing a fine job and I hope that Congress can continue to help him propel America forward," replies the Senator from Oregon. The applause gets louder and louder. They love him!

Giles raises his hand. He's acknowledged by the Dean and stands up. I cringe, upset that I didn't even make an effort to stop him. This could be bad. Mary tosses a mischievous glance in my direction, her lips curled in a grin. Aidan smiles in awe. He must think Giles will aid the propaganda.

"Mr. Senator," starts Giles. He pauses. Thankfully his drink is on the floor. "What is your favorite type of pie?" There's a few scattered laughs, one of them belonging to Mary. Otherwise, the crowd is silent, in anticipation of his answer to the important question.

The Senator laughs, though he sounds flustered. The laugh sounds faker than it should. "You've thrown a hardball at me sir, but I would have to go with rhubarb." A chorus of gentle applause ensues. I wonder if his answer cost him any donors. Giles nods and sits down.

"What the hell was that about?" I ask. Giles reaches over me to receive a fist bump from Aidan. He looks at me like I'm the one who asked a ridiculous question. "Brother, have you been listening to the questions these people have been asking? I merely wanted to know if he was the real deal. Pie is important. 3.14. The center of fucking civilization. That's all." Bullshit.

I can hear chitchat all around us. People want this to be over so they've eased up on the unspoken rules of decorum. I guess I can entertain Giles' line of thinking. "Well, what did you think of his answer?" I reply. Rhubarb. I don't know what to make of that. He says, "A very interesting choice. I was expecting apple given his blatant patriotism. Though we're close to Florida and he wants to look like a Southern sympathizer, so key lime wouldn't have been out of the question. I can respect rhubarb. It's a polarizing flavor. You either love or hate it. Rhubarb takes a stand. Rhubarb matters."

I roll my eyes. "Shut up. You're making me hungry." The pre-speech cocktail table was severely lacking in the munchies department. I hope they'll have some calamari, or, at the very least, some mini-hotdogs. I bet Aidan wants those. America.

A few more people ask our treasured guest questions. None of them have much value to anyone. I suspect this can be blamed on a lack of information about this guy. People didn't come to see him. They came to be seen. I guess someone can tell someone else they were here. Like that matters.

How would we know anything about this senator from a state most of us have never even been to? I would be very surprised if more than five people counting the Senator and his security have ever made the trek up to Oregon. It's not like he's tearing up the Senate floor either. He's just here because that's what people do. He gives his speech and life goes on.

Keeping up with appearances. Mary isn't the only one who values that. Mother would have loved this man. I suppose that's good to see. It doesn't matter if things are good as long as people think they are. Perception.

I wonder how intoxicated my little posse is. Giles, yes. Aidan, probably. Mary, probably not. Odd. Me, heavens no. I should be. I take another sip of my drink. There isn't any good reason why I shouldn't be a little tipsy at this point.

The Senator steps down from the podium and we all stand up to make our way toward the hors d'oeuvres and the free cocktails. I check my watch to see what time it is. My watch isn't there. Fuck, fuck. I must have left it in my room when I was getting ready. No doubt the fault of my brother. Such a distraction.

I don't need my watch. Not really. I don't have anywhere to be. The bar eventually. Or not at all. The choices, the humanity.

"Come now," I say to the group. No one moves. Testy, testy. "Aidan, come with me to get another round before the crowds swarm the bar." That got his attention. A simple matter of knowing what buttons to push. He looks alert as he walks over to me.

"What did you think of the Senator?" I ask. Part of me wants to gauge the true intoxication level of my friend so that I can take a fucking chill pill. If he's particularly wasted, it might be a good idea to be on our way sooner rather than later. Giles' question ensures that no one will forget that the Moores were at the function to welcome Senator McIntyre of the great state of Oregon. Anyone who cares.

"I thought he was good. It's funny how politicians are," he replies. A much more thoughtful answer than I was expecting despite its simplicity. "What do you mean?" I ask.

"Well, some of that was canned, obviously. There are some things you just can't say. Even if you want to. Nixon never knew that and that's why so many people disliked him. One of the reasons I guess. There are things they have to say. I get that. But what he chose to say was interesting. He tweaked the script a bit." Aidan doesn't appear to be too drunk. He's functional at least.

Was this guy interesting? I certainly didn't think so. Giles didn't either or at least he didn't suggest that he did. So, what to make of what Aidan said? Perspective.

Or not. Time to order some drinks. We order the same as before. I briefly think about ordering Giles a coke just to curtail his liquor intake but I stop myself. That would send a bad message to Aidan. Besides, do I really care? Let them eat cake! Now, Marie Antoinette, *she* knew how to cater to the people. Where's my cake?

Giles' question wasn't any stupider than any of the other questions. The difference was that he was aware of that. I was aware of that. There was minimal effort taken all around to prevent others from being aware that a mockery was being made, taking the form of an innocent pie question. Therein lies the problem with what he did.

Is the knowledge of Senator McIntyre's favorite thing about being a senator more important than his favorite type of pie? Not really. No one asked about the Soviet Union. Of course not. That would be out of place.

But why? He isn't our senator, but he does work in Congress. Hence, he does work for us in some capacity. He represents us to the rest of the world when he travels. Who really cares about that, though? Collectively, Georgia and Oregon both face the same concern regarding the behavior of our Russian friends. So why can't we ask him what's going on? That's what matters, not pie.

The answer is simple. It isn't conversation you have at functions like this. Lectures are for fluff when you aren't in the classroom. Not for key issues. That's what town halls are for. But town halls have similar softball questions. So when do they get asked, if ever? Never? I don't know.

It appears as though we missed an opportunity to do something truly memorable tonight. What? Something. Better than pie and college football, if that's not considered blasphemy punishable by death.

I want to see what Aidan thinks about these sorts of thoughts. "Why don't you think anyone asked him about the Soviet Union?" I ask my closest friend. He stops in his tracks, presumably pondering the question at hand. Yes.

"Why would they? People don't want the truth, they just want to be told things that will make them happy," he replies. "Isn't that why you didn't ask the question yourself?" he adds. He gives me a charming grin right after, showing that he didn't intend to be completely philosophical with his delivery. Interesting.

It is true. I didn't ask. I could've stood up and asked a question that was more out of the ordinary than my brother's question regarding the Senator's preference of baked goods. I didn't. It hadn't crossed my mind. I did nothing. Maybe it didn't cross anyone else's mind, either. We'll never know.

Giles and Mary are talking to an elderly couple. I always enjoy seeing elderly couples. Two humans who successfully made it through the game of life, who are now enjoying the tail end of it together as God intended. That sounds morbid, but that would eradicate the beauty of it all. It's supposed to be marvelous. Life is filled with such displeasures. It's nice to have someone to share those times with.

Giles waves for us to come over. "Ah, Jacob, Aidan. Come meet Mr. and Mrs. Bourcier, all the way from New Orleans. They received an invitation from a friend of the Senator and decided to make a grand trip of it. Isn't that lovely?" Giles is in a better humor. Maybe he always was and I just misread him.

"Welcome to Georgia," I say as I shake hands with them. I hope they weren't disappointed by the bullshit spewed from this West Coast senator. That'd be a shame.

"That's some brother you've got there," Mrs. Bourcier says. She's smiling. I'm happy she appreciates Giles when he's drunk. She probably wouldn't like him when he's sober.

Mr. Bourcier opens his mouth to chime in. "Congratulations to you both on being so close to graduation. I hope the future is bright for you. Aidan, I hear you want to start your own business." Jesus. How long were we gone?

"Thank you. I try to dream big," Aidan replies, who clinks drinks with the old man. Mr. Bourcier pulls out his wallet and takes out a card. "Let me know if I can do anything to help. I might be a little old now and far away from most of the action, but I've been in the game for a long time."

So Aidan gets a business card from a man Giles met in casual conversation. What is this world coming to? Something just doesn't feel right. Or maybe it does. Giles might make Aidan's operation plausible. He's got a knack for canvassing a room. Better than I do. Maybe he really should join our little operation once it gets off the ground.

The Bourciers leave us to converse with a group they appear to recognize. I think to ask Mary how she's doing when a commanding voice appears. Oh wow. It's quite radiating.

"That was some question, good sir. I was terrified that I wouldn't be able to answer it properly." The Senator. He's talking to Giles. Aidan looks starstruck. I am, too. A little bit. About as much as Mary, probably. Giles looks as calm as ever.

Except he isn't calm. He rarely likes to show what he's

really thinking. "Pie says a lot about a person, Senator," Giles replies. "What would we have said if you'd picked apple?"

The Senator is drinking white wine. Odd choice for a place like this. I look at Mary watching his glass. What to think of that? Mary probably thinks he's a fruit. White wine is more popular for men on the West Coast.

The Senator laughs. That voice of his is built for laughter. Loud and full. Controlled. I'm sure he's used to faking when he has to. People are more inclined to give you what you want if you laugh at their jokes. In this man's case, that's probably money. Not with us, though. We're students without any money to give just yet. He's more genuine than I gave him credit for during the lecture. Or he's planting the seed for future donations. Clever bastard.

"What's wrong with apple pie? Don't you have any love for your country old sport?" asks the Senator. He hasn't asked us our names. Is that unusual or just insincere? He appears to be only interested in Giles.

Which is exactly what Giles would want. He says, "I'm Giles Moore, by the way. These are my siblings, Jacob and Mary, and our friend Aidan Davies. I'm a junior and these three are seniors."

We shake hands with the man from Oregon. He says, "Seniors? Congratulations. Big plans for next year?" There's a pause. I wish people would stop congratulating us on having our lives flipped upside down. Don't they know we want to stay in college? Who wants to leave the cave? Plato was full of shit.

I assume Aidan wants to take a stab at continuing his luck by discussing his little plan. I give him a nod and motion with my hand to go ahead. As if he needs my approval. Well, he does. This is my show. Mary looks more attentive than she has all night.

"Well, sort of," begins Aidan. "I want to start an investment business eventually. Hopefully with Jacob. We'll need some experience and some capital before that can become a reality, of course. Do you have any advice for how we can make that happen?" I give Aidan another nod showing my approval. I worry about his behavior sometimes, but he's good at what he does when he manages to get on a roll. He seems to have a script developed.

The Senator gives us a smirk of questionable authenticity. It's less acceptable than his laughter. "That's a big idea. I'd say the same thing I said in my speech. Work hard and pay your dues and it'll all turn out right. You might want to include Giles in on this little plan. He looks like the real winner. Excuse me." He walks away.

Oh dear. That didn't go as well as it could have. Quite the contrary. What an asshole. Work hard? Yeah, that advice was real fucking helpful the first time he said it. He shouldn't have said anything at all if that was his only fucking line. Aidan looks hurt. Or disappointed.

Mary speaks before I can. "I don't think you made a believer out of him, Aidan. Politicians are full of shit. I wouldn't listen to him. Asshole."

"Yeah," I add. "His speech was fake and it's no surprise that he was like that here, too. Don't let it get to you, Aidan. People have loved what you've been saying all night."

How could he not let it get to him? "Little plan." This is the problem with so many of these older shits. They don't want to give you any advice that isn't generalized nonsense and yet if you try to pick their brain on something that's genuinely innovative, you're belittled like you're not worth shit. They fail to realize that their little clichés do more harm than good. Or maybe they just don't care.

I shouldn't lump the whole of America's upper class into that lot. We've seen plenty of people who genuinely want my generation to succeed. I don't know if Senator McIntyre does or doesn't. It's not fair to say.

But what he did was obnoxious. Aidan is a man with a dream surrounded by people he's intimated by. I don't care enough about them to let it get to me. I also didn't have my dream belittled by some shithead here to make buddy-buddy with a bunch of Southerners. You can bet I'll be telling Father to do precisely jack shit for this asshole.

"Ignore him, Aidan," I say. "You've done good today." As if he was here to do anything specific. One would think he didn't come to have his dreams crushed. Maybe I'm making too big a deal out of this. He nods, but he still looks sad. It's clear it's still getting to him.

Mary holds her glass up to a waiter in an attempt to solicit another cocktail before turning to Aidan again. "Aidan, you must understand that this is how these people operate. They don't care what you have to say if you can't give them anything. All you need to do is figure out which people have value to you and work from there. Play their game. Don't worry about one shitty conversation. You'll need to develop a thick skin if you want to get anywhere in this damn world." Whoa. Mary. Trying to make him feel better. Her compassion is more refreshing than a wine spritzer.

What's surprising is Giles' silence. The man has hardly said a word since the Senator left. He's doesn't appear to be paying attention at all. Giles always pays attention.

I sense it is probably time to go. We've been seen. We did what we came to do. That's good enough. There's probably a few more conversations worth having, but they don't need to happen tonight. There will be other dinners. I don't need anything from them right now and Aidan isn't going to get any more business cards looking all dejected. But how to motivate the troops? And where should we go?

Ah, yes. "Old Barn anyone?" I suggest. Aidan's face lights up. He looks to Mary and Giles.

Mary downs her newly acquired drink and replies, "Sure, but not just yet. I need to get my handbag and maybe some of the girls. You boys would like that, wouldn't you?" Ouch. Of course I'd like it. But Mary should know what Aidan wants. Aidan wants Mary. We turn our attention to Giles, who continues to ignore the outside world. What the fuck is he thinking about?

Noticing the attention, Giles shakes his head. "I think I will stay here and assess the scene some more. I'll catch up later maybe. Or maybe a nightcap at my place. Play it by ear."

We hand our empty glasses to a passing waiter and head off. Mary bids adieu and goes one way and Aidan and I take the road that leads to The Old Barn. Off campus. That's nice. You can often forget that life goes on outside of the college bubble. I certainly do. It tends to breed a sort of exclusionary mentality and definitely makes going home feel a bit weird. I just usually want to lay in the pool all alone like that scene from *The Graduate*.

The problem is that Mary and Giles want to do the same thing. Less is more in that instance. Mary can wait. She'll be just like Dustin Hoffman in a few months. Floating around in a pool, waiting for someone older to take her away and show her the meaning of life.

I hope Aidan isn't bummed. He was the only one who was actually looking forward to this night. "Did you have a good time?" I ask my friend. He smiles and hands me a cigarette. "I did. Thanks again for inviting me. It's great to see how those people conduct themselves. I always feel like I learn a lot just by being there." Perhaps that was a backhanded compliment toward shitheads like the Senator. Or maybe it was genuine.

That's what baffles me, I guess. Aidan went there to learn. The Moores went to drink. Giles might have gone to people watch. And to drink. He's still there. Weird. Maybe not. Giles does weird things.

"That senator was just as bad as I was expecting," I say as I light up a cigarette with a match. Aidan lights his with a lighter. "Arrogant, superficial, pompous. Pompous and arrogant are sort of the same thing but fuck that guy." I might have brought it up to make Aidan feel better, but it's definitely true.

"What do you think about Mary and me? If that's not out of line." Guess he's already moved on from the Senator. If we were back at the house it might be inappropriate. The circumstances are a bit different this time. He needs a boost and she did come to his defense.

"What do you mean?" I ask. Weird question that calls for an elaboration on an awkward question. Wonderful. I know what he means. I just don't know the context. In general? Tonight? I don't want to presume in case he thinks I'm on board with this crap. I don't know if I am just yet.

"I mean, I was getting a lot of mixed signals. She seemed to be supportive, maybe even impressed, at some points. And then just like that, it would go away and she'd snicker or something. I don't know, maybe I'm just being insecure. That senator did kind of throw me off." Maybe. But his description of Mary was spot on.

"Look Aidan, Mary is a complex person. Believe me, that's always been the case. She never thinks and does the same thing. You just kind of got to work with that. Sometimes it's in your favor and sometimes it isn't. But what you really need to know is that she isn't going to change." Fair assessment.

Aidan puffs away at his cigarette. I'm only vaguely sure we're going the right way. "So, what do I do to win her heart?" Fuck. Over the line. Well, maybe not. Not tonight. He gets a pass.

Only sort of. I still get to question him. I am her brother. "Why do you want her heart?" Shit, that came out wrong. "I mean, that's important to know. She can see through that crap. She's like Giles. She constantly picks apart people with her mind. That's why you're so frustrated by her. She jumps around with her emotions so that you're constantly guessing in an effort to keep up. It's impossible. It's a real pain in the ass, if you ask me." True. She is a big pain in the ass. What can Aidan say to that?

He doesn't answer for a while. I suppose he's thinking of alternatives to the obvious reason. Marrying Mary means marrying into the family and that bodes well for the future business. That's been apparent to me, and even to my siblings. It isn't fundamentally wrong, but it's at the point where it's almost too obvious. He should take his time with the answer. I have a duty to my sister and to myself not to let her marry someone who really just wants to marry me. Gross. That better not be the case.

"That's a tough one to put into words. Not because I don't have plenty of reasons. It's weird. She's not the affectionate type but that's okay. I've been out with those girls and they can smother a guy to death. But not Mary. She's sweet, sometimes at the perfect moment where you're reminded who she really is. There's something about her. You and your brother rag on her all the time, but she's special. You see that when you compare her to the rest of the girls who live in that house. I wouldn't have a tough time taking any of them out, but I don't want any of them. I want Mary."

Touché Aidan. I didn't think he could be sincere after all the booze. Or sincere at all talking about Mary. Alas, I was wrong.

He cuts me off as I try to brush off the mushy crap. "It's not like I want to marry her just yet, either. I don't know. But I'd like the opportunity to find out. Graduation is right around the corner. Who knows what's going to happen next year. But I don't want May to bring an end to all of this. You know what I mean?"

Fuck. When did Aidan get like this? "Say something man. Don't make me spill my heart out to a brick wall," he adds. Shit.

"Uh. Yea. That's all fair, Aidan. Sorry if I've been distant. I got some news about my father earlier. He's pretty sick, apparently. I don't know, that might have been Mother being melodramatic to guilt me into feeling bad or whatever. Who the fuck knows, but it worked." What the fuck is going on?

How much have I had to drink that all this shit is

spilling out? Shut up. Puff, puff. I didn't want Aidan to know before I tell Giles or Mary. Puff, puff. Shit. Shut the fuck up, Jacob.

He puts his arm on my shoulder. "I'm sorry, Jacob. Your father is a great man. So are you. You'll get through it. I'll be there to help. This is all going to be okay."

Is it? Is anything ever okay? Or do we just grow up to be like the Senator? We get to a point where we don't care because we don't need to. Life's figured out by then so it gives a big "fuck off" to the dreamers. But what did he figure out? What does that miserable shit have that got him to that point?

The Old Barn is in sight. What a stupid name for a bar. We should probably wrap up the sap lest we ruin the mood inside. "Thanks Aidan, you're a good friend. I probably don't tell you that enough."

He smiles and pulls out his flask. He offers it to me first. I take it, mostly in appreciation for the gesture. "Nah, I know. It doesn't need to be said, brother."

Eerie. Brother. That didn't sound like he meant frat brother. Does that go without saying? What would Giles think? Where is Giles?

The Old Barn is unusually quiet for a Thursday evening. Which means it's packed, but you'll still be able to hear yourself think. It's a popular college bar. We see our group spread out over a couple tables. A huge waste of space, but why not? The owner doesn't care as long as the drinks keep flowing. At his prices, that's never a problem.

I'm hungry. I should probably order something. Or have another cigarette. Puff, puff. That'll solve everything. Just a little food. Yum.

Our friend Charlie brings us a pitcher along with two

glasses. "How was the fancy cocktail reception?" he asks in a sly voice. Apparently drinking with distinguished members of Georgia's upper class is something to scoff at. Clearly Charlie is too focused on the fancy element and not enough on the free booze aspect of the event. Free booze is presented to me here as well and I shall drink it. A win for Jacob.

Oh look, a bowl of mixed nuts. That'll satisfy my hunger for a bit. Almonds, cashews, and the big ones that taste weird. What're they called? Macadamia. That's not right.

"Here, pick out the Brazilian nuts and put them in this bowl," says an unfamiliar voice. I look over and see a girl who looks to be around my age with dirty blonde hair and green eyes staring at me. If I didn't know better, I might think she was trying to flirt with me.

"You don't like those kind, either?" I ask. Well, that's a starting point. Something we have in common. A hatred of ethnic nuts. I don't hate them because of their origin. In fact, it's rather discriminatory that they're singled out because of where they came from while the others manage to escape that designation. Are they still Brazilian nuts if they're grown on American soil? What country did the almonds come from and why isn't that important to know?

She gives me the sort of smile I get from Mary's "sisters." Feels weird even calling them sisters. At least I like my "brothers." I'm out here drinking with them. Where is Mary? The girl is still looking at me, smiling. "Nope. They're too big and they taste funny. You reach into the bowl and that's all you get. Some big shitty nut that no one else wanted."

Good point. But who cares? Switch the subject, Jacob. Not more talk of nuts. "You're quite right. I'm Jacob, by the way," I reach out my hand. She accepts with a firmer handshake than I would have expected. "Raeanne. Pleasure." Now that's a Southern name if I've ever heard one.

"Raeanne, you say? What part of the world do you happen to call home?" What an awkward question. Get a hold of yourself.

She chuckles. "Abbeville, Louisiana. You probably haven't heard of it." I have not, but I smile as people often do when they're presented with things they're unfamiliar with.

"That's quite a ways from here. My friend Aidan is from Alabama. Hey Aidan," I call out. He comes over with the pitcher. I doubt he paid for it. Thief!

"Come meet Raeanne," I say. "She's from Louisiana." Aidan smiles. Raeanne waves at another girl who joins our little congregation.

"Jacob and Aidan, meet my friend Holly. We're traveling through on our way to Boston."

That's interesting. These girls aren't students. Well, not students here. Are they outgoing or in search of something from us? Aidan gives me a look that suggests he's thinking something along the same lines.

It might seem snobbish. It is snobbish, to an extent. But there's a potential problem here that we must at least acknowledge. If these girls are from bumfuck Louisiana and are frequenting a college bar such as this here Old Barn without any other students, chances are they're here for a reason beyond a just a drink. Sex. And a free place to stay.

Aidan and I find ourselves in different roles than we might normally occupy should a situation like this present itself. In a different setting, Aidan would be all over the opportunity to take these girls back to the house to show them how real university men live. But we just had a heart to heart about his intentions regarding Mary. He needs to tread carefully or he'll lose me as an ally.

I give him a closer look. The Jacob of yesterday might have suspected that Aidan wanted me to help him with this conquest. It doesn't look too difficult but his glance is more of a "Are you thinking what I'm thinking?" with regards to their potential intentions. We must convene privately.

"Aidan, I think Charlie wants that pitcher back," I say as I usher him away. "We'll be right back," I add to the girls. They smile politely.

As we walk away, Aidan says, "Those girls are hunting for a place to crash, Jacob. And maybe a bone. That's what you were picking up on?" He confirmed my suspicions. It wasn't wrong to wonder if those girls wanted more than a nice conversation.

No. They're hunting for some cock and a bed. What a foul word. Cock. A-doodle-doo.

"It looks that way," I reply. "But, looks can be deceiving." I fill my glass back up to the top even though it's not quite empty. When in doubt, more beer. You never know who will be buying the next round.

"Do you want a wingman for the Anne girl?" he asks. "I can keep the other one busy until Mary gets here. Or you could get someone else. I'm sure any of the boys would be happy to take Daisy." That's not her name, is it? I thought it was Holly.

Look at Aidan trying to set me up with that girl without a care for himself. No silly, he's thinking about himself.

He knows that if he shows concern for your libido, you won't mind as much when he makes moves on Mary.

That won't end well for him. Aidan thinks Mary is coming to this bar. He should know that the odds aren't great. I am ninety-five percent sure that she will not be making an appearance. The five percent is really just a safety net, in case I'm wrong.

There are two logical paths that Mary could take to get to this bar on this night. Neither of which are particularly plausible. She could get home and tell her roommates, but that wouldn't be like Mary at all. Mary doesn't plan things. She goes with the flow. Unless she doesn't like the flow. Then she doesn't go anywhere at all.

Which takes us to option two. Mary gets home and discovers a plan already in place for an outing to this very place. That's probably the most likely scenario that would lead her here. Then it becomes a question of timing and sobriety. If they leave too soon after Mary gets back, she'll feel awkward having not had time to have another drink before departing. If they leave too late, she'll start to get tired because she'll have been drinking for a few hours already. There is no such thing as perfect timing when it comes to Mary. She isn't coming.

"Do you want to shoot some pool until Mary comes?" Aidan asks. "I'm sure there's someone from her house that doesn't mind what happened with Katherine. You can just shack up with one of them." Ah yes, Katherine. Poor girl. Made the mistake of thinking I'd be the answer to all her fucking worries. The girl I chased away. Indirectly. How lovely.

"Sure," I reply. "Let's shoot some pool until Mary arrives." I need to give him some time anyway. I can't just say "Mary's not coming, I'm leaving, bye." Aidan deserves to have some hope.

We walk over to an open table. It's been free to shoot pool here ever since the coin machine broke back in the seventies. Fast Eddie would love it here, especially with all the rich college kids. You don't see generosity from an establishment like that much anymore. People want to charge you for everything in life. Next thing you know, they'll be charging you for the very air you breathe. That's life. And that'll be twenty-five cents.

Aidan sets up. I take a few more sips of my beer. The beer should hydrate me more than the hard shit has even with the mixers tossed in. How much have I had to drink? Time feels like a blur. I take a handful of nuts from the bowl on the table next to the pool table. Some Brazilian nuts in here. I wonder if Raeanne really gave a rat's ass about that. Probably just a conversation starter.

My game is off. My mind is off. I lose. We play again. I lose again. Aidan smiles. He's sorry we're not playing for money. I challenge him twice more. I win the first one because he scratched going for the eight ball. It's funny how that works. He does everything right except for one tiny mistake at the end and then he loses. I win because I was at the right place at the right time. Passive yet victorious. What is he left with?

David comes by looking to play. I hand him my cue. Aidan deserves some real competition while he waits for my absentee sister who isn't coming. Some consolation prize.

Those two girls are back. Raeanne and Holly. They sort of look the same. That's helpful. It certainly doesn't explain how Aidan mixed up their names. Daisy. A flower.

Holly. A flower. Ah, that makes sense.

I light a cigarette. "Can I bum one of those?" Raeanne asks. Of course she wants one. Want, want, want. I hand her one. Shit, now I only have one left. I knew I should have rolled more. Never leave the house without a full case of cigarettes. This is simple shit, Jacob. That's why cigarette cases were invented. Because you always need more than one.

"Thanks, where did you and your friend get off to earlier?" she asks. "I thought you were coming right back?" Desperation. Ugh. Go away.

"We got a little sidetracked. It's been a busy day." Damn right it has. To think the morning was so peaceful.

She rubs her foot up and down my leg a couple times. This might be erotic if I didn't have trousers on. Now it's just weird. Help.

"I know just the thing to help you unwind." Gross. Well, not gross always. Contextually gross. Same thing. Right? I can't rule out the possibility that this girl is a prostitute. I wish I could. You never know at a place like this.

I change the subject. "What are you going to do in Boston?" I ask. The other girl has disappeared. Maybe she found some lone wolf to sleep with. I might be drunk.

She removes her foot from my trousers. "We're going to visit Holly's sister. I don't know where we're going from there. Wherever the wind takes us."

Gypsies? No. Maybe. You can never be sure. What kind of girl starts a conversation over mixed nuts? A strange girl.

"Isn't it pretty cold up there this time of year?" I ask. Not very flirtatious. More like obnoxious. Don't be rude.

I'm not in the mood to have any coitus right now, especially not with this strange lass. She'd probably steal from the house and wreck my relationship with Jeremiah. We can't have that.

She looks confused. "Are you making fun of me?" she asks. No. Not really, but I can see how she arrived at that destination. Weather isn't very interesting.

"I am not," I reply. She smiles. "Good," she says. "I was hoping to have some fun with you tonight."

Ugh. No. Maybe a different night under different circumstances. Not this one. I am not in the mood for this bullshit. I'm not bringing some passing barfly over just to save her the indecency of having to sleep outside. What are the chances she has the clap? Definitely not zero percent.

What time is it? Late. Time to go. Aidan can sit here and wait for Mary all night if he wants. Won't do him any fucking good. I'm going home. I've had enough of this day.

"I need to use the restroom," I say. I head in that direction and make a sharp left toward the exit. Thank God.

Freedom. It's dark out. Real dark. How long was I in there for? Too long. Puff, puff. That's better.

Which way is home? Take a second and get your bearings. You know the answer to this question.

"Is everything all right, Jacob?" Fuck. Aidan found me. Why must he be on his game tonight? Do something stupid, Aidan. Please.

"We were right about those girls," I reply. "They just wanted a place to crash for the night. That won't be at our place. I'm headed home. I'm beat."

Aidan doesn't look disappointed. "Want to go to

Giles' place for that nightcap?" he asks. What's this? Aidan is ready to go, too?

I guess that could be managed. "Sure, but what about Mary?" I reply. He can't possibly think to abandon my sister even if the writing's on the wall. Something deep inside him has to give him hope. I know him.

"You know as well as I do. It's late. She's not coming. Probably never was. She's in her bed listening to some depressing music while she reads an Oscar Wilde novel or something."

I don't know what to say. "I'm sorry, Aidan." Sorry for what? Sorry you didn't get to have premarital sex with my sister? Gross. Definitely don't say that.

He pulls out a cigarette and lights it. "Don't be. I'll wait a day or two and ask her out formally. The proper way. With flowers and shit. She won't say no. Today was a success and we should toast the night with a drink at your brother's. Let's go." He knows the way.

There's a convenience store still open, but all the fast food places have shut down for the night. It could be after midnight. Jesus. I should go in and get some more cigarettes. No. You don't want that kind. Maybe later.

Giles' place isn't too far away. He lives off campus. Mother thought it was strange when he wanted to go off by himself, but he said he could get the best of both worlds. Comes in handy right about now, being out here in the wilderness already. Giles can come and go as he pleases. Peace and quiet. Isn't that nice?

I should probably tell Giles about Father tonight. I told Aidan. It's only fair.

No. What would that accomplish? Telling him now when it's late and you're drunk and tired is a terrible idea.

Drink his sherry or wine and go home. No misery to-night. It can wait until tomorrow.

It's probably for the best that Mary didn't come for that very reason. She was on to me earlier. If she decided to share her suspicions with Aidan, he might have spilled the beans. She'd freak if she found out that Aidan knew before she did. A patriarch's life is never easy. I suppose that's the way it's supposed to be.

The walk is quiet. Almost too quiet. I'm not really sure what that's supposed to mean. Two college seniors with their cigarettes making the not-so-strenuous trek to Giles' house. Some adventure.

We should've brought the girls with us. They could've slept on Giles' floor. He would've had a field day with that. Gypsies in his apartment. He'd wake up the whole neighborhood with his yells. They're probably better off soliciting at The Old Barn. Someone's bound to take them home.

Why did Giles stay at the lecture? That's a stupid question. We left a perfectly good party to go and drink with degenerates. Why didn't we stay is the better question? It's certainly one that I don't have an answer for. We could've just enjoyed the evening off by ourselves.

Giles lives in a building that is only half-occupied, which is sort of why he picked it. He likes his peace and quiet. A few old people live there. A few more used to, but they died. I see it up ahead.

The door is locked. Fuck. "Should we yell for him?" Aidan asks. I think about it for a second. No. Bad plan.

"No, hang on," I reply. I grab the doorknob. I start jiggling it back and forth in a slight yet consistent motion. After about fifteen seconds, the door opens. Progress.

"Good on you man. How did you figure that one out?" Aidan asks. "Giles calls it sleight of hand," I reply. "He figured it out one night when he forgot his key and wouldn't stop bragging about it the next day." We both toss our cigarette butts on the ground. I don't have a key for Giles' door, but that shouldn't be a problem. We're past the danger now.

I remind Aidan to keep it quiet as we make our way up the stairs. Giles is likely not the only person who enjoys this location for its tranquility. Disrupting that could be bad for my brother and vicariously bad for me. Giles can have a nasty temper.

We reach his room at the end of the second floor. I don't think anybody lives in the apartment next to his. Without thinking, I reach to do the same jiggling motion with his door.

Unnecessary. It opens. It's dark. Something isn't right with this picture.

I flick on the lights. Giles has a loft style apartment without a proper bedroom. Apparently the lack of structure is called modern. There's a rustling and a few disgruntled noises. Shit. Giles is in trouble. I rush in. Aidan follows.

Oh boy. I certainly wasn't expecting this. Giles is in bed with another man. Wait. No. It can't be. Impossible. Senator McIntyre? Holy shit.

"Get out!" Giles exclaims, in a muffled half scream. Even in a dazed state, he knows not to spout out disgruntled rage in the middle of the night. The police would have a field day with this if they saw who was in his bed.

A flashing light. No way could someone call the cops this fast. We haven't done anything wrong. Wait. The flash came from inside the apartment. Another flash. And another.

Aidan is holding a Polaroid camera. He's taking as many pictures as he can. The flash keeps blinking with no sign of letting up. What the fuck is going on?

"What are you doing?" I call out, to no one in particular. That isn't helpful.

"You need to leave right now. Both of you." Who said that? Giles. He's shirtless in his bed. The Senator looks like he's in shock. He's probably naked. Gross.

Giles puts his hand on the Senator. He resists, brushing him off. Flash. Another picture. Aidan, what the hell are you doing? I should beat the shit out of him for this. I don't. Why? What is going on?

"That's enough, Aidan," calls Giles. The Senator stands up. He's got some underwear on. I suppose I should consider myself lucky. He's staring right at Aidan. He looks like he's about to charge.

"I'd sit back down if I were you, Senator. This can all go easy or it can be very, very unpleasant. I have no desire to have a scuffle with you and I can guarantee you won't enjoy it a fraction as much as you enjoyed sodomizing a student, of all people. Be smart, Mr. Senator," Aidan says. His voice is stone cold. The Senator doesn't move. "I said sit down, you old fuck," Aidan repeats.

The Senator sits down. Silence. The ambiance feels like a shootout in a spaghetti Western. All four sides trying to determine how they get out of this unscathed.

Why don't I react? Alcohol. No, I feel sober now. I'm waiting because I want to see what comes next. I need to see what comes next before I do anything.

"Were you safe?" I ask. That's all I can think to say at

this point. To the Senator, I must look like a real piece of shit standing next to the wannabe paparazzi over there, but what does that matter? Giles' safety is still paramount.

Giles lets out a nervous sort of noise. Part sigh, part squeal. "Yes Jacob. I was safe. Jesus Christ, what are you two still doing here? Leave."

The Senator looks angry. "What do you think I have fucking AIDS or gonorrhea like some hoodlum?"

"Shut up," I reply. Simple. There you go. Nice and firm. Aidan starts to pick up the pictures that litter the floor. The Senator looks at Aidan, his arm slightly raised. He doesn't move.

"What now?" asks the man from Oregon. Good question. Who knows? Who gets to decide what comes next? Aidan does, but he's not talking. He continues to gather the pictures. He studies them, smiling. "What do you think you're going to do with those?" asks the Senator.

Aidan glares at him before returning his gaze to the picture. The Senator looks pale in the light cast by the ceiling lamp. It's easy to contrast him to Giles in this particular instance. Giles looks embarrassed. The Senator doesn't. Uncomfortable, yes, but it goes beyond that. He's trying to keep his composure. You can see it in his eyes. I suppose he's used to having to do that.

"That's up to you," Aidan replies. "No one needs to see these pictures. You have the opportunity to make them go away. For a price. Five hundred thousand dollars."

A felony has been committed. We're reaching the point of no return. Aidan, the man who wished to court my sister, is extorting a United States senator. This is no isolated move, either. He started doing it as soon as he saw him in the bed. Is Aidan showing his true colors?

IAN THOMAS MALONE

"You homophobic worthless redneck fuck," calls out the Senator. There's anger in his voice, but a sense of restraint as he pauses, gritting his teeth. Is he holding back in the name of civility? Or Giles?

Aidan laughs. That's more than mildly disturbing. "You're right about most of those things, Mr. Senator. But you got one wrong. This isn't about sodomy. You think I care if you're a faggot? You think I didn't know Giles was gay? Hell, I don't give two shits about that."

"Bullshit," the Senator says. Aidan shakes his head. He says, "No. This isn't a matter of gay or straight. It's about infidelity. I see that ring. You broke your marital vows. However you came to acquire a wife in the first place is beyond me. And now we find ourselves with an opportunity. You like that word? Opportunity, motherfucker."

"You shut the fuck up about my wife," replies the Senator, standing up.

Aidan pockets a few of the pictures. "You sit right back down, Mr. Senator. I'm going to raise the tax by a hundred thousand for that outburst. That's twice now you've acted out of line. Once more and we might have ourselves another problem."

Is this why Giles stayed? I want to ask what the hell is going on, but I'm afraid to get involved. I'm only a witness right now. I don't have to commit a crime. But if I said anything against Aidan, we'd look weak in front of the Senator. Something that cannot afford to be done if I end up taking my friend's side. We must be united or this piece of shit will eat us alive. He didn't get elected by being weak.

"Alrighty then. Let's just hear each other out and we can see what we can do." The Senator speaks like a man resigned to his fate, ready to worm his way out of the mess. I care less and less about his misfortunes every time he opens his mouth. Hear each other out, my ass.

"You're an asshole," Aidan says. "A purebred bona fide asshole. I mean that with no irony, given what's been done here tonight." Giles starts to laugh. What the hell? Aidan pauses until Giles is finished. The grin on Aidan's face is scary.

He looks at the Senator again. "At one point in your life, you chose the path of darkness over the path of light. You spew lies and bullshit all in the name of power. You forsake your vows and oaths because you don't know what they mean. You can't, because you're an asshole. And assholes don't see the error of their ways. They squirm on out to the next victim of their narcissistic bullshit. That's all you're good for. Loads and loads of shit."

The Senator spits on the floor. Gross. He pulls out a cigarette of his own. I reach into my case. Shit. I forgot. I'm out.

"And I suppose you're the Angel of Light? Here to cast judgment on the wicked homosexuals? How noble of you."

Aidan looks at me and then at Giles. He wipes sweat from his brow. "You don't get it. This isn't about justice at all. The fact that you're getting what's coming to you is an added bonus. But you're missing the point, you old fuck. It's about opportunity. A man tonight told me to create opportunities where I could see them. That's certainly better than the nonsense you spoke from your podium and to us afterwards. The side of a cereal box could give me better advice than a fucking politician. You're scum and you've done a bad thing against God and the American people. You've lied. I doubt this is the first time. Now you are going to pay for it. I take the reward because I can. Why the fuck not if it screws over a bad person?"

The disgruntled senator reaches for his shirt and then his pants. We're all quiet while he gets dressed. He catches Giles' eye and asks, "What about you, boy? You're going to sit there and do nothing while your little buddy rips me off?"

I haven't had a chance to think about Giles' silence. He's not really one to keep quiet if he sees something he disagrees with. This is his home. But he's done nothing to stop this madness. He could. Free to intervene at any time. I hope he knows I wouldn't try to stop him. I stand with my brother above all else. Family first.

And yet he's quiet. Could it be that he's thinking about the future ramifications? Should I be thinking about that as well? Does Giles see an opportunity here?

I find myself struggling to disagree with Aidan and his whole plan. What does that say about me as a person? My friend extorts someone who was having sexual relations with my brother and I've stood here like I'm watching a play. I feel sick.

But why do you continue to do nothing? Answer that, Jacob. Do you agree or disagree with Aidan's actions? You don't know. Fuck. I wish I had a cigarette. I don't think I can ask the Senator for one. I could, but what would that do to the mood? This whole operation is hanging by a thread as it is. The Senator won't cooperate if he doesn't fear Aidan.

Giles gets out of bed and walks toward Aidan and me. Neither one of us move. Giles starts to pace around the room, stopping to bring his hand to his chin. He's thinking. Good.

"You know what I think?" he finally says. "I think you shouldn't have mistaken my pie question for sexual innuendo. You know what I really meant? I was making fun of you and the whole damned event. You probably don't realize it anymore, since you do so many of these little talks around the country. It's all shit. Everything you say is nonsense. You are a bad person. I can disagree with what my friend here is doing without taking a stand against him."

I don't think that was what the Senator was expecting to hear. "I see. This is a dark road you're heading down. You don't care that you could be hit in the crossfire?" he replies.

Giles picks up the pictures off the floor that Aidan didn't pocket and gives it a look. "Do I care? Yes, of course I have an opinion on this matter. But I'm not worried. Six hundred thousand dollars is nothing to you. That's a small price to pay to save your career and your legacy. Make it back on a book deal. To Aidan, that's a start on his dream. You sinned. I didn't. That's the difference between us."

Silence follows. All eyes turn to me. I haven't said much. I don't know what to say. How to feel? Giles' position surprised me. I guess it makes sense. Giles is an opportunist, just like Aidan. He's smart enough to know he wasn't necessarily being used. We came for a drink. We found a senator. When life gives you lemons, you make lemonade.

"Well," says the Senator. "Are you going to stand by and let this transpire?" Good question. Why shouldn't I? How would it benefit Jacob Moore if the Senator got to walk free? My future gains clarity down one path. The other leads to alienation from my brother and my best friend. I won't have that.

"You said earlier to work hard, Mr. Senator, and we'll be rewarded. It looks like the reward is coming a little earlier than we expected." Aidan and Giles both smile. "Your loss is our gain." There's no coming back from this. You've made your choice to embrace the darkness. It's better than infidelity, but extortion is no venial sin. We're doing something wrong and we know it.

But it won't always be wrong once we make a living out of this money. I always said I'd follow Aidan if he could present the opportunity. Here it is. To ignore it would be foolish. A grave mistake. I cannot let this pass me by. This is my future right here. Right and wrong exit the equation. This is the here and now.

Aidan claps his hands twice. "Well Senator, it appears as though you have a choice. You can pay your penance for your sins and pray that you can find your way back to the path of righteousness. Or your legacy can burn once news of this leaks out. You've been terribly unlucky tonight, but there's hope for you yet. Pay the piper his due and that can be that."

The Senator sits back down on the bed. He picks up his jacket and takes out his wallet. There's a card and a pen in his hand, which trembles slightly as he takes a drag of his cigarette.

He stands back up and puts the jacket on. He puts his shoes on. His socks lay discarded on the floor. A memento for Giles of the night our lives changed.

"Here," says the Senator, handing Aidan the card. "Call this number tomorrow. It's long distance, but I'm sure you can stomach that with the funds that are coming your way. The person there will tell you how to collect the money. Now this will take a few days, so don't do anything rash. It can't be any faster. Believe it or not, I'm not used to this kind of shit. The front of that card has my office in Washington's number. If there is a problem, call that number. Be discrete. I'm being cooperative, you must understand." He's serious. He knows the stakes at hand.

Aidan looks down at the card and nods his head. "No funny business. There are three of us. You try to send anyone after us and we'll fucking plaster this shit all over the papers. You understand?"

The Senator laughs. "I'm not the hit man. You are. Now if that's all, I'll be leaving. I hope you all understand the severity of your actions here tonight. You won't answer to my people, but there will come a day when you face your hour of reckoning and you'll look back on this moment and you'll see where it all went wrong." He speaks not with rage, but with a sense of peace, like he knows what he says will come to pass. I hope he's wrong.

He walks out the door, forgetting his socks. The three of us stand there, silently. What's there to say after that? The nightcap that changed our lives. We didn't even get the drink.

"Giles," Aidan starts to say. Giles looks stoic. He's been through a lot, even if he doesn't care to show it.

He looks down at the floor as he responds, "Look, I don't want to talk about this tonight. We'll meet for breakfast at ten in the cafeteria. That's all for now. Just go." I can't get a read off of him. He was so strong just a few minutes ago. Maybe he's just tired. I'm tired.

"Giles," I say to my brother. He smiles at me. It's a faint smile. "I'm all right, Jacob. I just need to be by myself for a while." Fair. He was just embarrassed in front of his brother and a member of Congress. If the extortion didn't get to him, that certainly might.

I give him a hug. That feels like the brotherly thing to do. We depart in silence. There's no sign of the senator as we exit the building. Not surprising. I wouldn't stick around either. Aidan starts to walk toward home. I stop. I'm thinking of something I want.

"Are you all right?" Aidan asks. He's dropped the tough guy act and is back to his normal self. "Yea," I reply. "I'm going to the convenience store to get cigarettes." He pulls his pack out of his pocket.

"No thanks," I say. "I want to go for a walk by myself." I smile so he doesn't think I'm worried. I'm not. It's just one of those times where being by yourself is the only thing that makes sense.

"Okay, Jacob. We're going places, brother. This is just the beginning. Tonight, we rise. We're going straight to the top." He extends his hand. I shake it and we go our separate ways.

Good and evil. It's funny how people's perceptions of these two concepts work. We fail to understand them because we try too hard to see the world in black and white. Maybe morality doesn't even factor in to what happened tonight. It could just be that three boys saw an opportunity in someone else's misfortune.

Aidan isn't a bad person even if he did a bad thing. The Senator is a bad person who did a bad thing. That's three-fourths bad right there. I don't know what that means. I don't know where Giles and I fit in. I'm tired and I need cigarettes.

If I handled tonight, maybe I can handle taking charge of the whole family. One day. Opportunity came. I didn't seize it, but I didn't shoo it away, either. A learning curve. Maybe the next time, I'll be a little more proactive in deciding my own fate. Passivity could get me in trouble. Now we have money and that matters.

I cross the street. Well, I start to. I think I see those girls off in the horizon. Raeanne and the girl with the flowery name. I wonder if they found a place to stay.

Oh, look a light. It's so bright.

Friday, April 2, 2010

Giles

AROUND THE TREE, OVER THE TOP, AND THROUGH THE loop. God, I hate ties. Women's fashion is so much more interesting. With men, all you get is black or blue, and a long piece of fabric that hangs around your neck like a fucking noose. At least you get to pick the color.

Oh, but there are so many different ties. Yea, okay. If you wear a different colored suit, they assume you're gay or on drugs. Only one of those is true at the moment. I should swing by Mary's and load up on whatever shit the doctor has given her this time.

They should really tell me that kind of stuff. I know she's a grown adult, but she's not. Never has been. She's nuts. She was nuts before Aidan went missing and now she's even worse. The only difference is that now she's my problem. Fuck.

Should I put the jacket on now or later? Chomsky's coming to the house. I don't think he would care if I had a jacket on in my own home or not. Caleb might think it was weird. Does that matter? Hmm.

"Giles, do you want some French toast?" Speak of the

devil. The devil is me these days, according to the papers when there's nothing else to talk about. Funny how that works.

I haven't had French toast in a while. "Sure. That would be lovely," I reply. Something's missing. "Thanks honey," I add. Yikes. Could that have sounded worse? Probably, but it's the thought that counts.

No jacket. White shirt. Blue tie. I want to wear red ties now but everyone tells me not to. "Don't look aggressive," they say. Right. A red tie is certainly the sign of the alpha male and public enemy number one of Moore/Davies Capital. I wonder if the judge will strike Davies from the name when the trial begins so I can truly face the monsters alone. Not that I'm not alone already.

I walk into the kitchen. It's nice and modern. Just the way Caleb and I wanted it when we bought the place. Chic would be the better word. The key is the island with the marble countertop. At some point in life, that became a thing that everyone wanted to have. I had the money to have it so there it went. Lovely.

"What's the occasion for the breakfast?" I ask. Normally the answer is yogurt—Greek yogurt these days. I wonder what's next. Uzbekistani goat yogurt with two more grams of protein? Stick protein on fucking anything and people will eat it. Talk about ten percent increases on mutual funds and people go crazy, too. People go crazy for the stupidest shit. Buzzwords, motherfuckers.

Caleb gives me a strangely cheerful look. "Don't you know what day it is? It's Good Friday. Our Lord and Savior Jesus Christ is set to die today around three. Right after *As the World Turns*." That'd be real torture. Having to watch a soap opera right before your execution. Better not say that too loud or that'll be my fate.

I return Caleb's skeptical look with an indifferent one of my own. "We used to make French toast on Good Friday when I was little back home in Michigan," he continues. "You can't eat meat, but I guess eggs were okay. I'm not sure if I thought eggs went to heaven back then." He laughs. Neither one of us are religious now, but we grew up in relatively God-fearing homes.

Gross. Eggs and Heaven. What the hell is wrong with him? Don't ask. "Your family was religious, but we're not. So why can't we eat meat on Good Friday?" I ask while he puts the egg soaked bread in the pan.

We can eat meat. There's no mystical being waiting to strike us down if a piece of bacon slips down my throat. I see no point in honoring some archaic tradition. I haven't stepped inside a church for anything other than a funeral since Jacob passed. I wonder if Mary even remembers church. I only remember being bored.

"It's about sacrifice," he replies. "You're giving up shit in honor of Jesus' salvation or something like that. That doesn't really bug me. It's the notion that Easter is on a different day each year."

I see a smile grow on his face. That cute one when he knows how that simplistic shit bugs the hell out of me. "I'm sure you know why that is," he says. He flips my toast over.

"Of course. Lunar cycle. Passover is the same way. The Christians piggyback Passover with Easter, despite what those evangelicals say. To your average person, it makes Easter a bit too much like Thanksgiving. A bank holiday rather than a religious one. Set on a different day for convenience sake. The Jews are at least consistent. All of their holidays fit the Jewish calendar. The Christians jump around for whatever reason they please. Good Lord." Oh, the irony.

Caleb gives me my French toast and a cup of coffee. How nice of him. He hasn't been able to get much consistent work since shit hit the fan, but he's kept his complaints to himself. Caleb never needed consistent work anyway, but it kept him busy while I played with my investments. Until he started looking into adoption, which seems like a waste of time at this point.

"Big day?" he asks. I suppose my tie fails to give that away. I'd wear a tie to sit on the couch all day. One should always look professional.

"Sort of. Chomsky's coming over in a little while to talk about the deposition. Well, more about delaying it. Depends. Then I have to meet the PI to talk about Aidan. Then I suppose I should probably go and check on Mary. See how close she is to completely falling off the deep end. Busy for a Friday, I suppose. Even busier for a holiday, but Chomsky is Jewish and we're gay. Where does Jesus fit into our agenda?" We both start laughing at the same time.

Laughter. Joy. That's actually fairly significant. I can't remember the last time both of us shared a good laugh. Normally, one of us laughs in a foolish effort to cheer the other one up. This was genuine. I hope.

I only put a tiny bit of syrup on my French toast. Caleb didn't skimp on the butter. "You could've been a decent short-order cook in any Southern diner you wanted," I say. He smiles again. "Weird how that's a compliment," he replies. "I guess those people need to be pretty damn good at what they do."

Caleb is on to something here. Memories. "Father had a funny theory about that. He always said diners were about consistency rather than quality. Which is why you should always order what the waitress recommends, as long as it isn't seafood since pushing fish is a dead give-away that it's about to spoil. But anyway, he said that the cooks always had a system that they almost never deviated from. So you'd get one diner that had great hotcakes but shitty grits and another could make a mean omelet but slathered too much butter on the toast. And this would happen every time. If you get a bad meal at a diner, chances are, it's your fault. Because that's the way they need the diner to work."

There's a twinkle in Caleb's eye. He likes when I go on rants explaining bizarre theories I've either heard or concocted over time. Maybe when I'm in jail and he gets paid to write his memoir to save the house, he can write about the day I told him about proper diner protocol. That can be my positive contribution to humanity.

"If Chomsky is coming over here, why did you need to put a tie on?" he asks. Ugh. Don't snap. He just made you French toast.

But seriously. Why would he ask a fucking question like that? I stare at him, trying not to glare. I'm not amused. Who would be?

"Because I'm still a businessman and I'm conducting business today. You don't wear a bathrobe when you decorate houses, do you?" Sigh. That wasn't nice. Caleb turns away. Shit.

"You're right, I'm sorry." Ugh. Why did he have to mention ties at all? Doesn't he know the kind of stress I'm under? It's not some joke and I'm not playing house.

I need to look like I still care about how I present myself. Mary would understand. If she was still capable of having a normal conversation, that is. Maybe she will once she dries up.

"No Caleb, don't be. I'm sorry. It's hard." That's all I say. "I know," he replies. Caleb is a good man even if he forgets that I have the weight of our world on my back, now that my brother-in-law has run off with our stash of money.

I check my watch. One minute to ten. Which means that in a minute, Mr. Chomsky will be here to discuss strategy. Punctuality. How fun. Maybe we should offer him some French toast.

The doorbell rings. Caleb says, "I'll be upstairs." He's wearing sweatpants that don't exactly reek of casual Friday. Not with me wearing a tie. I walk to the door.

"Hello Mr. Chomsky, come on in." I don't need to wish him a happy Good Friday. His messiah hasn't come yet. Where's mine? Do Christians even wish each other that? It would seem to be a morbid greeting. Happy Good Friday? I don't think so.

"Can I get you a cup of coffee?" I ask as we head to my office. I have the real office. The one on the ground floor. Caleb's office is in one of the bedrooms. We have four bedrooms, but we only use one for sleeping since we don't have any children. Chomsky shakes his head, declining the coffee.

"Any word on your missing business associate?" asks my lawyer. Weird question. His wording is funny. He represents both of us, but with Aidan's disappearance, the waters are a little murky.

I should hire another attorney or two in order to

properly prepare for the case. Chomsky warned me about that already and will undoubtedly do so again today. There's a slight problem with that. More lawyers will put an excessive strain on my finances. Aidan is not helping matters.

"No. I should have more information later today," I reply. Chomsky first put me in touch with the private investigator nearly twenty years ago when we wanted to check in on our old friend Senator McIntyre, but nothing criminal is said out in the open. Not that we're even in the open right now. Less is more, according to this attorney.

Chomsky doesn't even like to meet in public anymore. That I can at least understand. That woman in Starbucks who came up yelling about how I'd ruined her whole family. The whole thing caused quite an unnecessary scene, so now we meet here in my home. I never told Caleb about the incident. I'm surprised it never appeared in the paper. Everything else does.

That whole ordeal was so déclassé. The woman was just begging for attention in there. I wanted to tell her the same thing I told that man in the supermarket who asked me if I felt bad about what happened. I wasn't trying to be a criminal. We were simply taking some risks that those who are put in charge of regulatory laws and all that nonsense said we couldn't take. What do they know? Fucking politicians.

We weren't thieves. Investments don't always work out. Risks are risky. That set off a chain reaction, which is quite unfortunate and we should have seen it coming, but that's life.

You know what isn't life? Putting money you don't have into the hands of people like Aidan and me. You should never invest money you can't afford to lose. It's funny. I told that to the man at the tavern and he bought me a drink. Rule number one is that there aren't any shortcuts in this business. If there are, they disappear fast. That's how it goes. If you don't like it, you find another job.

Why? Because the government is filled with fuck-ups and criminals who are put in charge of sticking their noses in my business, thereby preventing me from doing my job. It's illegal to buy alcohol in the state of Connecticut on Sundays. That shows you how arbitrary laws are, and yet people scream and scream about investment fraud. Crime is subjective.

You can't say that to a screaming woman in a coffee shop. Who would take my side? No. We had to leave. People glared like I was actually responsible for the destruction of that family. Not a single person told that woman to take responsibility for her own poor decisions. I know what they were really thinking.

"Are you optimistic?" Chomsky asks. Optimism. Aidan. Ha. Don't laugh. Chomsky's one of the few from the good old days who hasn't taken off. Because I'm still paying him. For now.

"Optimistic? That depends on what happened to him and what condition he's in if he's found." Yuck. How morbid.

Chomsky lets out a sigh. I don't know what he's thinking. "I take it you don't think he ran off with certain things then?" Certain things. Money? Women? Both?

"No," I reply. "I have a long list of complaints to levy against my brother-in-law, but Aidan is a family man. If he had a mistress, I'd know. He and Mary had their rough patches, but he wasn't like that. Especially not after Jack was born. Something happened to him. He didn't run off."

Do I believe that? That's a tough one. Yes. I don't want to believe that Aidan is capable of that kind of betrayal.

Infidelity. That was the catalyst that set off this nonsense. Father's demise gave me some more capital to put in on my end, but we wouldn't be working together if it weren't for the Seventh Commandment. Did I commit adultery? Or did I just participate in it? I wasn't with anyone at the time. And if I was, I don't think God was talking about homosexuals when he was dictating his rules to Moses. I think my hands are clean of any wrongdoing, at least on that night.

I didn't think about whether or not he was married. When Jacob, Mary, and Aidan left the party and he came up to me, I knew he was looking to have a little fun. It was dark at that point. You don't go by the ring on the finger. No, you watch the eyes. It's simple, really.

Power lies in the eyes. I had the power to see that a man of stature wanted to have a romp around with me. I went for it. Who wouldn't? The allure of bedding a senator back in those days would have been too hard to resist, even if I had been in a relationship.

"The prosecution wants to revoke bail. They're worried that what happened to Aidan might befall you as well." Chomsky looks like he's the reaper coming to pick me up and drag me to Hell. Might as well. So what's the danger?

"How can they do that?" I ask. "Don't they think he ran off? I've already surrendered my passport. I think it's pretty clear that I wasn't in on any escape plans or else I wouldn't fucking be here." I am not going to prison. Not yet. Not until I've explored all my options.

Another sigh from Chomsky. He doesn't want to be doing this anymore. I can't say that I blame him. This isn't in his wheelhouse, but he's content to defer certain payments while the cash flow is tight. Who else would? God bless him.

"I told the judge those shits can't have it both ways. Either they think something happened to Aidan or he ran off, but both cannot reflect back on you. Just one or the other. The judge didn't seem too amused by their antics, but I don't know how much longer I can keep them at bay."

Tick tock. Fuck fuck. "How much time do I have before we have to be back in court?" Why does that sound so morbid?

"Sunday is Easter so I got it pushed back to the end of the week. Friday maybe. I could try on Wednesday to get it moved again, if you want. Make up some shit about needing to take care of your sister. The prosecution knows they're in a precarious position with the two of you. They don't want to be rushed into making a mistake, but we're running out of time. The public wants blood."

I hardly need to exaggerate about Mary's condition. She'll start to lose it when she finds out she can't make local liquor purchases. A preventive move on my part. So was taking her car away. Very embarrassing, but that's what happens when you can't hold your alcohol anymore. The DUI with the mailbox says it all. Always have your back covered, Giles.

"I'll let you know," I reply. There's a question that I don't want to ask. "If they're prepared for next week, they must have something?" Why couldn't that news have waited until Monday? Can't I enjoy my weekend?

Chomsky puts his hand on the arm of the chair. He's about to say something I don't want to hear. "Unfortunately," he says, "they've been meeting with Mrs. Ramsey. Your old bookkeeper."

Shit. Aidan hired that old hag despite my pleas that a reputable company doing business in the Big Apple should employ someone slightly more qualified than a single mother from Alabama.

Of course there was logic behind it. She was smart and not particularly outgoing. She didn't let the big city get to her. She came up with her son, who was attending NYU at the time, and said the change of pace did wonders for her hip. Whatever that means. At least our clients loved her. When the going was good.

"How did she crack?" I ask. She knew things weren't always done in the proper fashion and that was perfectly fine. If the police hadn't given her husband all that trouble down in Mobile, she might have cared. Said he was never the same after that. The marriage was ruined. Our crimes didn't bother her. We were good to her.

"She has a granddaughter with cancer and her son is out of work. The economy got to her. I'm not a hundred percent sure what the deal was, but her cooperation comes with some treatment at some fancy hospital." Chomsky bites his lip. How is it legal that her grandkid only gets saved if I'm betrayed?

Figures. The old woman betrays me for her kin. Makes it hard to curse her. Cancer is a bitch. An expensive bitch.

"Where does that leave us?" I ask. No point in discussing the possibility of getting to her. I've done some bad things in my life, but Ramsey won't need to fear retribution from me. Family is family.

"The problem isn't so much what she knows about the case. She can connect some dots, but the real issue is that she can place you at the center of the action. We can manufacture stories for who did what, considering a certain someone isn't here to contradict your version, but this woman can fuck you."

Ah. Chomsky is offering unethical advice here. Well, maybe unethical. He's only hinting at it. It's hard to say at this point. He wants me to throw Aidan under the bus and save myself.

"I see," I reply. I can't think of anything else to say. I don't need to say anything else. This decision won't be made now. Not just yet.

Chomsky knows my hesitation. Aidan and I are very different people, but we work well together because we know how to operate as a unit. The best way to avoid getting caught. Until he ran off.

He says, "You know how you can get out in front of this. There's a great narrative to paint. You're a gay man who grew up in the South, pressured by some hotshot Gordon Gekko wannabe friend of your dead brother who married your lunatic sister. Fucking brilliant. Money drives people mad, but you're not the one who needs to take the fall. Aidan left. He fled. You can be the victim if you start talking. You come clean and if the media gets behind you, you're golden. You don't have to go down with the ship."

He's right. Aidan is fucking me over with this shit. If his idea of a grand escape didn't include his wife, child, and business partner/brother-in-law, then fuck him.

Especially when that brother-in-law could easily make this the most interesting fraud case in recent memory if he chose to talk about the Senator. I could bury that piece of shit.

But that requires me to be sure that he did in fact, run. I wouldn't be able to live with myself if I sold him down the river and it turned out he kept his mouth shut. You can't be sure he wasn't taken out by someone. But who?

Does that really change anything? It's been a month. He's dead one way or another. No one would keep him locked up for that long. We never did anything that sadistic.

Unless they know about the money. The twenty million he was responsible for moving. Twenty million. Big number. Unless you're in my business. Then it's not so difficult to hide.

He told me countless times he had it under control and that it was better if he was the only one who knew where it went. Better for whom? He had the nerve to think that I could break? Jesus Christ.

Paranoia. That's what all this Aidan crap boils down to. Even if you're right, there's no reason to think anyone would target you like this. You're not Bernie Madoff, and it's not like anyone went after him like that anyway. What we took is chump change in the grand scheme of things. We're just what's interesting right now. True financial analysts would be bored by the simplicity of our operation. But not the reporters and the CNBC pundits. I'm thankful I don't get Fox Business. I wouldn't enjoy what they'd have to say about me.

He didn't take his car. Someone must have driven him. Or he was abducted. Either way, something is definitely not right with the circumstances surrounding his departure. You don't need to make your decision now, but you cannot try to sugarcoat the grim nature of what lies before you.

Chomsky is staring at me. He knows I'm conflicted. What was he saying? Ah yes, Gordon Gekko. He's only half right about that. Aidan always had those dreams, but our plan was already in place when *Wall Street* came out in '87. That just fueled his fire. I'm pretty sure he wore through his VHS copy of the film. I bet he still has it. I should tell Caleb. Some sick fuck would buy that off eBay in a heartbeat.

Aidan Davies' broken copy of *Wall Street*. Starting bid at a hundred bucks. Cha-ching. I can afford better lawyers if I just start taking advantage of the situation.

Chomsky looks bored. I can tell he wants to leave. Everyone does. Except Caleb. He says, "You don't have to make a decision now. I know it's not going to be easy, whatever you decide. But you need to understand that this window is closing. This whole remanding ploy is a scare tactic. But it's also a wake-up call. You're a sympathetic figure to the media – until they've got you on better charges. People will love that old Southern woman up on the stand. She'll be like the courtroom *Driving Miss Daisy*, all proper and authoritative. Don't laugh. I'm serious. They want somebody to hang for this. They'll take Aidan if you give him to them, but as soon as you're in their crosshairs, they'll take the shot. A body is better than a memory."

Can he stop with the death metaphors? I know what they want. They want me in the courtroom standing before them, guilty of my crimes beyond a reasonable doubt.

I'm no fool. I've seen enough *Law & Order* to know that once my case starts to come undone, I'm finished. There won't be any fluke surprises unless my brother-in-law is found. Where are you, Aidan?

"You're not making me feel any better, Chomsky," I say. Maybe if I can stir a laugh out of him, he'll quit being so depressing.

Nope. He looks even sadder. "I'm sorry, Giles. I don't think you're fully processing that you're running out of time to get ahead of this mess. I'm not qualified to handle a lengthy trial. Neither are you." He puts his glasses on. I fear our meeting is coming to an end.

He means something else that he doesn't quite care to say. My financial situation can't handle this much longer with the way things are going. Three weeks ago, I successfully retrieved two million dollars of stowaway money I'd left in Georgia near campus, thanks to the help of my brother's old fraternity caretaker Jeremiah. He changed careers and became a barber. Opened his own shop. Good for him. He was always meant for more than that shitty house occupied by perpetually intoxicated students like Aidan.

To think I ever felt bad about hiding it in the first place. But fifteen years ago, when we first started to make the so-called "big bucks," and I decided that Aidan wasn't a basket I wanted to put all my eggs in, it made sense to find somebody whose trust I could buy. Jeremiah was always good to me. They say a good man is hard to find. I just doctored some forms and sent them along to Mrs. Ramsey, who cleared it without a second look. Aidan never once questioned where it went. Maybe he wasn't so good at his job after all.

Aidan's nest egg was different. Our "get-out-of-town-quick stash," as he called it. Kept it buried in a safe behind a shed in his backyard. The same day he let most of the staff go, he took it and said he needed to move it somewhere safe where no one would think to look. I don't know how the Feds could've found it there, but I didn't argue. That was step one.

Step two was all about assessing the damage. Running was never really an option with Mary and Jack to think about. A drunk and a two-year-old on the move would have been impossible. Plus, we'd have to replace Regina and how would we go about that?

His plan wasn't all that bad. Chomsky agreed that if we could just show them where enough of the money went and pay some of the people back, we could maybe escape jail time and all would be well. We got hit at the worst possible moment. Timing was the big difference between a couple of fines and a life behind bars.

We underestimated the thoroughness of the United States government when it came to putting the blame on someone else. They're the ones who created the system we took advantage of. I could've handled a couple years away, but they came after us too hard. The market dropping left us like the emperor when he realized he wasn't wearing any clothes. Naked, with the whole world laughing. Fuck.

It was some miracle when we didn't get hauled off straight to prison in the first place. People love blood, even if the crimes we caused only affected a few people. It's not like we robbed any charities. Only assholes. That makes it okay, right? If only.

I need to stop daydreaming with Chomsky still in the room. He's tired of this crap. I bet he retires after this case.

Why did we work with so many old people? Did Aidan need to be sure he could be ahead of absolutely everyone? Of course he did. You did, too.

"We'll talk on Monday. Have a good Easter," Chomsky says, as he stands up. He pauses and adds, "Some say Easter is a time of rebirth. I never had much need for God in my life, but maybe that can help you somehow." Maybe. We shake and he leaves. I don't walk him to the front door. No need for that kind of formality. I sit back down. I'm not ready to talk to Caleb just yet.

I miss the days when Aidan, Chomsky, and I would sit in that shit office in the wholesale district and talk strategy. Chomsky didn't know shit about investments, but he'd sit there and smoke his pipe and occasionally tell us if what we were doing would attract unwanted attention with his nods and his stares.

Attention. Aidan's love affair with that word is nothing shy of legendary. Mary would talk about how he was obsessed with being a big shot, but that was only part of the puzzle that is/was Aidan Davies.

We never would have survived if Aidan hadn't grown up poor. The yearly car upgrades, golf club memberships, and island resort getaways weren't his style. When we made our first real money, we had a sit down to discuss how we would proceed.

In the long run, that conversation might have been more important than the one following the Senator McIntyre incident after Jacob died, when a business partnership wasn't looking like a very good idea. It certainly solidified my faith in the man. "There's a difference between reaping success and reaping excess," he said. Reaping. Funny.

It made sense, which is probably what didn't make any sense. We had a moment to live. Aidan had just gotten married to Mary and I was still single and sort of out of the closet. I suppose it would've made sense if we spent money on expensive shit, but we knew that was what got people like Jordan Belfort unwanted attention. And we chose not to do that. Much to Mary's chagrin. It wasn't that we didn't have any fun. We just didn't empty the bank accounts in the process.

Aidan looked like the hot shot compared to me. Most people do. As we got older, his tastes in suits got a little more refined while I retained the flare of my youth. Sort of a cross between my Southern heritage and my natural affection for color. Unlike Aidan, I wasn't ashamed of where I came from. My upbringing was a far cry from his though, and just about every New Yorker with a strand of common sense could see that.

Somewhere along the way, the line between security and prosperity became blurred. After Jacob's death, my father's death, my mother's suicide, and the formation of the business partnership between us, Aidan felt an extended sense of duty toward the Moores. I suppose he probably felt responsible for what happened to Jacob.

It only sort of adds up. I saw how Jacob was that night. He was practically in shock the whole time. His silence could be attributed to Aidan, who was on a roll that night. McIntyre never got credit for recognizing that he was pretty fucked right after Aidan started taking those pictures. Aidan thought it had to do with his speech on good and evil, but my partner should have been able to see that he'd won long before he uttered that nonsense.

The tides had turned and that was fairly obvious. The

Senator had plenty of experience with that sort of stuff through his partisan bickering on the Senate floor. When you've lost, it's better to brace for landing than to grasp at strands of air, hoping for a parachute that isn't coming. Not enough people know how to lose.

Maybe Jacob knew that and didn't want to fuck things up. Most manmade disasters happen when people try to fix something that isn't broken. Jacob didn't have my book smarts, but he wasn't a stupid man.

Sure we can figure out why he was quiet, or enough of why to satisfy any lingering curiosity. But that doesn't explain the cigarettes. Aidan told me that Jacob was going to buy cigarettes. He smoked a ton, but he always rolled his own. Always. He never bought a pack in his life.

And Aidan knew that, too. Never tried to hide it from the police, me, or any of my family. He said it was odd and that he offered Jacob one of his own. They checked his room and found his pouch half full. He didn't need tobacco or cigarettes. Maybe he went for Aidan's sake and he just didn't have the balls to tell me. Typical.

Yet he wandered off into the street and got plowed by a fucking bus. Where's the sense in that? A life wasted for a pack of Marlboros or Newports. What kind did Aidan smoke?

I can't remember how drunk he was that night. Not with any sense of accuracy. He was tense. I was hammered. That's what you're supposed to do at cocktail parties. You drink free booze and you go home. There's nothing in there about getting hit by a bus. Things should be different.

I walk into the kitchen to get more coffee. I don't particularly need energy, but that bitter taste gets the mind moving. Coffee is meant to be consumed black. Maybe with a little milk if you've got a stomach that can't take the acid, but never with that syrup crap. Caleb disagrees.

Caleb is back in the kitchen. Wearing workout clothes. Sexy. For a thirty-seven-year-old, he looks pretty damn good. Blonde hair that shines without salon treatments. He's a little short for a top, but that's okay. That's what the gym is for.

"How did the meeting go?" he asks. That's not a question he wants to ask, but it's something that needs to be said. It's nice to know he cares.

"They want to revoke my bail," I reply. Is that the most important thing you took away from that? Don't be such a drama queen.

Color vanishes from Caleb's face. "How can they do that?" he asks. Good question. I'm not sure I know.

"They're worried I'll disappear like Aidan. Or that I'm in danger. Whichever is most convenient for them at the time. Chomsky has them at bay. He thinks it's just a scare tactic." Good old Chomsky.

I sit down on the seat at the island to brace for this unpleasant exchange of words. Unpleasant for me. Caleb reaches his hand across the countertop so we're almost touching. That's nice. He's sort of there.

"A scare tactic for what?" Ugh. Stop with the tough questions.

I take a sip of my coffee. More French toast would be nice. I don't think I'll be getting any. Too bad there aren't any Waffle Houses in New York.

"They want Aidan. They don't want me. I'm what they have. The prosecution wants progress and the status quo isn't working for them so they're stirring the pot in an effort to get me to give him up."

Caleb looks sad. Betrayal is sad. So is jail. There are a lot of things to be sad about. Maybe I should mention Mary. That would make the conversation even sadder.

"Did you reach any conclusions with Chomsky?" Caleb asks. His wording shows his reluctance to just ask me what I'm going to do. Etiquette. That's nice, but I wish he would just be forward with me. That's what I like about Chomsky.

I reply, "Yes," without thinking about what should come after that. Words, words, words. I haven't really come to any conclusions. Caleb touches my hand with his finger. How erotic. He's waiting for me to elaborate. I don't want to. Why can't he be satisfied with what I've given him? I don't want to talk anymore.

Eh, I might as well be blunt with him. He is my partner after all. "He says I have a little less than a week to decide whether or not I'm going to throw Aidan under the bus. Our next court date is for later in the week, contingent on the decision, of course."

Caleb pours himself a cup of coffee. Oh dear. Why isn't he leaving for the gym? I could use some alone time. Maybe watch *The View* or whatever else is on TV. I'm still pissed that PBS took *Mister Rogers' Neighborhood* off the air. I fear for the future of America.

"Are we going to talk about what you're going to do?" I'd rather not. Why should I have to right now? Chomsky just left and I didn't give him an answer. I don't have an answer.

"I don't know what I'm going to do. One tries to think about life-changing decisions before one makes them." Don't be rude. You were rude.

And Caleb knows it. He says, "Yes, and one also talks with one's partner about decisions that affect said partner." Fair. I say nothing for a little while. I'm losing my edge. Growing soft in my old age.

"Yes Caleb. That is fair. Talk away. Tell me what you think I should do." Drop the condescension. I add, "I'm sorry. You know I value your opinion and it's good to have someone trying to talk to me about this who isn't Chomsky. That was a lot to handle." Now you're being vulnerable. Stop that.

Looks like it worked. Caleb looks sad and maybe slightly guilty for his part in my rudeness. Good. I'm under a lot of stress. "I'm sorry," he replies. "I know you've got a lot on your plate."

I could end this conversation now. Caleb wouldn't try to push. But that's not fair. He has a right to voice his opinion about the mess I've made.

"I was being serious before. In my own way. I would like to hear your thoughts. This decision affects both of us." That's better Giles.

Caleb doesn't look happier. I guess we can't win them all. "I think you need to distance yourself from Aidan and let him take the fall. He fucked us when he took off. Now he gets what's coming. When he isn't even around to see it. You need to think about the future."

Ouch. Poor Aidan. Is Caleb wrong? I guess we don't know the answer to that, do we?

I ask, "Can you honestly say with complete certainty that he took off? Because I can't, Caleb. I know Aidan and I know that this isn't like him. Something's not right and I'm not ready to stab him in the back until I know all the facts. There's the future and then there's right and wrong.

You don't forget the latter to make the former easier. He's my kin. Our kin."

Caleb's face tightens. He's struggling. Arguing with me is never easy, so I hear. I don't know why.

"What difference does it make if he took the money and ran or not? It doesn't change anything. He's gone. You're not. Let his ghost burn for it. You think his legacy is going to be any different? He's been missing for a month. Aidan is not coming back."

Ghost. Yikes. I guess I've always acknowledged the idea that Aidan could be dead. Hearing it said is different. Especially from Caleb, the eternal optimist. Well, he's an optimist compared to Mary and me. Anyone is.

Mary would lose it if she was here right now. No one can tarnish Aidan's name but her. That's a good point, actually.

"What am I supposed to do about my sister if I go public with accusations that this was all Aidan's doing? Do you really think I'll still be able to keep her quiet? Aidan isn't going under any bus with her around. Mary would blab and blab and blab once she realized what I was trying to do. That'd bring her back from La La Land." Yes, Caleb. Process that one. That'll buy me some more time.

He replies, "She still has something to lose. And we have something to gain." Maybe I was wrong. Is Caleb coming to the dark side?

Jack. Not John, Jack. Stupid right? What's even stupider is that he's named after Jacob. Jack sounds like Jake, which also isn't a real name. Only a nickname. Aidan told me he suggested Jack for the memory, while avoiding the problem of Mary freaking out when she's in one of her moods. That makes sense right? No. Of course not.

"You really think we should move forward? Try to take custody of Jack at a time like this? Caleb, I know things are shitty, but that's somewhere we don't want to go right now." I rub my eyes. The coffee isn't helping.

Caleb starts pacing around the room. He's thinking of ways to try to get through to me. I wish him the best of luck with that.

"Don't you get it, Giles? Now is the perfect time. There isn't going to be a better time. You make a play for custody of Jack and then come forward blaming Aidan for the whole mess and they'll listen. They'll have to. You'll give then what they want. A perpetrator. Someone to blame. And you give me what I want. What we want. A child. How else are we supposed to get one?"

We were looking into adoption agencies for a few months before this all began. Things got complicated. I don't really understand why that matters so much, since apparently all the foster homes are full, yet no one seems to be able to adopt any of the children. Why should we be blacklisted just because I committed a few white collar crimes?

There's all sorts of types to choose from. I don't care what the kid looks like. I want to see what the problem is that keeps all these children away from loving homes. Unless people are just stupid. Never take that option off the table. Human stupidity.

This isn't the first time Jack has been mentioned as an alternative to adoption. Mary is a terrible mother who shows no affection for the little rascal who came out of her womb. Regina is more of a mother. Which almost makes things easier. She could come work for us. I'm taking care of her fucking salary anyway.

Adopting a kid is basically out of the question for the time being. I suppose Caleb could try on his own without mentioning me. That could work. We're not married. Not yet. From what I've seen of those agencies, they'd never put two and two together. Unless they did a Google search. I wouldn't hold my breath.

It's not about them, though. It's about us. Could we survive if Caleb did something like that by himself, even if I gave my blessing? It's an admission of expendability. No, you can't allow that. You're too important.

Jack represents the best case scenario, anyway. He's my own flesh and blood so Caleb can't have him without me. That'd be nice. Unless I went to jail, but I'd be able to live with that. He's also two so he doesn't have far to go before he can shit in a toilet. Who needs a newborn?

Caleb's proposition is still problematic. "Are you prepared for the inevitable shit storm that will come if we try to take Jack away from Mary?" I ask.

He shakes his head. "I don't see why she'd care. He could disappear for three days and she wouldn't even notice. She'd care for as long as it would take her to get her next drink. Although that's harder for her now. Maybe waking the dragon wasn't such a great idea."

It's true. Mary would care out of principle, which isn't the same thing. Jack is little more than a prop to her. We could give him an actual home. Maybe. If things go our way.

Who knows? "I'm not sure I can do that to Mary. Aidan is one thing. She's my sister and this isn't her fault. He screwed her, too. Is that a just reason to take her kid away?"

Screwing over Aidan is wrong, depending on how

you want to look at it. But Mary? I've got little love for my only surviving sibling, but there are lines a man shouldn't cross. It's hard to spin betraying your blood like that, even if I only need to convince myself.

"Yes. You said it yourself earlier. If you tried to pin this on Aidan, she'd go berserk. How is that not a reason?" Oh, Caleb. You were doing so well. But you can't make truth out of lies and betrayal.

I take a deep breath, trying to remember to maintain civility as I explain the flaws in Caleb's argument. "Who would be at fault if Mary took offense to my public execution of Aidan's character? You want to talk about justice? We can't, because we don't know the facts. Mary doesn't, either. If she were to speak out in defense of her husband's name, how could I blame her? That's the real kicker. I think you're forgetting something in all of this."

No. Don't go there. Too late. "What's that?" Caleb replies. He doesn't look like he wants to hear the answer, standing there with his arms crossed.

"I was with him every step of the way. I know you don't want to hear it. I know I didn't say anything because – what was there to say? We did bad things. Well, I don't think they were that bad, but that's beside the point. We moved money around knowing that it wasn't entirely legal. We dipped our toes into things we shouldn't have touched when it all started to go south, trying to save the business. We broke the law. Aidan did. I did. Why must he answer for the both of us? And why would Mary put up with that?"

Do you fight fire with fire? Do you still fight if you don't know whether or not the fire did anything wrong? Billy Joel could sing fire songs about Aidan if our crimes were bad enough. Does he still write new music?

Caleb is silent. I think he's upset that I've admitted guilt. Spousal privilege is a bit of a gray area here. Chomsky doesn't think that it will be much of an issue. Putting Caleb on the stand would draw too much sympathy for my case. They need more than him to get me, anyway. That's probably why they want me to rat out Aidan. It's simpler that way. Beyond that, saying it out loud makes it real. I'm in trouble.

"What are you guilty of?" Caleb asks. There's a small smirk on his face. Could he be joking with me at a time like this? I've known the man for close to six years. Is this in line with his character?

Yes. Yes. He must be going insane. Or he's trying to win me over.

"Being guilty is not the same as feeling remorseful, Caleb," I say. He stops pacing. He knows he's dealing with vintage Giles now.

I'm not remorseful. Those regulations are stupid. I wasn't operating a Ponzi scheme. I was using money to make more money. That was my job. It was fun. Until questions started being asked. Then a bad day became a worse one. They thought I was robbing Peter to pay Paul. Little did they know I had already robbed Paul. Paul McIntyre. Oh, the Senator. I wonder what he's up to right now. Laughing about my state of affairs.

Caleb comes over and kisses me. How passionate. I forgot what that felt like. I try to return his gesture, but I feel a bit silly doing so. Stress can alter your libido.

"Thanks," I say. Awkward. That's okay.

"Don't think I don't see what you're trying to do," he replies. What is he talking about? "You're making excuses for why you can't let Aidan take the fall. You're not afraid of Mary. You just want to be afraid of her. That way, you get to keep your moral compass. What does she even know?"

Nothing. I am afraid of her. She's reckless and dangerous. Maybe he's right. I'm not ready to cede that. "You've made your point, Caleb. I'll talk to Mary later today. It'll beat trying to talk to Regina over the phone, though her English has improved over the years. I'll stop over there after my meeting with the PI."

Aidan didn't confide in Mary. He confided in me. He trusted me. No one else. I might not know where he went, but I know he never told Mary about the Senator. I took Jacob's spot. He wouldn't be stupid enough to tell her about our business endeavors. She wouldn't understand it, anyway. She barely even knows how to read anymore with all those pills.

"I'm late for the gym," Caleb says. "Late?" I reply, "How can one be late for the gym in the middle of the day? Is it in danger of closing?"

Caleb puts his mug in the dishwasher. He's smiling. "I already missed one pilates class. I can get there now and run for a bit before the next one starts." Oh, Caleb.

I should be thankful that he's still around. You tend to write that kind of stuff off when you're in a long-term relationship, but this shit would have scared off anyone else. And we're not even married. If he decided that this nonsense wasn't for him, I'd understand. I'd probably end up like Mary without him, but I wouldn't blame him.

Where's my phone? In my pocket. It's getting close to noon. I'll need to head to the Chestnut Street Tavern at twelve thirty to meet with the PI. Mister Smiley he calls himself. What a stupid name. He's good at what he does. Chomsky recommended him, which has to count for something.

I think I'll go outside for a bit. The backyard should be looking nice and clean. Not like the Rubinoffs next door with the dog pissing everywhere. The brown spots would drive me insane. I'll bring a cup of coffee. If we still subscribed to the *Wall Street Journal*, I'd bring that, too. Can't read that anymore without the office.

Fuck reporters. To think they've done all this digging and yet none of them have come close to finding out the real juicy tidbits of the adventures of Aidan and Giles. Well, now it's just my cross to bear.

I would have thought that would have been the craziest night of my life. After all this, I suspect that night is still to come what with prison and all. Caught having intercourse with a United States senator by my brother and his frat buddy. That alone would make for an unforgettable evening, but then the frat buddy extorts the Senator for six hundred thousand dollars and then my brother gets run over in the street. Now that is something you write about.

Aidan deserves credit for not demanding too much money. He started at five hundred thousand and only raised the number by a hundred thousand when McIntyre tried to go all politician on him. A million got you a lot farther back then, but he would have paid. Greed would not have suited us at that moment. Aidan knew that.

Would it have ruined him? Probably. There was that Mississippi representative who got arrested for having sex with the janitor who worked in the Library of Congress. Charged with sodomy. What a joke. A life ruined because he put a cock in his mouth. The owner of said penis even consented. McIntyre had to know the stakes.

I guess Aidan was right. He still had an extramarital encounter. I've never done that. Nor have Aidan or Mary, to my knowledge. Aidan had plenty of chances. All those conferences in Vegas and Newport Beach. He kept it in his pants. Good for him.

Am I supposed to have sympathy for the Senator because he was gay? No. Being gay doesn't mean you get to be a cheat. Even back then. It certainly doesn't mean you have to marry a woman. People like McIntyre give the rest of us a bad name.

There was a simple solution. Don't be a senator. Go have sex with all the men you want, wherever you want to have it. Provided you're not in a committed relationship.

That's the thing about doing bad things. People hide behind ridiculous excuses. It's okay to cheat because you're a closeted homosexual? Bullshit. That guy's poor wife and kids. Who wins in that scenario?

Maybe he was bisexual. To my knowledge, his life wasn't ruined by what we did. Served two more terms and retired in '04. Not a bad life.

If I saw him again, the only thing I'd really want to ask was whether or not it was worth it. Not the sex with me. I was frisky in my youth, but my ass ain't worth six hundred grand. Maybe four.

I have a hard time believing he felt his altruistic calling to elected office justified living a lie for all those years. The lie he's still living. He wanted what they all want. Power. That's where corruption comes from.

But why does power need to come at a cost like that? What's it worth? Aidan and I could've expanded our business. We could've been swimming in money like Scrooge McDuck and that vault of his. We might have been caught quicker, but that's what happens to corrupt people.

I never lived a lie and I never chased power. People knew I was gay, even if they were afraid to admit it, because I did a job that I was good at. That's all that matters. There was a time where I was afraid to admit it. I went on a few dates with women. They never moved past the first stages. Why? Because that kind of life isn't worth living. The lie becomes you. You talk about bullshit on podiums that you don't even believe. You don't believe in anything because the lie is all you are.

Moore/Davies Capital is something I believed in. We were good, even when we were bad. We had a fucking code and it was morally sound. Sort of.

I might've paid the people back if I could, though I maintain that they knew the risks involved and are not entitled to reparations as a result of this situation. But I can't so that might be bullshit. Most of them don't miss the money. They miss it because it's gone and it was theirs, but that's greed. There's plenty of money to go around.

Like that woman in the coffee shop. Her husband chased dollars he didn't have. So he put what he had in the wrong places. Tough fucking shit. I always made sure I had a stash in case I needed it.

I do need it. Two million doesn't get you very far when you're dealing with people who make it their mission to avoid run-ins with the law. That's only part of it. Two million doesn't get you very far when you don't know how far you need to go.

What if I need it to do something really fun and

scandalous? Like run. That's what I really want to do. Caleb and I can get fake passports and get the fuck out of here. Caleb wouldn't need a fake. Mine is in the possession of some federal judge. What's his name? I don't even remember. Oops.

Let's go to Asia. Tokyo is nice. So is Singapore. Singapore is clean. You'd like that. You also might get discovered there. That wouldn't be good.

Then there's Canada. Or a Scandinavian country. Cold might do me some good. That's why the Russian prison is in Siberia. Cold brings clarity. But then what?

Or something simpler. Doesn't Caleb have a cabin in New Hampshire that his uncle left him when he died? He was probably gay, too. We've talked about going skiing up there for years. I don't know how to ski. You only need to hide for a little while. People forget. You're not that interesting.

Caleb would like that. For a while. He'd become a criminal, too. I'm not a criminal yet. Only after a conviction or a confession. Good luck getting either of those from me.

I think I defend Aidan based on the principal of it. Giving into them means giving into fear. I'm not afraid.

I don't want to go to prison. Mostly because of the food. The sex might be nice. Might being the key word. I hear they test for diseases quite frequently so I wouldn't need condoms and I wouldn't be afraid. I don't think the pillow talk would be very interesting. If they even have pillow talk. Savages.

That also makes running more appealing. If I'm fucked, why not have some fun? Jail will be there when I get back. And if not, then oh well. A beach somewhere would sure beat a jail cell, even if it meant I could never come back to the good old USA.

Roman Polanski can't come back. He ran after some statutory rape charge that hasn't really impeded his career. He still made *The Pianist.* Maybe I can flee to wherever he is and help him finance his next film.

Not being able to come back would bother Caleb. I wouldn't care. I've hardly been back down south since Mother overdosed on those pills. I don't blame her. She loved Father and Jacob more than she ever loved Mary and me. And we were all that was left. Not a fun world for her anymore. That's how it goes. When life isn't fun anymore, you give up. Why not?

Who cares really? Your family, yes? But if people you cared about were still around, you wouldn't give up. That's why I'm still here. What would Caleb do if I offed myself? I can't take the easy way out after all of this.

I have no thoughts of that. Too much excitement lies just over the horizon. The trial might actually be fun. I could make faces at Mrs. Ramsey so she can understand the gravity of her betrayal.

Caleb might actually be interested in running if we could take Jack along. Two affluent-looking gay men and a baby running all over hell and creation. That wouldn't last long.

Caleb should get Jack. It's only fair. Eh, he's got alternatives. If I go to jail, he can always move to someplace where no one knows who he is. Problem solved. Maybe that's why he's still here.

If they want to fight gay marriage, then maybe they should consider that someone like Caleb could start over while a married woman would be hampered down by her husband's crimes. As soon as you start to consider the negative baggage, opposing it becomes far less appealing. That's how we work. Logic.

I've never been a big gay rights advocate. I'm for it, of course. That should go without saying. But the whole marching thing isn't appealing to me. Draws too much attention. I don't have the right shoes. I'm gay. So what?

Aidan and I used to do good cop, bad cop when we were looking for investors. Aidan would be all gung-ho about their potential and I'd sit there and scowl while I looked through the portfolio. I didn't always need to act. We were right to stay away from a lot of those people.

We made a lot of people plenty of money. I hope they come to my trial. They probably won't because popcorn and soft drinks won't be served in the courthouse. Testifying in my favor would be a big detriment to their business. I couldn't ask them to do that.

That's fair. Fair is a funny word. We use it when we're kids to justify entitlement attitudes. My turn on the swings. No? Well, that's not fair. Says who? You? Being the arbiter of your own fortune might not be fair, either. Who's to say who gets a turn on the fucking swings?

Plenty of people don't get to pick. Outside circumstances dictate it for them. Sure, they could pick up and leave. Many of them do. Me? No, not I. Fate? Yes.

I could decide now, as long as Caleb was willing. When Jacob died and I found out about Father's deteriorating condition, I had a responsibility to Mary. Maybe I still do. That doesn't make a whole lot of sense. She was Aidan's problem for two decades and now she's mine again. I was the one who had to take her to the hospital.

What to do, oh, what to do? There is a simple answer

to all of this. Just do whatever the fuck you want. You're going to Hell, anyway. Enjoy the warm ride down to Hades.

That's no way to live. Why? Rules. People love rules. They're only there to keep people from doing bad shit. Where rules fail, people have excuses. Words to justify their own intentions for this shit storm we call life.

Breathe Giles. No need to get all worked up over life's greater issues. You've got plenty of your own to worry about. Much simpler. C'est la vie!

You made it this far because you were always ahead of the rest. Even Aidan. You had to conform to him a bit, but that didn't mean you had to get on his level. Adaptation. That's what will get you through this.

Adaptation to what? Does an animal survive in the wilderness by tripping its kin so that some other animal eats it? Maybe? If given the chance, would the victim turn the tide? It would only seem fair.

Another question you don't seem to know the answer to. Fuck. You're letting things slip these days. You can't have that. You must be in your prime.

Time to head over to the tavern. Time flies when you're sitting outside drinking coffee, trying to decide if you're going to betray your brother-in-law. I wonder if Aidan thought about this as much when he took off. I doubt it.

I get up. Ouch, my creaky legs. That's probably stress. Not age. I should probably go to pilates, too. That wouldn't be good. Caleb can disappear in crowds. You can't.

My jacket. Yes. Keeping up with appearances. Mary would be proud. Mary will be proud when I see her later today. If she still remembers what appearances are. Pills are a nasty way to take solace in the misery of life.

The mirror. Take a look. Hairline's receding. Still skinny. You look good, Giles. That's probably a bad thing. Makes you an easy target for the media. If you looked a little gaunter, you'd probably get off with no trouble. Stiff upper lip, there's a good man.

Blue BMW. Not a Ferrari, but you never needed one of those. You can't drive it anywhere around here. A BMW is safe. Doesn't attract as much attention in this part of the world. Or you could take Caleb's Porsche.

I'd hire a driver if I could go back in time and do it all over again. That's the one thing I regret. Not that I needed one. Especially with the train. It's just a representation of class that's all but disappeared from this earth. That would have been nice. People don't have drivers anymore. Except for the really rich folks. What is this world coming to?

Caleb and I could cuddle up in the back seat on I-95, with the windows tinted while some old fuck drives us around. Dreams do come true. Maybe you didn't enjoy your money enough while you had it.

No, stop that. Turn the ignition on. You enjoyed your twenties and most of your thirties for that matter. You traveled. You kept Aidan from getting all caught up in the big world with its endless possibilities. Life was good.

And then when you got older, you settled down. Too many people think a gay man has to run around copulating for his whole life like some voyeuristic savage, like the Senator. Doesn't want to live a normal life. You showed them.

But do they know that? No. They only care about one thing. The present. Where you stand now. Who says you can't forget the past? The past doesn't affect where you are in the here and now. It's just some comfort from a time that's over. It's comforting when you look at something you can't fix.

You can change the present. Live the life you want to live. Think of it now.

Move to the West Coast. Some San Francisco suburb. Caleb can find work catering to the faux tastes of the bourgeoisie and I'll write my memoir. Sounds arrogant, but people love that shit. Belfort made all that money. Some wolf he was.

Then once we get some money I'll invest it and we'll make more money. Not a bad life. Certainly more realistic than Lennie and his rabbits. Of mice and hedge funds.

All yours if you can sell your soul. If you still have one. Tell the Feds and collect your pardon and your book deal. Thirty pieces of silver? Nah, that would make Aidan a Christlike figure. He'd love that, wouldn't he?

Oh look, it's Roxburgh Wine & Spirits. I was in there just yesterday to talk to a man about my sister. That wasn't very nice. Some things just have to be done. Mary can undo much of my good fortune with that mouth of hers. Not that she has a fucking clue what's going on.

That's the funny thing Caleb can't seem to understand about my sister. She might not know anything. But she knows that knowledge isn't necessarily where she draws her power. All she needs to be is convincing. Mary can do that.

She doesn't need to know where the money is to be a problem. All she needs to do is point her finger at me, and boom. I'm done. She can be just as much a sympathetic character in all of this as I can. Even more so.

Would she? Depends on the alternative. That's why I

had to cut off her booze supply. Not only does she need to be able to think clearly, she also needs to be shown the line between reality and the dream. Escape routes can cave in. The bottle can run out. Well, I made it run out. Let's see what she's really capable of without Regina to help her get drunk.

The Chestnut Street Tavern isn't on Chestnut Street. It's on Lake Street. Which isn't near a lake. Some people hate that. I think it's kind of beautiful. You can be anything you want to be. All you need to do is tell the world what you are.

Who would have thought a little gay boy from Georgia could grow up to commit major financial fraud? Only in America. Maybe Canada.

I don't know what kind of car Mister Smiley drives. I suppose he likes it that way. He probably switches his car every time. Some people are just paranoid.

Should I be worried for my own safety? No. No one is coming for me. If somebody got Aidan, that's enough. He knows where the money is. I don't, and no one else does.

The tavern is occupied by a few of the barflies. I like them. They don't scoff at my presence. I didn't rip any of them off. None of them could afford my services. Now, now, don't be rude.

It's only noon, but it's also a holiday for some businesses. Mary wouldn't bat an eye. I am in a bar, though. It's rude to not order something when you're using the establishment to meet with a shady PI. I don't need anyone talking about my presence here, and they're only going to do that if I give them a reason to.

"What can I get you?" asks the bartender. Why are they even open? Because there are people here, that's why.

Business moves with the customer. You know that.

Hmm. What do I want? "Tom Collins," I reply. How lovely. Very popular in the South. Father used to love them. He said they were invented in Savannah. I don't think that's true.

A good Tom Collins is hard to come by in the year 2010. People don't order them much anymore. Which means that bartenders are often bad at making them.

That bothers me. It's a drink that has ties to the old days. How many drinks are there really? And yet, bartenders fuck it up all the time.

Too many people lack pride in their work. It's "beneath" them. Fuck that. If you're employed to do a job, do it right. That's how you climb up the ladder.

But then of course there's the old counterargument: entitlement. Which can happen to anyone, independent of status or wealth. All you need is an attitude.

Father blew a lot of his money on amenities in his last few months. Mary hated that more than anyone else because she couldn't understand why. She was worried about what was going to happen to her. It wasn't like we were left empty-handed, even after Mother faded away.

But what if we were? What if Father decided he wanted to give all his money to the Church or some other charitable organization? Or if he wanted to have a month-long party with top-shelf booze and debauchery. Stupid, yes, but who am I to say anything about it?

Make your own way in life. You never know if someone is going to be there if you fall. I was lucky to have some cash to help our little business get off the ground but much of that was my own doing. If I hadn't, I just would have had to work harder.

The bartender returns with my drink. I put a couple of bills on the table and I take a sip. That's good. "Cheers. It's a fine drink," I say. The bartender nods.

Off to the back booth. Only one of them is occupied. By a man. I wonder what the rest of the people in this place think of that. Eh, don't get ahead of yourself. Don't assume that people give a rat's ass about your business unless you have something they want. Or if they're a bunch of gossips. Barflies don't have much else going on.

Mister Smiley looks up at me. He's an older man with thinning gray hair. He looks older than Chomsky, but he's in better shape. I still wouldn't want to go against him in a fight. He's wearing a jacket with no tie. Classy, but you probably wouldn't take a second look at him walking down the street. All by design, of course.

"Hello," I say. I don't call him Mister Smiley. I refuse. He can have his alias all he wants. I don't begrudge him that. I won't be entertaining that narcissism, either. Only my own. He should go by his real name. What's he afraid of?

"Mr. Moore," he replies. He's got a cola on the table. I doubt there's any alcohol in it. I feel stupid for ordering a cocktail.

"I figured I'd order a drink since we're in a bar," I say, feeling self-conscious. I've barely taken a sip of it. Does that make it worse?

I expect him to laugh. I don't know why. I don't know the man. He replies, "It's not my place to be concerned with your public behavior. That's on you." Ouch. I think? Getting a read off this guy is impossible.

He doesn't seem like a man who likes small talk. Who really does? I don't have any small talk to give him. I don't really know what to say. It's not often that I can't size up a conversation. That's probably how he squeezed ten grand out of me just to poke around. At least Chomsky approves of him.

"I've made some progress on the location of your friend," he says. What he's doing is perfectly legal, and yet he neglects to say Aidan's name. I guess he hasn't lasted this long by being careless.

"And?" I ask. And isn't really a question. I hope he doesn't think that's rude. My mouth is a little parched, but I don't want to take a sip of my drink.

He smiles. Odd. "Social media did us some good," he says. "There was a tweet the day he went missing about a man on a train with a suitcase that matched his description."

Bullshit. No way this fucker went digging through month-old tweets. This old fart would have trouble digging through tweets from an hour ago.

I don't say anything. He says, "If the police saw, they must not have thought much of it, but one of my associates took interest since the tweeter in question was a business student at Colombia. Naturally a tweet about a local financial criminal caught our attention." Okay. You've got my attention, you old fuck. He called Aidan a criminal. How dare he?

I relax a little. I have to. I say, "Impressive," neglecting to ponder what exactly is impressive about this. He smiles. "Well, that's only part of it. Maybe someone noticed the tweet and didn't know what to make of it. We checked around the local car rental shops to see if he was trying to skip town. Took a little persuading, but we got what we were looking for."

No fucking way. Why does this guy keep stopping? Spill the fucking beans. "You found him?" I ask. Why would this man keep me hanging? Doesn't he know this is life-changing shit?

"No," he says, keeping up his cryptic nonsense. He pauses. Maybe this is just how he is. These people are weird. Hell, people are weird.

You can't push these kinds of people, either. They're not businessmen. Their job is to take care of things without causing a scene. Pushing him would be causing a scene. I must play his game.

"So, your friend goes into the place and gives the attendant an ID with the name Jacob McIntyre. Does that name mean anything to you?"

I'd be surprised if he didn't know that Jacob is my brother's name. He could be good enough to figure out McIntyre. Does that need to be said? Maybe he's trying to see if I'm lying. I'm not giving everything away.

"First name belongs to my deceased brother and my associate's old roommate. Second is a party joke. Do you think he could be leaving a trail?" Good. You asked him a question. That'll throw him off.

"Doubtful. Probably just laziness. Not evidence the police can use for anything. So anyway, the attendant thinks the ID is a little suspect, especially since your buddy never used their service before and looked a little frazzled. Of course, he's got no idea who he really is." I don't know what to make of this. What was Aidan doing?

"So your friend pulls out twenty-five thousand dollars and tells the attendant that he wants the car without filling out any of the paperwork. Mr. McIntyre says he only needs it for a day or two. He's making a little journey to see someone, so the attendant says. Naturally the attendant wants the money so he takes a copy of the fake license and fills out some bogus paperwork himself in case the car doesn't come back. Didn't seem like the brightest kid I ever met."

"I see," I reply. He doesn't need to know what I think. This is confusing, anyway. "So why didn't the car rental place call it in stolen?"

Mister Smiley folds his hands on the table. "That's where it gets really interesting. The car was returned in Maine. Portland. So this attendant gets the best of both worlds. He gets the money and no one is going to look into a car that isn't missing. He didn't even ask me to pony up any money for that information. Said it was the weirdest thing he's ever seen." I'll say.

Maine. What the hell is he doing there? Is? That was a month ago. He could be anywhere now. Surprised Smiley ran into the same attendant at the car rental. That place must have a high turnover rate.

"So, what happens next?" I ask. "And any idea who he went to see?" I cringe. I try not to be too pushy with these sorts of people. Can never tell whose side they're on.

He takes a sip of his drink and exhales. Definitely no alcohol in there. "I've got some people there looking into it. No luck so far. I know a guy who has an in with the Canadian border patrol, but we don't have much to go on without a car or a date. If what our other mutual friend told me is true, wasting resources is not in your best interest."

Chomsky. Why the fuck is he telling creepy PI's about my finances? What happened to attorney-client privilege?

Chomsky is almost as secretive as this guy. Doesn't

like to admit when he's broken the law. Probably because he doesn't do it very often. That's the thing when you don't know what people are doing. You never know what they're doing.

It doesn't help me to get all defensive with this guy and he knows that. I don't need to pretend I have unlimited funds when he knows I don't. "No, it isn't," I reply. "Thank you for using your best judgment," I add. I don't want to stroke this guy's ego, but he's done good work so far and I need him. I don't have too many allies.

He gives me a smile. More like a pity smile. "Do you know why they call me Mister Smiley?" he asks. Because you wanted to be a lame superhero when you were growing up? No. Be nice.

Don't entertain him. Show him you've got balls. "No," I say. "My father always told me never to ask questions I didn't need the answers to." Snarky, but funny. Good work.

He laughs. Ah, you've gotten through to him. Excellent work, Giles. Maybe I can take a sip of my drink now. "Your father was a smart man. I got that name because of my ability to deliver information faster than anyone else. Always puts a smile on their face. Makes sense, right?" I nod.

"Well, I mention that because we're at a crossroads. I don't know how much more I'll be able to deliver. You build a reputation with consistency and you build respect by being upfront with your clients. I can keep looking for your friend, but this is basically a cold case at this point and that's problematic beyond what I can fix. If this were some relatively unknown name, I'd have more hope, but this guy knew people were coming and he was prepared. I cannot say with confidence that I will be able to find him. The question is whether or not you need to know more than what you know already. If so, we can keep going, but I needed to make sure that you knew where we're at."

Damn it, Chomsky. You better not have told him about the looming decision. If he thinks this coercion will help, he's out of his mind. I need new attorneys.

Stop being paranoid. That'll completely unravel you. What's left of you. Nice and calm.

"Thank you. I guess you're right," I say. I'm not sure what else needs to be said. Or what else I can say at the present moment.

Mister Smiley takes another big sip of his drink. "I'll have my people poke around Portland a little more and see if they can find anything that resembles a trail. If you need anything else, contact me through our mutual friend. Good luck." He leaves without shaking my hand. Rude.

Well, I can't really say it was rude. He did say he'd continue the search. I wonder why he's so skeptical. He found Maine through a month old tweet and dumb luck. Isn't that a trail? Why is he so convinced that lightning won't strike twice? That's rational. I guess it's his job to know, but he's looking a little fishy with that unexplained certainty.

You're questioning Mister Smiley because you don't want to process the obvious. He's gone and you're the only one who doesn't care to realize it. Take a sip of your drink.

Aidan screwed you over. Say it one more time. Aidan screwed you over. Another sip. He took the money and ran.

Why would he do that? Why did he need all the

fucking money, anyway? At least leave some behind for your wife and kid, you fucking fuck. God damn.

How could you not see this coming? Your entire business was founded on a scam. He used you right from the start. It was all okay because you played it cool. You were "in on it." Fucking dipshit. That's how life goes. It's all fun and games until the feces start getting tossed in your general vicinity.

It doesn't make any sense. Even if he was running, he could've said, "Look, I'm leaving. Here's a few million for my family. Pin this shit on me and get yourself out. Bye." Would that have been so hard? No, and that's what's so strange.

Maine makes sense. It's the opposite of where they'd look for him. I know the Feds looked for him in Alabama and Georgia. They were basically obliged to tell Mary that, given that he's technically a missing person and all. Not that she cares.

But why do this to me? What does he gain by tossing me under the bus? It would've made more sense to kill me so that he could be sure the McIntyre incident never got out. I should fuck him on that one, too. God, what a piece of shit. Good thing there's no one around because I'm about to lose it.

He's probably sitting in some bar in Halifax drinking Canadian Club and laughing about his life, devoid of any moral sanctity. Here's to Aidan Davies, the swine who screwed the Moores. He killed one, ruined another by marriage, and left me to burn in the wreckage.

Where would I be without him? People usually ask that when they're thinking about loved ones. Not destroyers. Aidan would probably like that term.

But seriously, I could have been anything. Look at what I did in finance after only taking an economics elective. No formal education. Political science major. I built an empire. I could have done anything with my life.

You were the smartest in the whole family. You needed to be. You didn't have Jacob's people skills or Mary's looks. That's why the partnership was so fucking appealing. Convenience. But you didn't have to do all the heavy lifting.

Why did you ignore the red flags? You knew they were there. You can't tell anyone about the Senator because they'd all ask the same question.

Why would you have gone into business with that man?

It's simple really. I wasn't going to be the victim. If I shared the reward, you can't say I was a victim.

The better question to ask would be why didn't I lock the door? I can't answer that one. I didn't think they'd come over. Who would? Aidan would end up with some girl and Jacob might, too. But they wouldn't come over to my place even after I'd suggested it. Why was Jacob such a stick in the mud that day?

It's funny. Even though I'm filled with rage for Aidan right now, I can't hate him. I had fun with him. Jacob's death could've torn us both apart, but we rose from the ashes. The fact that he betrayed me hurts more than I can comprehend right now, but it doesn't change the fact that he was my business partner for my entire adult life.

Now a new chapter begins. One that doesn't involve him. It might involve his kid and maybe his wife. That's for me to decide. And Caleb. That's the big difference. Aidan shut people out so that he could rule his fortress of solitude. I, on the other hand, learn from my mistakes.

I finish my drink. That was good. Mister Smiley's drink is gone. That's weird. I don't remember him taking it away. Maybe he's a ghost afraid someone would steal his DNA. Or maybe you were just too caught up in your own thoughts to notice. That's more like it.

I should give my glass to the bartender. He'd forget we were even back there, all by ourselves. That would be the courteous thing to do.

This place has great lighting. It's not too bright, but not dim enough that you'd walk outside and be blinded, forced to come to terms with how you spent your day. I wonder why Mary never comes here.

A man seated at the bar looks at me as I approach the counter. Maybe he's a fan of my work. I put the empty glass down. I call out, "Thanks," to the bartender and turn toward the exit.

"Get this man another drink. On my tab," says the man, turning on his stool to face me. Interesting. What does this guy want? Scruffy beard and a baseball cap on his head even though we're indoors.

You must be careful with these sorts. They don't want to be your friend. No one wants to be your friend, anymore. That's what happens when you get arrested. He's a reporter or a lawyer.

But Father also told me never to turn down a free drink. It's something the other person can never get back. If they want something for it, that's for you to decide. Smart man.

"Why, thank you," I say to the man. I sit down on a stool next to him. He's wearing a polo shirt. Maybe that's a golf shirt. I never cared much for golf. He looks to be in his mid-thirties. Not too muscular. Not like Caleb. I see a wedding ring. He's not gay. That's good. I'm not going to sleep with this man for a Tom Collins and it would be a shame to see him mistake me for easy.

There's a twinkle of awe in the man's eye. That's not just arrogance on my part either. He knows who I am. He wants something. I can see it.

"What brings you to the tavern on a Friday as good as this one?" he asks. Oh yes, he's searching for something. The small talk looks for direction. I don't have time for this. I still need to stop by Mary's. Now I actually have something interesting to tell her about her traitorous husband.

"Just catching up with an old friend." Semantically true. He's old and he does nice things for me. Friend? Sure why not. You need more friends.

The man's left eyebrow rises slightly. He doesn't believe me. I don't really care. "I see. That must be nice," he replies. I don't answer. What must be nice?

My drink arrives. "Cheers," I say to him. Might as well be civil to the man who gave me a drink. Even if he does look like a bit of a swine. We clink glasses.

"You're Giles Moore, aren't you?" he asks. He knows the answer to that question or I wouldn't be drinking a free Tom Collins. "I am." Civility and brevity often go hand in hand. He's getting straight to the point. I'm sizing up this man and he doesn't appear to be much of a threat. He's certainly not a reporter.

"Can I ask you a question?" Oh dear. Maybe he is a reporter. "That depends," I say. I don't care to explain that it would be foolish of me to talk about my case to a stranger in a bar. He should know that, and if he doesn't, fuck him.

He says, "Oh, goodness no! I wouldn't ask you about your troubles." He puts his hands over his face for a second. No, definitely not a reporter.

I'm at a bit of a loss here. How does one deal with such a peculiar man? I know. You finish your drink and leave. That's the perfect solution. I take a sip.

He stutters as he opens his mouth. Jesus. Somebody should take this man out back and shoot him. It'd be a mercy killing on this "good" Friday.

"I'm not sure how to phrase this so bear with me," he says. I'd rather not. "My wife and I got divorced last month. She left me for another man. I have a decent job in marketing. It's not flashy and I'm never going to hit the jackpot, but I thought it was a good life. You know? Well, you don't know because you made all that money. Which brings me to my question." Pause. "Does it change anything?"

I hate vague questions. If you can't figure out how to say something right, don't say it at all. Girls like to play guessing games. Guys aren't supposed to. No wonder his wife left him.

Compassion never killed anyone. Well, that's not true, but it won't kill you here. "I'm sorry to hear that," I say. Don't stop there. "Pardon me, but I'm a bit confused by what you're asking."

The man looks defeated. I don't really see why. Shit happens. At least this is happening to him in a place like this, where his wife and her new boy toy can't laugh at him.

"The power. Did it change you?" Well, there we go. Clarity. How does that feel?

This man needs a lecture. No, I need a lecture.

Whenever I was down in the dumps, I'd show someone how much smarter I was than them. Well, I found out my business partner betrayed me today and this man is looking for pity in the wrong place. I'll give him something to keep his mind off his wife.

"Take out a dollar," I say. I speak with authority. Nice and firm. Feels really fucking good. He gives me a funny look. He better not give me any lip. I'm not in the mood for bullshit that isn't of my own doing.

He pulls out his wallet and extends the dollar to me. I take it and put it on the table.

"I'm going to give you a little crash course on investments," I tell him. "Turn around." I make a whirly motion with my finger. I take a sip of my drink with the other hand.

The man turns around. His back is to me, and to the dollar. He's silent. Maybe I should just leave. No, this is fun. This is good.

"What are you thinking about?" I ask him. That might be a dangerous question. I don't really want to know what he's thinking about.

"The dollar," he replies. Naturally. "Of course you are. You can turn around now." I'd rather he didn't.

He looks confused. That's okay. "Was I supposed to be thinking about something else?" he asks. Your wife's pussy. Maybe then she wouldn't have left you. "No," I reply. He says nothing. I suppose it's on me to continue. Time to explain myself.

"What would happen if something happened to that dollar? Perhaps the bartender thought it was a tip or someone stole it for the jukebox. What would happen then? How would you feel about the loss of the dollar that was once yours?" Use your brain, sparky.

He's thinking too much. "I don't know, I wouldn't care. It's just a dollar, isn't it?" He thinks it's a metaphor.

"It is a dollar," I reply. "Let me ask you another question. What is the value of that dollar to you?" Now I'll stump him.

Think, think goes the man. Much ado about nothing. "A hundred cents," he replies. "Is that right?"

I've attracted the attention of another patron. Watching me from the other end of the bar. An audience. You love those. Don't disappoint them, Giles. Give them a show. I take a big sip of the drink. Maybe too big.

"That can't be right. You just said you wouldn't be worried if something happened to it. That dollar has no value to you. It's expendable. You don't need it." Maybe you will after the divorce.

"I'm not sure I follow," replies the man. The sad confused man. Why doesn't he understand? This is simple shit. I sigh. Eek. Don't sigh, that's rude. Elaborate.

"People have a misconception about money. If you follow foreign currency at all, you'd see that while a dollar might be a hundred cents right here, its value fluctuates. Obviously a dollar doesn't get you what it used to when you were little, but it goes beyond that. Do you follow?" The man nods.

"That's only part of the equation. An easy part. You can look up the value of a dollar relative to the euro or the pound on your phone. But what about to the individual? Your perception of a dollar is different than mine, and anyone else's in this room. It may not be much different since we're only dealing with a dollar. But what about a homeless man? You can't expect him to evaluate a dollar the same way that we might. He wouldn't stay idle if someone took his dollar." Oh no. I said we. Now he must think we have some fraternal bond. Yikes.

I take another sip of my drink. Boy, that went fast. As I bring my glass down to the counter, the man calls out, "Another round," to the bartender. He's giving me drinks for simple life lessons. If I didn't need an ego boost right now, I wouldn't care. But Giles needs his comeback.

"I think I understand what you're saying," he says. "The value of money differs so you can wield power by having a greater knowledge of it than someone like me." Oh boy. How did he arrive at that? He's obsessed with power because he doesn't know what it means.

I nod my head. "Well, that's probably true to an extent. But that's not what I was trying to say." He looks helpless and defeated. Maybe he should try harder. "Power hasn't come into play at all. We're strictly talking about the value of perception."

He picks up his fresh beer and raises his glass to me. Good thing we don't clink again. I don't want him spilling beer into my third Tom Collins, even if he paid for it.

He looks like he wants me to keep going. Eyes are perky like he's a dog anxious for a walk. "I assume you've seen a magic trick? Card tricks of sorts?" I ask. He thinks for longer than he should need to and replies, "I have. I don't know how to do any." No surprises there.

"Well, what I do isn't much different. Not pulling shit out of thin air, but making something arrive at a destination that people aren't supposed to be able to understand. That's the point. The power lies in the illusion."

He's still confused. I've attracted more attention. I guess that's a good thing. Hopefully from people who can actually understand this stuff. "So, you're like a magi-cian?" he asks.

"Sort of, except the trick isn't what should be focused on. It's the work that matters. Finesse. Could you perform a magic trick with someone staring down your neck the whole time?"

He sips his beer and looks around. Maybe he's thinking about how he's paying for the whole bar's entertainment. I should raise my prices. Or get a tip jar. That'd get me a new lawyer. At least I'm having a good time.

He answers, "I can't do one at all." Fuck. I give up. Nothing worse than a man who pities himself in public. No, others are watching. Continue your point or people will remember this day as the day you made a fool of yourself. You don't want people to remember you as being full of shit, do you?

"That's fine. You don't need to know how to do one as long as you get what I'm saying." He nods. "Good. That's the basics of investments. You want to move something from point A to point B and what you do along the way to make it profitable is your business. People like me excel at that when we're not being micromanaged. Money flows if you let it, but a stream can't flow if it's got a ton of shit in its way. If it was simple and out in the open, everyone would do it. And then it wouldn't work. Work quickly and efficiently and people won't care what your methods are. Results speak louder than actions and words combined." Simple, right?

"And a good magician never reveals his secrets," calls another man. This man possesses a strong deep voice. I look over. He's hiding behind a newspaper. What the fuck? Ah well, don't entertain his heckling if he can't show his face.

"Not unless he wants to write a get-rich-quick book," I reply. "And even then, it's mostly bullshit." The bar laughs. I think they like me.

The man who bought me the drink is looking down at the counter. This is clearly way over his head. There's little doubt in my mind that his wife left him because he is a complete loser with no hope for the future. I doubt his job was steady. He was probably about to be fired.

"So the power lies in the illusion," he says. It doesn't seem like a question. More like a revelation he accidentally stumbled upon. It's stupid, regardless.

"No, no, no," I reply. "The illusion allows you to perform your duties. You can't work with someone breathing down your neck, but you can't work at all if you don't know what you're doing. Power is an obsession that people have. It's a myth."

Silence. This is awkward. I must continue. "Well, it's not truly a myth. It's not quantifiable. That's where people go wrong. They chase power instead of excellence, and they lose focus on the task at hand. You gain power solely through people's confidence in you to carry out a certain task. That's why it fluctuates. You can't wield it with an iron fist if you can't back it up. Therein lies desperation. When people see other people's faith in them dwindling, they make mistakes because they're flustered. Risk needs to be controlled. Powerful people don't get flustered." My father taught me that. They don't need to know that.

"Then where did you go wrong?" The newspaper man. What the fuck? That voice.

There's silence, but it's an eerie sort of silence. "You,

get out. None of that in here." The bartender has come to my defense. I turn away. I don't need to face a man who can't face me. I hear a crumpling of the newspaper followed by the sound of the door slamming shut. All is right with the world again.

"I'm sorry about that," says the bartender. "Let me get you another drink."

Powerful people know when to call it a day. "No, thank you. I've had more than enough, but I appreciate the offer. Kindness has become a scarce commodity in my world."

Quit that sappy bullshit. Powerful people don't go fishing for sympathy, either. Maybe you've lost your touch. Aidan ran off with that, along with the money. You fool.

You can redeem yourself. Say something motivational. Like what you would say to the troops at quarter's closing.

"Look man," I say. I still don't know his name. It doesn't really matter. "It's tempting to be concerned with power. We see it all around us. But the winners don't become obsessed with it. Power is a slippery slope. It's best to spend your time excelling at your passions. That sounds like a lot of wishy-washy bullshit, but it's how you acquire believers. Apply that to your life and you'll find the peace you're looking for." I hope.

How do I know he's looking for peace? It's simple. He's in a bar in the early afternoon. Unless he met with Mister Smiley before I did, he's a pretty fucked up guy. Or a drunk. Or both.

I shake the man's hand and take my leave. I still think this guy is a complete waste of air. I don't want to be his friend. Or ever see him again. But he's pathetic and that's sad.

Oddly enough though, he helped me in a strange way. Not intentionally, besides buying me the drink. Some people need an audience. Like me. I need to be heard.

That's what hurts the most about Aidan's betrayal. After Jacob, he was my sounding board. There's Caleb, but Caleb could never call me out on my shit in the business world. He's biased because he's my partner.

Sometimes I have stupid theories. Everyone does. But people need others to tell them when what they're saying is ridiculous. Aidan knew how to do that. Caleb nuzzles his nose against mine and takes my clothes off. That might be nice right about now.

Where to next? Right, Mary's. Maybe that man helped me there, too. Best to approach my sister with a good buzz going.

I do feel somewhat responsible for Mary's role in all of this. It's doubtful that she would've married Aidan if I hadn't gone into business with him. But it goes beyond that.

She started to come around on the subject of Aidan a couple months after Jacob's death. That shows she's human anyway. With the state she was in, she wasn't getting many dates. With Father's deteriorating condition and Mary living at home, that wasn't likely to change.

It showed Aidan's true colors, too. Jacob and Mary had a bond that she'll never have with anyone else. I can't even describe it. It's a twin thing. They weren't always civil, but he understood her and that led to compassion that I didn't always care to give.

I don't doubt that Aidan felt guilty and there was a way to make up for that, through Mary. I'm fucking glad I didn't have to be around for that every day. God bless

Aidan for ever going back to that house after he saw what it was like.

Mother's death was quick. That's a relief in my book, but maybe not Mary's. She spent the better part of a year with those two as her primary company and then they were both gone. Who wouldn't be traumatized by that?

Mary and Aidan together was a relief for me, too. It allowed me to trust him in a way I couldn't before. I stopped looking over my shoulder, afraid that he would screw me over. I'd look pretty damn old now if I had to deal with that kind of stress every day of my life.

Or maybe I would've branched out. Simply Moore Capital. I was never one for putting up with a situation that didn't please me. I might not have broken the law if that was the case.

Mary and Aidan were happy together, for a while at least. In spurts. I think she was relieved. She was never meant for consistent happiness. In a fairly short span, her least favorite family member became the only one still alive. That would be tough on anyone.

I get to my car. No, I've been sitting against it for half an hour. Shit. Maybe I shouldn't drive. Ah, fuck it. Caution to the wind. Buh-bye.

Leave the radio off. You need a clear mind, Giles. For the ride and the talk that will follow. Keys, ignition. Reverse, drive. And go.

What was I thinking about? Ah yes, Mary. The root of our contempt. It's simple, really. Mary is a cold-hearted bitch. I might be a snob and a criminal, but there are people I care about. She's sort of one of them.

Mary's homophobia didn't help. That's a strong word. She likes Caleb. Perhaps I was the problem, not my sexuality. Her attitude has changed with the times. Does she get credit for that? Eh, why not?

It was all the "When are you going to go on a date?" questions she asked, even though it was pretty clear she knew. She gave Jacob the same bullshit. I bet she was worried he'd turn out like me. Fat chance of that happening.

She was cold to everyone. I'll never forget going down with the two of them for Aidan's fraternity reunion. Charlie gave that nice toast to Jacob and she got all pissed off, like she was the only one who got to care he was gone. Ten fucking years after the fact. We were doing fine. Get over it.

I wouldn't be surprised if her entitlement fueled Aidan's desire to break the law. Not that they needed the money, but he needed to show her that he was the best at something. Or that our company was the best. Seeking approval from someone who cannot be satisfied is a terrible idea. If I ever see Aidan again, I'll have to tell him that.

He could be dead somewhere. Guilt is stressful and Maine roads can be awfully slippery this time of year. Even worse last month.

Then they would have found him. And the money. That'd be a sight. State trooper pulls over to find a white-collar criminal and his stash in the middle of nowhere. I'd pay some of my remaining dough just to see that.

Shit. Mary's house already. That was fast. Be careful. She's got that long winding road leading to her house. Fits with her soon-to-be spinster image once she's all alone there. That's not nice. She used to have friends. Now she doesn't. You don't either, but you were the one responsible for the troubles. Mary only deserves it because she's a bitch.

Careful now. You don't want to drive on the lawn. Regina would curse you next time she goes to church. You don't need any more enemies than you have already. There's Regina's car. It was nice of Aidan to buy that for her. I guess she's the only person who will remember him fondly.

You made it. Put this death machine in park and be done with it. You're lucky you didn't run into any cops. A DUI might jeopardize your sympathetic appeal when you turn on Aidan. That'll be the day. Thursday. Maybe sooner. You should talk to Chomsky soon.

I walk in the house. I'm family. I don't need to ring the doorbell. Even if Regina is the only one who cares about my presence. Mary is probably asleep.

I hear a "Hello," that could only belong to one person in this house because it's coming from the kitchen. Mary couldn't find the light switch in there if her life depended on it.

"Regina, it's me Giles," I reply. No need to give her a fright. She doesn't have to worry about reporters peeping in the house. Nice and quiet back here down the road. Not that reporters are above trespassing. We should switch houses.

Jack is sitting in the living room, playing with his toy trains. They're probably a little risky for a two-year-old, but Caleb and I thought they looked fun. He seems to agree.

I go to my nephew first. God knows the kid could use a little love. "Hey there, Jack," I say as I lift him off the ground. He smiles. That's because I don't speak to him in baby talk. I only whip out that sort of lingo for his mother.

He's got Jacob's eyes. As much as any two-year-old could resemble a twenty-five-year-old memory. And that smile. What does he have to smile about?

That's pessimistic. He's got his trains. That's all he needs to be happy. You should adopt a similar simplistic philosophy and then you wouldn't be so grumpy all the damn time.

"How's he doing?" I ask Regina. She's cleaning up some shit. Probably just looking for something to do. Busy, busy.

"Bueno. I keep him busy. He's happy. He plays and he sleeps. Buena vida." Damn right. I'm jealous of the little guy.

I don't ask how Mary is. That will be painstakingly obvious the second I go into her room. Suddenly, I don't want to. Staying here with Regina and my nephew would be much more fun. Or I could just leave.

No. That's not the Giles who captivated an audience back at the tavern. You spoke with eloquence in front of a bunch of men. You can handle your sister in her home. Stop being such a baby.

I never did learn how to deal with Mary. Truly deal with her, that is. I was never much into horseback riding, but Mary is very much like that old pony Father used to talk about that couldn't be tamed. Clichéd, but true.

You could never convince Mary to do something. All you could do was tell her the facts and why she should do it. From there, it was on her to interpret what she wanted in her own little way. Threatening her never worked. She'd just get mad and throw things. Maybe a change is in order.

I leave my nephew to his trains. I should come over

more. Caleb does, but I suspect there's an ulterior motive in play there – fatherhood.

Sooner or later, a change is going to have to happen with Jack. This system where his only constant source of attention is a Colombian housekeeper won't do. Not that I have a single negative thing to say about the way Regina's handled all of this, but she's not his family. She doesn't need to be a surrogate when he's got an uncle to take care of him. Two uncles.

I can practically smell the booze as I walk up the stairs. Maybe that's some sort of cleaning liquid. Regina must clean this place 24/7. There's not much else to do when Jack is sleeping or watching TV. Mary isn't great company anymore, not that she ever was.

I knock on the door. It's a courtesy knock. I'm coming in regardless of what she says. "Go away Regina, I'll be down in a bit." I walk inside. It's dark. I turn the light on.

"You," says the shell of my sister. Jesus it stinks in here. I never knew a girl could stink up a place like this. Booze, farts, body odor. Every stench the nostrils could possibly dream up linger in this room. Fucking Jesus Christ himself would have chosen dying up on the cross over spending ten minutes in this room.

"Ever heard of opening a fucking window? You sure you're still alive? How can you breathe in this shit and not drop dead on the spot?" That's not a good way to talk to Mary. Don't let the booze go to your head like it's gone to hers.

She scowls. "If you don't like it, you can go somewhere else. No one invited you in here. Am I the only girl whose bedroom you've ever been in?"

Ah, she's trying to be insulting. "That'd offend me

more if I wasn't gay and if you weren't so pathetic. The answer is no, not that you care." Now now, Giles. Don't stoop to her level. This isn't middle school.

Silence. I'm getting dizzy. It's not the gin. It's the smell. I can't fucking bear it. Is there any spray around here? No, that'd just make things worse.

"I assume there's a reason you're here, Giles?" There was. What was it? Don't tell me you've forgotten.

Ah, yes. "I've come to check up on you," I reply. No, that wasn't it. You don't care.

She cackles. "Bullshit. I haven't seen you in days." Is that true? She takes a sip of the drink on her side table and lets out a moan of relaxation. Of course there's alcohol in it.

"Enjoying yourself there?" I ask. "Don't you realize how fucking sad that is? It's the middle of the day and you're drinking in bed in the dark. If a priest saw you he'd whip out a Bible and some holy water. Exorcize the fucking shit out of you. We've got a real Reagan MacNeil in here."

She takes another sip. "I don't see where you get off judging me. You're the one who created this nightmare. I can't go anywhere without people giving me dirty scowls like I'm some mob wife whore. You stupid shit. You caused all of this."

Is this really the time for family feud? I won't have my honor disgraced by this drunk. "Oh yeah Mary, it's all my fault. The only reason you married Aidan is because of me. We all know that you're quite the obedient twat. Maybe if you could've been domesticated like the rest of your sorority, Father could have found a better match for you before he passed on. But you pissed away those opportunities. It's only natural you wound up with swamp scum."

Rude? Yes. But Aidan can take it. He's not even here.

She laughs and laughs. "Oh Giles, how am I supposed to take that seriously? You got into bed with him as many times as I did. I guess I'm lucky he didn't swing both ways." Gross. Mildly funny. I'm surprised that Mary's wit isn't as dull as a knife at a food court.

I've always liked talking to Mary. That's about the only thing I like about her. The girl showed no passion for anything other than taking pot shots at whoever happened to be standing in her crossfire. For a snob like me, that could get quite amusing. It's a shame she never did anything with that wit.

She adjusts her place in bed, looking restless. She says, "Something is giving me a headache. It's either you or the light. Either way, you're a problem. So get to the point and leave, brother. I have things to do today."

That's funny. And sad. I hope she doesn't. "Yeah, I can sure see that," I reply. There's a bottle sticking out from under her bed. I retrieve it.

"Give that back. What are you doing, you pervert? Looking for my panties to wear?" And there goes the wit.

"Why would you even put this under the bed?" I ask, admiring the Grey Goose bottle. Oh right, you told Regina to take all her booze away. How did you forget about that?

I take a swig from the bottle. Ouch, that's harsh. "Give it back Giles or else," she warns. Don't go there Mary.

"Or what? You best watch your words sister. I think you're forgetting how few people you have left on this earth. Would be a shame if I had to take another family member away from you so I'd shut the fuck up if I were you. Disgusting wench."

She reaches for the glass and downs the rest of it. I've had enough of this. "Good. I hope you enjoyed that drink. Savored each fucking sip because that's the last you'll be having for a long time. You're cut off. The liquor stores won't sell to you. Regina won't buy for you. You're out. Last call for Mary Davies. No more drink to wash away your sorrows."

A tear falls from her eyes. "Fuck you," she says. I suppose I deserve that. I shouldn't be so hard on her. It's hard not to be.

I should also get to the point. I came here for a reason. Aidan. Mister Smiley. The money. Yes. Plans.

"We're running out of time, Mary," I say. Not I, we. Mary must feel like she's a part of this. If she's capable of feeling. I'm still here.

"The prosecution is getting their shit together. The window of opportunity to get ahead of this mess is closing." Come on you fucking drunk, you can see this just as well as I can.

She looks me straight in the eye and says, "So?" She reaches for the empty glass, scoffing as she adds, "What's that to me? Are you looking for my blessing to rat out my husband? You're not going to get it."

Fuck. I knew it. Of course she sees the writing on the wall. No matter what that shit has done, she's going to stand by him. Admirable, I guess. But stupid.

Does she still love him after all this? He takes off for Maine and she still won't renounce him. Maybe she does love him after all. I guess that's not too surprising for any couple. You'd have to really look to see it. I doubt anyone but me could. Appearances. For the public. Certainly not the bedroom. She cares too much about herself to be any good at sex.

She wants to be difficult. Fine. I'll give her all the reasons she needs. "I know it's hard for you to see clearly, since all you care about is the bottle in my hand, but try to tap into some of that common sense I know you have. You're a Moore. You're smart. You know what money you've kept from the Feds won't last forever. And what would you do if it did? You can't even cook a fucking meal. You need me. I'm all you have left."

She starts to lick the bottom of her empty glass. How pathetic. Why am I even bothering with this shit?

"Yes, that might be true," she replies. "But you're leaving something out, Giles."

Oh really? "What might that be? I'm in no mood for games."

She smiles. Her devious smile. I'm surprised she couldn't get more men with that look back in the day. She must not have wanted them.

"You need me, Giles. I can undo you. I might even know where the money is." What?

How does she know about the money? No way. Aidan wouldn't tell her shit. She's never known anything about our business. Does she?

"You're lying," I say. How to get it out of her? I must have the truth. It'll eat away at me if I don't.

Oh, now she smells blood. She sits up in bed with the devil in her eyes. "I'm his wife, of course I know. Now why would I tell you? I'd rather wield this over you, brother."

Think Giles. Give her a reason to give you what you want. "I'll give you your bottle back. I'm sure you'd like that. You seem to be a bit dry over there, sister."

A twitch. Then a blush. She's cracking. "It'll take more than half a bottle of vodka to get me to tell you. Nice try." She stumbles over her words. She's lying. I'm sure of it.

"Okay then." I open the bottle to take another sip. "I guess I'll pour the rest of this down the drain. Or I'll give it to Caleb. We can have it with dinner tonight. Maybe in a nice penne alla vodka. Oh, my mouth salivates at the thought."

She lunges forward in her bed and falls down amidst the piles of blankets. "No, I don't know where it is. Just give me another sip. Please Giles, just a drop. Please." That was easy.

I put the cap back on the bottle. "No. Fuck you, Mary. You think this is some big fucking game. All I need from you is to keep your mouth shut. There's more than one way to do that." She buries her face in her blanket. I'm getting through to her.

Cruel? Maybe, but that's the truth's fault. It's not a tall order. You're just doing the Lord's work for dear old Mary. She needs to hear this crap.

"Get your act together or I'm going to have you committed. Jack won't stay with Regina while you're gone either. He'll come live with Caleb and me. And he won't be coming back. I'll have no trouble putting you away with your pills and your booze. You want to fuck with me? I'll put an end to you, sister. Your husband's gone. You have no family but me. And you treat me like shit. No more. Be smart. We're doing this my way. You can hop on the train that gets us out of this mess, or you can try to resist and see where that takes you. I built an empire. People paid me millions of dollars to handle their finances. I can handle a miserable drunken bitch without breaking a sweat."

She cries. Crocodile tears. Mary isn't capable of re-morse. She doesn't care if I take Jack away. All that would ruin is her image of an ideal family. Which is gone any-way. She hangs on to the fragments of what's left.

Mary isn't stupid. If alcohol wasn't part of the equa-tion, this wouldn't be a problem. She needs to see that I'm throwing her a rope here.

Perhaps compassion might be the better approach. I sit on the bed. She growls and moans. I stand back up. Shit, how do I get through to this intoxicated woman?

"You're blind to the world around you because you're so numb under all those chemicals. There's a way out of this. Life fucked us. I deserved most of what came to me. You didn't. I can't change that. I can, however, get us past this." That's better, Giles.

She rolls over on her bed. God, she's like a fucking beat-up puppy. I almost feel a tear developing. "Us," she says, with a whimper.

You've done something right. All you need to do now is close. Make Mary understand.

"Yea. Us. You're my sister. Family. Don't forget that. We don't show our love and quite frankly, I like it that way. But I'm not going to weasel my way out of this shit without dragging you with me. Aidan bounced. Push has come to shove and now it's time to show the world what we've got. I'm still here. Hate me for that all you want, but please for the love of God don't sabotage me. We can see the light. Just open your eyes and see what we need to do."

That's all code for, "Let me betray Aidan." Good. That's the way it has to be. I don't like it, but that's not my problem anymore. My family needs me. I'm not going to prison for that shit unless they drag me away in chains.

She looks at me with a blank stare. That might be concerning for some, but the lack of rage is an important sign. She's coming around. She just doesn't like to show her true colors. Never has. Never will.

"Fine Giles, I won't stand in your way." A pause. "Just don't leave me behind." Fuck. Normal families would hug at this moment. We won't.

Is it over? What happens next? "Okay, you've made your point. Now go. And leave the bottle. I'll need it for my afternoon pills."

I toss her the bottle. A goodwill gesture. It could be shown as a sign of weakness.

"This bottle is it. I'm serious about cutting you off. If you're not going to be sent away to rehab, you need to clean up your act. You need your wits, Mary. People will see right through you if you're not sharp."

Mary makes a mischievous face. "Oh, don't worry, Giles. When the time comes for me to do my part, I'll be ready." What the hell does that mean? A problem for another day. "Goodbye," I say as I shut the door.

Why does talking to my sister have to be this brutal? It's not fair. Why did my sane family members all have to die? Crime would be so much easier if I could play this game with a full deck of cards.

I start to head for the door. Shit, I need to talk to Regina. Plans must be made for Easter. We must do our best to resemble a family. "Regina," I call out.

"Yes, Mister Giles?" No one has called me Mister Giles since Jeremiah. "We'll take Mary for dinner tomorrow," I say. I want to show Caleb that I have her under control.

"Yes Mister, what about Easter?" Good question. What to do? I don't wish to do any more planning today, even if it's just for a dinner. Let someone else handle that.

"I'll cook here for you and Mister Caleb," she replies. Excellent. Less trouble for me. I'll have a busy Monday ahead of me with Chomsky. I'll give it a few days before I call, lest he think that meddling with Mister Smiley was the straw that broke the camel's back.

Ah, Regina. "Yes, that sounds lovely. Something simple. From Colombia. Your homeland. Nice and easy. No stress. The Lord's Day." She smiles. I doubt that Mary takes much of an interest in Regina's home cooking.

"Will you come to Mass? You and Caleb. Spanish Mass. You'll love it," she says.

Don't laugh. I don't have any use for church. "No thank you, Regina. That's very kind of you to offer. God and I are not on speaking terms these days." I'm not sure she understands, but she nods and smiles. I wish Mary could take after her. She's so nice. I wonder if she knows what the rest of the world thinks of me.

I pick up Jack and toss him in the air. God, he's cute. I see why Caleb wants a kid so badly. Wait until he shits in his diaper. Eh, he's still adorable.

"I'll see you tomorrow, Jack. I'll bring you some more trains." What kid wouldn't love that? Too bad he can't understand me. Maybe he can. I'll teach him all the shit he needs to know later. Especially honor. Something Aidan never knew shit about.

Time to go home. It's almost dinnertime. Caleb will be worried. I check my phone. He hasn't called. I guess he's busy doing what normal people do. I miss the office.

I get in my car. Driving is easier without the weight

of my sister bearing down on my mind. I guess that was more of a detriment than those few swigs of vodka I took.

That stress is to be expected. Mary is the only one left who has to stick around. Child services can take Jack, and Caleb can leave. They won't and he won't, but we thought the same about Aidan, didn't we? Everyone can leave. But not Mary, because Mary can't take care of herself and child services doesn't take adults.

It'd be hard to actually have her committed. The court hearings. Doctors. No thanks. I mean, one look at her would show how necessary it was. But that would require someone to put forth an actual effort towards the wellbeing of another. That's why rehab fails. People are allowed to leave. Here, come up this long and winding road and take my sister away quick before more of her money gets frozen.

Driving is fun. If I can't get out of this, I really should just take the police on a high-speed car chase. Not like O.J. Caleb can come too. Run, run, run.

Don't be silly. You're going to get out of this. You point the Feds in the direction of the money. Mainly, the money Aidan ran off with. Once that's done, you double back in a whirly whirl that they won't understand. Because only you understand how years of fraud worked like this one did. They don't have the missing pieces to the puzzle. I do.

You don't even need to explain it all to them. Plant enough on Aidan and let them search for him. Get some hotshot lawyer who will pit you and your homosexuality against Mrs. Ramsey, and the media will back you. Who doesn't love a civil rights tragedy?

Community service will be gross, but you can escape jail time if you play this right. They can't take you away from Mary and Jack when you don't officially have a spouse due to the injustice of America. They need me. God, this is genius. I'm back, bitches.

I'm home. Caleb's car is here. I'm glad I bought him that Porsche. He looks so cute driving it like a little hotshot.

My stomach growls. I'm hungry. And horny. Tonight will be a good night. I can feel it.

I walk in the door. I'm tempted to announce that I'm back, but that's rude and arrogant. Caleb won't appreciate that. We should order Thai and eat it outside. It's a tad brisk, but the sun is out and now it looks with favor upon me.

"Hey Giles, I'm in here," calls Caleb. He's in the kitchen. "I'm making some tea. Do you want some?" he asks.

"That would be lovely. Let's chat in the living room." We never use that damn space anymore since people stopped accepting our invitations.

Caleb used to throw cocktail parties a few times a year. He tried cooking for one, but he burnt everything and filled the house with smoke. Not a lovely environment for a soiree. We catered the rest. Sometimes it's nice to splurge with all the money. I'm going to spoil the shit out of Jack when this is all over. Uncle of the fucking year. Every goddamned train in the toy store.

A few minutes go by. Caleb comes in with two cups and sets them on the table on top of the coasters. Good old coasters, protecting my fine wood. He sits on the couch while I take one of the comfy chairs on the other side of the table. Is it still a coffee table if there's tea on it? Eh, that's not important.

He's showered. What a shame. I love the smell of him when he's all sweaty. He hates it when I say that. Some compliments make people feel self-conscious. What a strange world we live in.

"So," he says, "how was your day?" Realizing that I had a day in which actual business was conducted, I feel extra happy that I had a tie on. Professionalism pulled through. But now business is over. I remove my tie.

"Excellent. Things are moving forward, Caleb. We're going to be okay." It's relieving to say that out loud and actually mean it.

But Caleb looks concerned. "Did the PI learn anything new about Aidan?" he asks. Why that question? Maybe if he'd asked it this morning, but I said things were excellent. Who cares about Aidan? If Aidan had been found, I would have said that. But I have good news and it's not that. Strange.

"Oh yes. It appears as though Aidan was taking a little trip up north." Caleb looks scared. Why? There's nothing to be afraid of.

"North?" he asks. "Yes, they found a rental car he'd borrowed under a fake name in Portland, Maine. That's all they know, but that's okay. That's all I need to know."

So I've said my intentions without saying the word betray. The idea was implied. Excellent. I don't need to come across looking like some swine to my romantic partner even if I'm filled with contempt for my business partner.

"Maine," Caleb says. It's not phrased like a question. He seems almost relieved. Weird.

I reach for my tea, forgetting how hot it must be after only a minute. Thankfully I don't get burned. "Yeah. Bizarre. He was probably on his way to the border. God knows why he decided to switch cars in Maine. A bit far away to be thinking about that. There wasn't any sign that the police were onto him."

Caleb lets out a deep breath. "So you're going to talk then?" he asks. Don't say it like that. It makes me sounds like a snitch.

"It's pretty clear, isn't it? He takes off with our nest egg. We can't all run to some island and live like Gilligan or the *Lost* people. Where is our smoke monster? We have no choice. I have no choice. It's talk, or go to jail." Tough, isn't it?

"That makes sense. He hasn't left us any options. You made the right call." I'm glad he agrees with me. I don't need to second-guess this shit anymore than I have already.

"What about Mary?" he asks. Of course. Thankfully, I have good news on that front as well.

"I've taken care of Mary," I reply. That sounded like something a mobster would say. Caleb looks slightly disturbed. "Taken care of?" he asks.

"No, not like that. I went over there and spelled everything out for that drunken cunt. It wasn't easy, but she'll come around. She doesn't have a choice. It's keep quiet or go to an insane asylum. When I laid out Mary's options for her, she saw the light. She may be a shell of her former shelf, but she's not a complete fool."

Now Caleb definitely looks disturbed. He puts his tea back on the coaster. Can't have spills where our guests might sit when they come back to us. "Jesus, Giles. You said that to her?"

Don't look like you didn't want that to happen. "I had to do what was necessary. Mary's stubborn. She always has been. It was clear that she wasn't going to be cooperative right off the bat so some threats had to be made. That's how you deal with people like Mary. You don't let them walk all over you. You do what needs to be done. That's what I do."

I sort of see how Caleb could be upset by my words. He's seeing a different Giles than he's used to. Work Giles. The Giles that made millions and millions of dollars. The scary Giles. The criminal. In the flesh. Right before him. What a treat!

This has to stop. I can't have him afraid of me at a time when I need to be at my best. I stand up from my chair and move over to the couch. I put my arm around him. I tell him, "It's all going to be okay. I'm taking care of everything."

Caleb pushes me away. He sniffs. "Giles, have you been drinking?" Way to kill the mood. Why can't I have a fucking drink? I'm not my sister.

I put my arm around him again and try to pull him closer to me. "Shush, let's make love. We haven't been intimate since Aidan went missing and now he doesn't matter anymore. Come on, Caleb. See the light."

He pushes me away and stands up. "Giles, you're drunk. And you drove home. What the hell is wrong with you? What were you thinking?"

Jesus fucking Christ I don't need this right now. It's never enough. You fix something and nobody takes a fucking second to appreciate it. It's always more. More. No wonder everyone's on pills. The only way to get some peace and quiet is to block out the world. I can't take it.

Swat goes the cup. Tea splatters all over our rug. Watch it fly. The Roxburgh Tea Party all over that expensive Persian rug that Caleb picked out. I'm sure he'll want that cleaned. Everyone always wants more.

"Giles, what the hell is wrong with you?" Caleb

screams. He's what's wrong. I don't answer. He turns away. He takes a step toward the door. Shit. Fix this. If he leaves, you're finished.

"You know what's wrong with me? I've got the weight of our world on my shoulders. That's what's wrong. It fucking blows day in and day out. And you know what? I'm dealing with it. I dealt with it today. Some guy at the tavern where I met the PI bought me a drink. He was complete white bread, but I didn't care. No one tells you how lonely it feels to be the villain. So yeah, I had a couple drinks. I drove a car. I also fixed the problem. Because that's what I do. I fix things. If I could have, I would have begged the government for two weeks to fix that fucking mess. I could've. I'm fucking good at what I do. But I didn't get the chance. They didn't listen. That's okay, I still get the chance to fix our problems."

I pause to take a breath. Caleb is crying. Maybe I've gotten to him. I don't feel so buzzed anymore.

"You know what I found out today, Caleb? I got confirmation that I was betrayed by the man who's been in my life longer than anyone else still alive on this earth, except for that miserable wife of his I call my sister. Aidan and I did what we did because we had each other to make it all right. We took care of each other. I couldn't sell him out because I couldn't accept the idea that he did that to me. But I have. And then I took care of things. Mary knows where she stands. I made everything okay. So all I wanted was some Thai food and a victory fuck with my partner because I haven't had shit to feel good about in far too long, Caleb."

That felt good. You're still back. Sometimes people aren't going to agree with you. And that's okay as long as you make yourself heard. Stand and be noticed, Giles.

I don't think any of this would've gotten to me if the four of us had just stuck together. People withdraw from each other during moments of crisis. That's a poor strategy. We need a fucking phalanx and then we'd get through everything like it was nothing. Instead, everyone ran to seek solace in one thing or another.

Except for me. I haven't been sure of much since Aidan took off, but I know that getting through this takes priority over everything else. I don't need booze, pills, or delusion. I stand strong.

Caleb sits back down. He needs to know that he can't fuck with me like this. I'm struggling. Isn't that obvious? I don't need added stress in my own home. My home. My name is on the fucking deed. Not his.

"You're right. You had a busy day and you solved a lot of problems for us. I shouldn't have shouted. I'm sorry. I was just surprised and scared. I'm scared all the time. People think that because we're not married, I can just pick up and leave like it's nothing. It's not nothing. I love you. So smelling alcohol scared because I don't want stupid mistakes to jeopardize our future."

He kisses me, his right hand slowly caressing my face. That soft skin. Thank God. Caleb is my tie to humanity. Ever since we met at that art gallery opening. The way he smiled at me even though I was tired and cranky after a long day dealing with other people's money. I love him. I need him. I don't know what I'd do if he betrayed me.

"You should've seen Jack today. He looked adorable with his trains. It's going to be okay. We're going to pull through." Damn right, we will.

Sunday, April 4, 2010

Regina

"IN EL NOMBRE DEL PADRE, DEL HIJO Y DEL ESPÍRITU Santo," said the Priest. "Amen," replied Regina, as she made the sign of the cross with Jack's hand. The little toddler didn't make a sound throughout the entire Mass. The same would not have been said for his mother if she had chosen to come. Her snores would have created a big distraction on such a joyous occasion.

Regina spent most of the Mass going through her prayer list. She prayed for the safe return of her employer, Aidan Davies, and for the health of Mary, who is rotting away in his absence. She prayed for Giles and his partner Caleb, two men who chose to spend their lives together.

Most of all, she prayed for her good fortune at a time when misery ran rampant throughout much of her world, both at home and in Colombia. Too many people suffering for reasons she couldn't understand. The cutbacks had taken a big toll on her community.

She worried that people neglected to understand the ripple effect that occurs when jobs are lost. The reconsideration of so-called luxuries.

Regina was thankful she still had a salary when Aidan

and Giles were arrested. Truth be told, they needed her now more than ever. Mary completely fell apart and there was no one else to take care of the boy.

Jack reached for her thumb with one hand, the other clutching his stuffed elephant. Her love for him transcended any semblance of duty. Jack's smiles meant more to her than any paycheck. A boy neglected by an alcoholic mother and a missing father. The line between employer and family member mattered little in an economic crunch, but the heart pays little attention to practical needs.

The arrest kept her up at night, crippled with the anxiety she had to bury whenever Jack was nearby. Not just for herself and her future, but also for the future of the family she'd grown attached to after all her years in their service. They weren't a big family. Not like the one that Regina left behind back home. She didn't have a choice. Times are tough when there are too many mouths to feed.

Some family scattered in Texas. A whole world away. There are always construction jobs for those who are cleared to work. And plenty for those who aren't. Regina visited a few years back, but the Davies were her real kin.

The love she never got to experience. The kind that she assumed Aidan and Mary felt for each other at some point in time, years ago. Dating wasn't impossible. It just wasn't something thought about in a serious manner, the kind of thinking that gets you off your feet, determined to make a change. Just a fleeting yearning every once in a while.

She kept her finances in good standing by living a modest, low cost life. She said her prayers every night in thanks that she didn't put any of her money with her employers. Regina didn't care much for investments. She didn't pay rent and the only meals she had to pay for were the occasions where she went out with friends. That hadn't happened much since the arrest. Jack took up too much of her time.

Regina prayed again for Aidan and vowed never to judge him for what he was accused of. She heard bits and pieces of what Mary and Giles said about him, which made her hands shake with rage. The man was courteous, respectful, and above all else, the patriarch of the family. People deserve respect just for that.

Regina would have preferred an Easter vigil or at the very least, a morning service. Latin Mass in Roxburgh didn't carry the same demand as the city, leaving her with fewer options. She could have gone to an English Mass, but that wouldn't do on such an occasion, not with her English in its current state. All the time spent around Jack and Mary gave her little time to practice.

A tear ran down her face as she looked around the church. People of all ages and nationalities were gathered in their Sunday best to worship on the most important day of the Church calendar.

She wore a purple and gold dress in honor of both the suffering and richness of Jesus' sacrifice. There were plenty of kids dressed in white, reminding her of Mass back home. Jack wore a red sweater because that's what he had in his closet. Mary never seemed to care about the state of Jack's wardrobe.

The Davies never showed much interest in religion, which surprised Regina given their Southern background. Aidan told her that his family back home in Alabama was religious at some point, but he stopped going to church once he wasn't forced to anymore. Apparently tradition didn't mean all that much in that regard.

They were all invited to join her, of course. Even Giles and Caleb. The two of them politely declined, though they would be coming to dinner later that evening. Dinner would be an exciting occasion. Mary laughed when she heard the news. Apparently, salvation was amusing to the perpetually intoxicated housewife.

The idea that a celebratory dinner might be considered rude crossed her mind more than once. Who could raise a toast with the patriarch missing and the family shrouded in legal trouble? Regina couldn't let a holiday like Easter pass by without at least offering to make something of the occasion. She found herself almost taken aback by Giles' receptive embrace of the idea, like she'd stumbled onto something missing. Joy. A night to forget, if just for a short while.

Regina looked forward to cooking something reminiscent of her home city of Santa Marta, even if it was just a simple bandeja paisa. A safe choice that they were bound to enjoy. Except for Mary. She would probably scoff at it and beg for wine. But that would be okay on Easter Sunday.

She thought about what the year had brought so far. April is a good time to reflect on that while it's raining all the time. Jack had grown bigger. He hadn't spoken much for a two-year-old. Not surprising. Mary rarely spoke to him and Regina's English was hardly ideal to learn from.

But Jack would turn out okay. She knew it. Even with a mother like that.

The music filled the entire church. Some people sang while others just smiled. A full band accompanied the organist and choir. Regina sang along. The feeling of home in a foreign land. Spanish Mass, not Colombian Mass, but close enough for today.

She checked Jack's diaper, which felt a little wet. She would have to change him before she went to the store. Changing him in a church would be sacrilegious, so she held him and enjoyed the music as the priest and procession walked down the aisle.

Seeing such a crowded church made Regina happy. She worried that people were forgetting God in their day-to-day lives. Having lived in the Davies' house for Jack's entire life, she knew he wasn't baptized. Just another example of the decline of morals in 21st-century America.

Regina considered having him baptized in secret. He shouldn't be deprived of such a simple and important sacrament because of his parents. Every time she thought about bringing the subject up to Mary, something always got in the way. She weighed the ethics of going to a priest behind her back, wondering who would think to object to such an act of love.

Thoughts of the night when the police and the men in suits came to question Aidan filled her head. The elderly lawyer constantly interrupted the interrogation, telling the police they were out of line. Regina was confused as she thought the two of them should tell the police everything they knew to avoid further trouble, but later she understood why. Certain illegal acts eluded the police.

Regina never suspected that Aidan was a criminal. She saw him as a businessman. He didn't have gold chains or fancy sports cars. He did buy her a Honda Civic, but the car served practical purposes. If he was such important criminal, why didn't he have more fancy things?

The end of Mass saddened Regina, watching enviously as the families around her excitedly headed off to their celebrations. She hoped the money she sent home had arrived on time. American money, since it always held its value.

The priest stood outside as Regina walked out with Jack and his bag of necessities.

Regina offered a simple, "Gracias Padre," to the priest. It was a beautiful ceremony filled with music and joy. Nothing else needed to be said.

The priest smiled. He reached for Jack's hand and said, "Dios le bendiga, mi hijo." Regina smiled as she waved Jack's hand at the priest. As close to a baptism as he would get.

She walked to her car, thinking about Jack's behavior in church compared to the other kids. The idea that he was somehow falling behind constantly weighed on her. She opened the back seat and put Jack down to change his diaper. Jack smiled up at her, clearly touched by the presence of the Lord in his life. She thought to remind herself to sign Jack up for the toddler gymnastic classes that Giles had agreed to pay for.

The crowded grocery store parking lot gave her pause, wishing less people were out and about on a holiday. Rest and family time were neglected at an alarming frequency these days. She wished someone out there could muster up the courage to simply sit down and take a break.

The seemingly endless aisles filled with food never ceased to amaze Regina as she pushed her cart inside. So many choices for so many meals. A whole world calling out for you to give it a chance.

Regina thought about what she needed to buy. Beef,

rice, beans, and vegetables. Plantains especially. She put Jack into the seat in the cart. He waved his elephant around like he was trying to show the whole world what he had in his possession. Regina laughed at his playful behavior, reminded of the good things in life.

Cooking became a tedious chore in the Davies household with Aidan gone. Jack's palette was rather limited and Mary never ate much. As she normally thought it would be improper to make a feast just for herself, tonight presented a golden opportunity to indulge in one of her passions.

An odd request from Mary came to mind. Something she'd never asked for before. Unusual for the bitter middle-aged drunk. A soda. Coca-Cola. No, Mountain Dew. The green one. Regina couldn't figure out why Mary would want something like that, but she learned to limit questions to matters of necessity.

She knew not to question Giles, either, when he forbade her from buying alcohol for Mary, even though the request put her in an awkward position between the woman she worked for and the person who now paid her salary. She wondered what Giles would think of Mary's latest request for a colorful soft drink.

A bag of Colombian coffee caught her eye as they walked down the aisle. Smiling, she picked it up to add to the spirit of the festivities. Mary's gloomy attitude couldn't spoil everything.

She remembered the cumin. Spices are important to any dish, but she couldn't capture her own native flare without cumin. Mary hated the stuff, but Regina thought she might be more amicable with her new beverage. An Easter miracle.

The next aisle was wide open, causing her to pick up speed for just a few seconds as the cart rolled along. Jack let out a shriek of excitement at the sudden rush of adventure. He laughed and laughed as he waved his elephant around. The sound of innocence.

Regina paid for the food with the credit card Aidan had given her for house purchases. She kept her wallet open as she extended the card to the cashier, remembering that you could never be sure with Davies' money.

The weather was mild for an April evening. The roads were empty, but the driveways were full. Regina liked to see that. People were together. It would be a shame to be alone on such a beautiful holiday. Like Mary was right now, but Regina would be home soon with Jack, freshly blessed by a priest no less!

Cooking would get in the way of their visit to the park, a Sunday ritual since before Aidan went missing. He used to love to take Jack for a ride on the swings, but now that was Regina's responsibility. She would have even taken him there in the cold weather, so long as he was all bundled up. Tomorrow presented an opportunity to make up for it. Jack wouldn't know the difference.

She called out, "Miss Mary, we're home," to no answer as she walked through the front door. The noise of the TV meant that Mary was probably awake.

She walked into the living room and put Jack down in his toy area. He immediately started to play with his trains without acknowledging his mother sitting on the couch. She kept her eyes fixed on the TV.

The Mountain Dew. "I've got your soda, Miss Mary," Regina said, as she pulled it out of a bag.

Mary's face lit up. "Ah, excellent Regina. Thank you.

Be a dear and pour me a glass. With some ice. Leave some room at the top. In case I need more. Ice." Regina thought nothing of Mary's pauses as she headed into the kitchen.

Regina poured the glass and handed it to her. "Thank you," Mary said, as she took a sip of the drink. "Was this the only color they had?" she asked.

Regina stood still, pondering the question. "Uh. Yes. That is what you wanted, right?" Regina picked up a toy train that lay on the floor as she tried to remember the soda aisle, confused by the unexpected importance of the drink.

Mary took another sip and puckered her lips, her tongue moving as if to absorb every last drop of the flavor. "I suppose you're right. Delicious, thank you. I must have remembered the color wrong." As Regina turned toward the kitchen, Mary added, "Regina, I think I heard a sound coming from the laundry room. Could you check it out, please?" Mary was acting stranger than usual.

Regina walked into the laundry room and scratched her head as nothing seemed out of the ordinary, besides the idea that Mary would have been in the laundry room. Upon returning to the living room, she noticed that Mary's drink looked full again. Ay, yi, yi, Regina thought to herself. Alcohol. That's why she wanted the soda. Regina didn't bother thinking about where Mary could have found some.

The thought of snatching the drink from Mary's hand briefly crossed her mind. Giles would appreciate her in-stinct. Mary would sulk for the entire dinner. Conflicted, Regina headed back to the kitchen, favoring a pleasant dinner over a sober Mary. She started preparing the meal even though Giles hadn't specified what time they'd be over. Normally, they could be counted on for a pre-dinner cocktail, but that was up in the air with Mary's current situation.

She started with the vegetables since the beef wouldn't take long to cook. She prepared a salad to go along with the main course. She hoped Mary would at least eat that.

The thought of overkill crossed her mind as she pondered how much food she was preparing. Shredded beef, plantains, fried eggs, sausages, beans, and rice. The salad struck her as unnecessary, except it was Easter. A feast needed to be had on the day of salvation.

Regina sighed as Mary came over and sat down at the kitchen island while she cooked. She worried that Mary's opinion of her changed on an hourly basis and that she showed no regard for her son, who continued to play quietly.

She watched her employer sip on her spiked drink as she chopped the vegetables. After a few minutes Mary asked, "Jesus, how much food did you buy?" Regina opened her mouth to remind Mary not to take the Lord's name in vain, but stopped, knowing that such an act would be pointless. Mary wouldn't care.

"Too much, Miss Mary, but today is Easter. We shall all have a little of everything." She pulled out the salad bowl and tossed in the vegetables. She reached into a cupboard, looking for the biggest frying pan. She started with the plantains, followed by the eggs, and finally the meat.

"How was Mass? Did Jack scream the whole time?" Mary asked. She laughed. "I'm sure the other people loved that."

Regina rolled her eyes as she replied, "No, no. He was perfect. He played with his toys and slept for a little while." Like a little angel.

Mary reached over and picked up a cucumber slice off the table. "No, I guess he doesn't scream much. Unlike Giles. He whined and whined for whatever the fuck babies cry about. He denies it, of course. Says I couldn't possibly remember that shit. I do." Regina stared blankly at the simmering food, hoping Mary would find another way to occupy her time.

"What does church do for you?" Mary asked. Regina looked up, confused. "Que?" she asked. She paused for a second, wondering if the English translation was needed.

"I mean, why do you go? What does church have that here doesn't?" Regina resisted blurting out the obvious answer. For starters, church didn't have Mary.

"You go to say thank you to God," Regina replied. She lifted a plantain up with a spatula, pleased with the progress. On to the eggs.

Mary polished off the rest of her Mountain Dew. She tiptoed back to the refrigerator. Regina sighed and took a deep breath as she heard the sound of a second bottle. No fighting today. Giles could break the peace if he wanted.

"Do you find it relaxing, being there? I've heard people say that church is relaxing. I never understood why." Regina did her best to tune Mary out as she cracked an egg.

"Very. You should come sometime, Miss Mary. I'll take you to Spanish Mass. You'll love the music. It's beautiful."

Mary laughed as she sat back down on her stool. "I bet it is. But I don't think I'll go. God doesn't want me. I've been a bad girl my whole life. It's nice of you to offer. You're sweet."

Mary's admission brought on a feeling of sorrow as Regina wiped her brow with her forearm trying not to think about whatever happened in Mary's past that made such a sad person.

The sound of the front door brought a much-needed end to the awkward conversation. "Hello!" Caleb called. "Merry Easter." He held his arms out to embrace Jack as he ran to his uncle.

"It's not 'Merry' Easter, it's 'Happy' Easter," Mary shouted, forming a protective barrier around her drink with the crevice of her elbow. She shuddered as Giles entered the kitchen and asked, "Oh my! What do we have here?" Mary growled before taking a long sip of her drink.

"Not that, sister—I know what you're drinking. I mean the food. Look at all of this. Smells great, Regina. Happy Easter."

Regina's face beamed, a wide grin stretching from ear to ear as she embraced Giles with her free arm. "Feliz Pascua, Mister Giles. And Feliz Pascua, Mister Caleb." She tossed the beef into the pan.

Giles began rummaging around in the cupboard, taking out a few plates. "We brought wine. Why don't you pour that sludge out and have a glass, sister? You don't need to dry out on the day the Lord has risen." Regina saw the beginnings of a smile develop across Mary's face as she gulped down the rest of her drink.

"No, no. I'll get it," Regina said, motioning for Giles to stop trying to help. Giles laughed and replied, "Nonsense. This is your day and you're already cooking the food. Caleb, can you get four wine glasses and some milk for Jack?" Regina took a second to embrace the moment. Everybody was happy. It had been too long.

The food only took a few more minutes. Regina prepared four big plates and one small one for Jack on his favorite *Thomas the Tank Engine* plate. Caleb brought the high chair into the dining room while Giles poured the wine. Mary sat and did nothing, as usual.

A silence followed the seating of the five guests. The thought of grace lingering without action. Regina, being the religious one at the table, asked, "A toast, anyone?"

The silence continued. Giles raised his glass and said, "To Jacob." The glasses were all lifted without words, a somber reflection for the fallen brother. Jack reached for his food, declining to toast with his sippy cup.

Caleb fed Jack while the others helped themselves to the feast. Giles said, "This is delicious. You've really outdone yourself, Regina," as he bit into his second plantain.

"Couldn't we have just gotten this at Taco Bell?" Mary asked. Regina sat puzzled, unaware of Mary's sarcastic intention.

"That's enough, Mary. That wine can be taken away just as easily as it was poured," Giles replied. "Let's have ourselves a pleasant meal."

The meal continued with fractured small talk. "How was Mass?" Caleb asked.

"Very good, Mister Caleb," Regina replied. "Jack was such a good boy."

"I'd like to join you someday," Caleb replied, smiling at Jack.

"The Church frowns upon your kind," Mary said, smirking at Giles as she sipped her wine. Giles shook his head and continued eating.

After the dinner, Caleb cleared the plates while Regina brewed the coffee. Realizing she forgot about dessert, she grabbed a carton of chocolate ice cream from the freezer. Three bowls for the boys plus four coffee cups, knowing Mary didn't care for sweet things that didn't contain alcohol.

"It's Colombian coffee," Regina said, with an added boost of energy as she walked in with the tray. "How wonderful," Caleb replied. "Has this dinner reminded you of home at all?"

Mary let out a laugh. "What do you think, Caleb? Serving food to a couple of white people. Yeah, this dining room sure looks a lot like Colombia. Let's whip out the cocaine and rave, bitches." She laughed and laughed at her own joke.

Giles rolled his eyes at Mary, folding his hands on the table and biting his lip, clearly struggling to resist a fight with Mary. "Uh, sort of," Regina replied. "Less chaos. Food isn't as good as my mother used to make. But this was nice."

Giles took a sip of the coffee. "That spice had a sharp bite to it. Delicious. You've done good, Regina. A real credit to the family." Regina's heart rose as she embraced the affection. Who knows when it would be offered again.

"Big plans tomorrow?" Caleb asked, to no one in particular. Giles looked up, being the only one who could provide an interesting answer. "Call with Chomsky," he replied. "Maybe a meeting. Should get busier later in the week. I suppose that's a good thing."

Jack yawned and rubbed his eyes. "Is the rain cloud finally moving away?" Mary asked, alternating sips of coffee and wine.

"If we're lucky," Giles replied, "I have a good feeling about this week. Tonight was a good idea. Setting a positive tone for the future. Our family is going to be okay."

Giles looked over at his nephew. "Regina, why don't you put Jack to bed and we'll clean up and have a night-cap." Caleb wiped the ice cream off Jack's face and lifted him up to give him a hug before handing him off to Regina. "Good night, little buddy. Sweet dreams." Regina struggled to maintain her hold on the child as he reached out for his uncle.

As she walked up the stairs she heard, "You didn't even say goodnight to him, Mary. How the fuck do you think that kid is going to live a normal life with a cold-hearted bitch for a mother?" Giles. Regina stopped on the stairs, not wanting to eavesdrop but unable to re-sist the delightful sound of Mary getting called out for her terrible parenting.

"All right, Giles. Put it on the list of improvements I need to make and I'll get on it in the morning," she re-plied. Regina recognized Mary's aggressive tone as the product of the confidence given to her by the bottle.

Regina continued up the stairs. She put Jack into his pajamas and brushed his teeth, hoping that the ice cream wouldn't keep him up.

Music. Jack should have music tonight. She walked over to his stereo and picked up a CD she recognized as a gift from Caleb. The disc read *Rockabye Baby: Lullaby Renditions of The Smiths*. Mary always liked listening to that record in Jack's rocking chair.

"Good night, sweet prince," Regina said, as she kissed him goodnight. Despite the ice cream, Jack's eyes quick-ly closed as his head hit the pillow, reminding Regina of his mother. "Tomorrow will be a new day filled with new adventures. Te amo, Jack." She pressed play on the stereo and exited the room, taking caution to leave the door slightly open so he wouldn't be scared by the dark.

Regina paused on the stairs, unsure of how quickly she wanted to return to the dining room. Fearing another fight, the idea of a long hot bath sprung into her head. The thought of Caleb being forced to endure Giles and Mary's bickering alone kept her from retreating to her room.

The front door began to open as she reached the bottom of the stairs. She rushed down to greet the presumed guests of Giles or Caleb before she saw something out of the ordinary.

"Dios mío," Regina cried out. A man appeared, carrying a gun in one hand with an especially long pointy end. A silencer. Two men followed him inside.

The man with the gun put one finger to his mouth while he pointed the gun at her with his other hand. His command was ignored as Regina fell backward, hitting her head on the foot of the stairs.

The man with the gun headed for the dining room, followed by one of his colleagues. The other hovered over Regina, offering no assistance to the startled woman.

"What was that?" Caleb yelled. "Regina, are you okay? Holy shit!" A plate smashed as it hit the floor. "What the fuck!"

"All right, that's enough screaming. Let's be calm people, and this will all be over soon," said an unfamiliar voice belonging to one of the intruders. The voice was deep, with an unrecognizable accent.

"Michael, bring Regina into the dining room, please," said the voice. Regina trembled at the sound of her own name. The people couldn't be normal robbers or the police.

"I said sit down, Mr. Moore. There's a right and a wrong way to do this. Unfortunately, it requires some thought on your part to tell the difference, so let's all put our thinking caps on."

Regina walked into the dining room to find Caleb, Mary, and Giles seated. The man called Michael stood just inches from her, his breath causing the hair on the back of her neck to stand upright.

For the first time she noticed that all three intruders were wearing black suits with black dress shirts. The man with the gun wore a purple tie.

The leader pushed his long blonde hair out of his face. A muscular Asian man with black hair stood close to him, facing the family. The man called Michael was black, bald, and wore a thick moustache. A diverse group of intruders.

Regina stepped off to the side of the room by the door and took a seat in an extra chair, used for larger parties. Michael motioned for her to join the rest, but the long-haired man said, "That's fine. She can sit on the sidelines while we take care of business."

Giles grit his teeth and said, "Listen up, tough guys. I know this might come as a big surprise to you, but we don't have much for you to steal. You may have heard, but our company isn't really doing all that great. So help yourself to whatever you care to take and kindly get the fuck out of here." The Asian man hit him on the back of the head with his pistol.

"Giles, how dare you invite them to rob my home," Mary said. She looked at the man and added, "Don't you dare think about hitting me, you chink. Yea, that's right.

Racism. If you don't like it, you can march your sorry ass back to China, or wherever the fuck you came from."

Giles chuckled. Caleb's face lost all its color, a white palette of despair. The long-haired man stood still, looking around the table before kicking over Jack's high chair. The sound of broken wood made Regina tremble.

"Don't hit him again, Tron. We need him fully conscious." Giles rubbed his head.

"Tron?" Caleb asked. "What does that make you, Jeff Bridges?" The long-haired man laughed. He wore the smile of the devil, casually waving his gun around.

"No, it makes me Gabriel. Can't you see my wings?" He extended his hands up in the air, pointed toward the sky. Giles reached for his wine.

He said, "Michael, Tron, Gabriel. Those are all names of angels, Caleb. I suppose they're here to do the Lord's work. Fucking adorable."

Gabriel took a bow and holstered his gun. "Precisely Giles. We're here to perform a cleansing of the wicked. It seems as though we have a couple of very bad people in this room. Sinners. I see two before me. This one I'm not so sure about," pointing at Caleb. "Guilt by association, perhaps? Unless you've got a crime you'd like to get off your chest?"

Tron and Gabriel continued to hover around the room. Michael stood between Regina and the doorway. Regina sat despondent, resigned to helplessness.

"Your act gets an A for effort. I'll give you that, angel boy," Giles said. "Though the lack of prosthetic wings sure is disappointing. I guess there wasn't enough room in your budget? Care for some wine? It's white, so I guess that would make it Christ's piss rather than His blood.

Fitting for someone like you." Giles extended the bottle before taking a sip out of it.

"No thank you, but it's very kind of you to offer. I suppose I should explain why we've come. I have it under good authority that there's quite a bit of money stashed away somewhere. Care to share with me where that loot might be, Giles?" Gabriel took out his gun again and waved it around in Giles' general direction, causing Regina's heart to beat rapidly.

Giles' jaw clenched. A forced smile quickly followed. "I hate to disappoint you, but none of us know where the money is. I have some of course, but it's not very much. Barely covers my legal fees. Not worth the hassle of a production like this. My partner ran off with the jackpot. If you find him, let me know and we can hound him together."

Tron tilted his head to Gabriel, who nodded in reply. Tron walked out of the room. Gabriel said, "It's funny you should mention that, Giles. We've brought a surprise for you."

Giles stood up. "Okay, I've had enough of this theatrical bullshit. You obviously know who I am. You know I've got people working for me who can make quick work out of amateurs like you. Now, I could say leave and I won't do anything, but we both know that would be a lie. I'll hunt you down and shove that silencer so far up your ass the guy behind you could still bury his full cock inside your overstuffed butthole. But that's as far as I'll take it. A visit to the ER and you'll be as good as new. I'm sure you're familiar with Mister Smiley?"

Giles started pacing around the room, stopping as he made eye contact with Michael. A mixture of smug pride and defeat lingered on his face, his half grin and piercing eyes telling two very different stories.

"Oh, I'm familiar with Mister Smiley. I saw him at the bar with you, remember?"

Mary yelled, "You're the guy who told off the reporter. Now I see why. You had to have us for yourself. Selfish prick."

"A real man doesn't hide behind newspapers and pistols," Giles said. "What a voice though. I'll give you that. About the only thing you've got going for you with that Fabio hair. The '90s have been over for ten years, you piece of shit."

Gabriel snapped his finger. Tron returned with another man, sickeningly skinny with a patchy beard. He tossed the man on the floor. The man groaned as he rolled over.

"Aidan," Caleb gasped. "You're alive?"

Giles and Mary stood up to have a better look from the other side of the table. Caleb dropped to the floor next to him. "Jesus Christ, what have you done to him?" Aidan mumbled inaudibly as he tried to move his arm.

"All right, that's enough tender love, Caleb. Back to your seat," Michael said, pointing his gun at Caleb's empty seat. Caleb stood up, trembling. Aidan remained on the floor.

"We have quite a bit to catch up on, everybody," Gabriel said. "Where to begin? Michael, where do you think we should start?"

Giles interjected, "You don't know where he hid the money, do you? He didn't tell you. You haven't got shit."

Gabriel gave him a dirty look, his eyebrows raised as he pouted his lips. "Now, now, Giles, it's not your turn to speak. I asked Michael a question. It's his turn, not yours.

Now Michael, where should we begin?"

Michael took his time to answer, grinning as he looked around the room. "I think we should start with the big one so we're all on the same page." Gabriel's face lit up as he brought his hand to his chin. Regina held her stomach, growing sick from the pleasure the intruders drew from all the suffering.

"Excellent choice. There are some old family secrets that Giles and Aidan have neglected to share with the rest of you. Who wants to spill the beans? Giles? Aidan?" Neither of them spoke. Giles sat glaring at Gabriel, barely even blinking.

"Okay then, I guess I'll just have to do all the talking. It's a shame really. Two first-person accounts available and yet I'm the one who has to tell the story. Though of course, I have some original firsthand information pertinent to how I came across this lead. You see, when we first caught wind of Aidan's scent, we had no idea what to make of the name Jacob McIntyre. Obviously the first part refers to the late, great Jacob Moore, but was the last name a coincidence? A lazy person might say yes, but we were quite thorough."

Giles yelled, "Shut up." Gabriel waved his hand. A loud whack followed the swing of Tron's pistol.

"I thought I told you to leave his head alone," Gabriel said as Giles groaned, grabbing the back of his head with his hand.

"Oh, well. Don't do that again, Tron." He paused, taking another look at Giles, who clenched his mouth to stifle his whimpers. "Ah yes, where were we? McIntyre. Yes. So we did some digging. It wasn't easy, but perseverance can yield its reward. Three of you at this table and Jacob attended a cocktail party held for Senator Paul McIntyre in Georgia the same evening Jacob was hit by a bus. Significant? Of course. But was that all? It wouldn't seem likely."

Gabriel paused as he looked around the table at his audience. The barely conscious Aidan on the floor. The guilty-looking Giles, sitting at the table, avoiding eye contact with anyone. The nervous Caleb, whose body shook every few seconds. The indifferent Mary.

Gabriel smiled. "Where was I? Right. So we paid a little visit to Oregon to meet with the retired senator. Treated him to a nice lunch. He was happy to have the company, until your names came up. Apparently, there was a little heist that night. The two of you extorted a United States senator. You should have seen the look on my face when I learned the truth. The crime that started it all. The original sin." His voice raised as he finished his statement, forcing a few boisterous laughs.

Caleb opened his mouth to speak. It took a few stutters before he managed to ask, "Is that true, Giles?" Giles looked away. "Your lover asked you a question, Giles," Gabriel added. "Have you forgotten how to have a conversation? You were so full of chatter just a minute ago."

"It wasn't planned. Jacob and Aidan walked in on me having sex with the Senator and then it all came together." He paused and added, "I went along with it. I'm sorry, Caleb. This isn't something I ever wanted you to know."

A woman's laughter. Mary, in hysterics. "So *that's* why you stayed at the party. You wanted to bed the Senator. Bravo Giles. Greed and sodomy destroyed two lives in one night. That poor, old, confused man *and* our brother." She continued to laugh, only stopping to take another sip of wine.

The sound of a whimper came from the floor. "That had nothing to do with it. Jacob was in on it, too," Aidan wheezed, grasping his chest.

"He lives," Gabriel said, clapping his hands. "I was so worried that our dear friend would miss out on all the fun. Michael, help him up so he can sit with his family while we figure this out."

Michael holstered his gun and picked Aidan up off the ground. The ease with which Michael lifted Aidan's bony frame sent chills down Regina's spine. She wondered when he'd last been fed.

"I must thank you, Giles. I never knew that part. Aidan hasn't been very talkative this past month. He doesn't like to give us information. It's rude, really. We kept him housed for all that time and this is the thanks we get? Our little house is certainly better than Rikers or whatever prison they'd haul his ass off to." Regina took another look at Aidan and disagreed with that assessment.

"So wait, if you don't have the money, how do you have Aidan?" Giles asked. Gabriel smiled.

"What—you can ask questions, but you get all annoyed when I try to? How is that fair? Oh well. I'll indulge your curiosity. We were a day or so behind on the trail. We wasted too much time tracking you when we should've been focused on Aidan, the real brains of the operation. He was driving south through New Hampshire when we finally got a lead on his plates. Picked him up at a rest stop and lugged him to our safehouse in Vermont. One of those old abandoned timeshares. Fearing the police might make their way up north looking for him, Tron brought his car to Maine. Lot of good that's done us. Aidan doesn't seem to like us, do you champ?"

Giles and Aidan made eye contact, glaring at each other as their decades of corruption unfolded before their eyes. Mary turned to Gabriel and said, "All right, so you got him and he wouldn't rat. So you brought him here and now what do you expect to happen? You're at a dead end. Oh well." She poured herself more wine, offering the bottle to Tron, who waved it away, chuckling.

Gabriel let out a loud sigh. "Mary, you're pushing this along too quickly. I haven't had a chance to ask nicely. But since you're so impatient, I guess we'll just have to move on to the messy portion of the night. Sad really. I thought we could do more with this exchange. Tron, who should we start with?"

Tron walked around the table, stopping to hover over each of the four choices. Looking unsatisfied, he turned his gaze to Regina. "The beaner."

Gabriel clapped. "Bravo. Thinking outside the box. Well, we certainly have a winner. Do you want to do the honors?"

Regina screamed. "No!" Caleb yelled. "I'll tell you where the money is. Just don't kill her. She's an innocent woman for fuck's sake. Takes care of the kid. She's got nothing to do with this."

Giles turned to look out the window, silent, growing sweatier by the moment.

Gabriel smiled. "Well, well, how unorthodox. I will say Caleb, I was not expecting this. You'll have to be extra convincing if you expect me to spare anyone on your word alone. The Moores aren't very good at keeping their promises."

Aidan moaned. Caleb looked away from Giles, toward Mary, whose gaze remained fixed on her wine glass. "You were close. My uncle left me a cabin in East Madison. About ten miles north of King Pine. I told Aidan to bury the money there. I can give you the address, but put the guns down first." Gabriel waved, causing the assailants to lower their weapons.

Aidan let out another moan as he tried to speak. "You stupid faggot. Now we're all dead."

"Those words aren't very nice, Aidan," Gabriel said. "Caleb, is the house in your name?" Caleb nodded, looking down toward the floor.

"Congratulations. We'll spare Regina as promised." Caleb gasped. Mary shrieked with laughter. Giles remained silent. "What the hell does that mean?" Caleb asked. "You got what you wanted. Now leave us alone."

Gabriel waved his arms in the air and shook his head. "I've got some of what I wanted. Remember what I said earlier. I've come to do a cleansing of the wicked. From the looks of this table, there's an awful lot of wickedness still here. That just won't do."

Silence. The laughter ceased. The aura of foreboding lingered.

"You fucking son of a bitch. You told Caleb. What is this, some perverse way of getting back at me for not being Jacob? Twenty-five years, you fuck, and this is how it ends. God, what were we doing all that time? And you still can't trust me?"

Aidan looked Giles in the eye from across the table for the first time that night. "It wasn't about trust." He took a deep breath, his body shivering at sporadic intervals.

Giles lunged across the table. He knocked Aidan over in his chair, both hitting the floor. Caleb stood up, but Tron grabbed him and held him back.

Giles wailed on a defenseless Aidan, raining blows down on his skeletal frame. "You ruined my life, you shit. You fucking ruined it." He started to choke him. Aidan looked up, his eyes devoid of anger.

"You're a man now, Giles," Mary said, from across the table. "Finish him." She took some pills out of her purse and washed them down with what remained in her glass. She tossed her pill bottle on the table.

"Giles no!" Caleb cried, his voice weak. Giles didn't look up. He kept his strangle hold on his brother-in-law until the choking sounds grew faint. Giles let out a few grunts and released his hold. Aidan lay dead on the floor.

Giles collapsed next to Aidan's body, panting as he caught his breath. Regina stared at the floor, praying that the silence would last forever. After a minute Gabriel said, "Sit up, Giles. Let's talk. Help him up, Tron."

Tron moved toward Giles, who got up on his own and slowly took a seat. He kept his gaze on the window, ignoring eye contact with Mary and Caleb. "How did that feel?" Gabriel asked. "Your first kill?"

Giles didn't answer. Sweat dripped from his forehead down past his eyebrows to his chin, creating the illusion of tears on a remorseless man. "You got the money. What else do you want from us?" Caleb asked.

The million-dollar question. Gabriel sighed. "My hands are tied, Caleb. You see, Giles threatened to send a very bad man after me. The only way to ensure that the bad man doesn't come after me is to take his bone out of the fight. You see where I'm coming from?"

A snort. "Cleansing of the wicked my ass, you're as full of shit as he was." Giles spoke without emotion, as if he had just uttered an irrefutable statement of fact.

Gabriel circled around Aidan's body glancing over it to make sure he wasn't still breathing. "That's not fair Giles. I haven't misled you. Here's the problem with what you've done. You took matters into your own hands – quite literally. Right Aidan?" He kicked the corpse before he continued. "

"You wrote your own book on justice. I'm sure you came up with some fancy reason for why extorting the Senator and ripping off all those people were fine ways for an educated man to earn his living. They didn't need the money? The restrictions were unnecessary? You could fix the problem? Excuses. All excuses. Once you made it okay to change the rules of this very game we all have to play, you invited people like me to swoop in and do as we please. That's where you made your biggest mistake. You have no moral code."

Caleb's face turned red, sweat making his complexion resemble the raw beef Regina had prepared just a few hours prior. Everything changed.

Caleb said, with a stutter in his voice, "What are you - some - grade A - sociopathic stalker?" Michael hovered over his chair, touching Caleb's shoulders.

Gabriel replied, "No. Why do we have to call each other names? I'm good at what I do. I smelled blood and I pounced. Fortune might have helped me out along the way, but even the best poker hand needs a little luck."

"Like this." Mary swung the wine bottle at Tron's head. Glass smashed, sending pieces everywhere. Caleb picked up a knife and moved toward Michael. Giles barely twitched. Regina sat still.

Caleb paused, his hand shaking. He took a deep breath and lunged at his attacker. Michael grabbed his arm with ease and threw him back. He lost his balance briefly, his left foot skirting around the floor. As he moved toward Michael, Regina heard the sound of two muffled gunshots. Smoke rose from the end of Gabriel's weapon as Caleb fell to the ground.

Regina screamed as Tron moved closer to Mary. "Keep her alive," Gabriel said, keeping his composure as he moved over to Caleb and kicked him over. Caleb grunted and coughed, barely moving a muscle in his entire body.

Gabriel looked over to Giles as Caleb spit up blood. "Aren't you going to say goodbye? He might have spilled the beans, but he was your lover."

He motioned his weapon toward Caleb and Giles stood up. His knees buckled, causing him to fall on the floor next to Caleb. He held his head in his hands, his lips trembling, though no words came out.

Cough, cough. More blood spurted out of Caleb's mouth as Michael moved in to kick away the knife.

"I love you," Caleb said, in a muffled spurt. He opened his mouth, but nothing but a screeching noise came out as his head tilted over in Giles' arms. Regina let out a wail. Michael walked over to hand her a napkin.

Mary looked away, seemingly emotionless. Tron hovered over her, his eyes fixed on Caleb's body.

"He was brave, Giles," Gabriel said. "Many people talk about going out in a blaze of glory, but it's rare to see someone who understands that talk is cheap without action. You want to know the funny thing?"

"What's that," Giles replied. He spoke without the rage or fear one might expect in such a situation. Regina recognized this tone as the one he'd use whenever Aidan and he disagreed on a business decision, sitting in the living room drinking bourbon. A false sense of toughness, projected to keep up the illusion. Simpler times.

"Neither one of them betrayed you. I'm sure it feels that way. You were obviously harboring some resentment toward poor Aidan. Saved us from the guilt of another body on our hands. But think about it. Were you better off knowing where the money was? What would that have changed? You and Aidan were goners. It was only a matter of when."

Mary picked up a bottle off the ground. A bottle of gin. She took some more pills and washed them down.

Giles and Gabriel engaged in a long stare down. The man from Georgia looked beyond broken, aware of his limited time. "What about the boy?" he asked.

Gabriel put away his weapon. "I see nobility is contagious. Let me ask you this: in a perfect world, what would be little Jack's best option moving forward?"

Regina said, "Please, please." She tried to stand up. Michael put his arm on her shoulder, causing her to scream, the napkin falling to the floor. Giles shook his head at her and put his hand up. Her screams ceased, but her tear-stained face and a tremor of her hand served as reminders of the fear still present.

"She'd take care of him. She's basically his mother anyway. Loves the kid." Some authority returned to Giles' voice. "That sounds fair," Gabriel replied.

"You best not fucking joke about that boy, you sick fuck," Giles said, looking over at Mary to see if she had anything to say about her child's future. Eyes closed, Mary let out an audible sigh.

"Who said I was joking? If what your lover said was true, there will be plenty of money to ensure that the boy gets an education and lives a relatively normal life. Enough damage has been done tonight to the Moore/Davies clan." Gabriel stood with a blank stare on his face, making a slight shrug with his shoulders.

Giles laughed. "You can't expect me to believe that. You're going to let Regina walk out of this after all she's seen?"

Gabriel sighed. "You don't get it, Giles. You're a bad seed. Mary is a bad seed. Aidan was a bad seed. Caleb was unfortunate collateral damage. I have to live with what I did to him. I can't change that. I can make amends. I told him I wouldn't kill the woman. I made a promise. She doesn't need to die. The world is better off without you, Giles. It's better off without Mary. But Jack can turn things around. Your family's line can live on. He's got good genes. Never said any of you were stupid. He can be a force for good. I'm willing to make that happen. Tell her not to fight this." Gabriel motioned toward the chair where Regina sat.

Giles closed his eyes for a few moments, leaning against a chair. He turned to Regina and said, "You hear that? They're going to let you take him. Promise me you'll take care of him. All of this, forget it. You need to take care of Jack. You're all he's got. Promise me, Regina."

Regina's tears stopped as she looked up at Giles. "Promise me," Giles shouted. "Yes," Regina whimpered. "I will."

Giles turned to Mary. "You've got nothing to say? Of

course you don't." She downed the rest of the gin while continuing to avoid eye contact, not even looking in his general direction.

"You told me on Friday you had things under control. I don't know if this is what you had in mind, but good job, brother. Where would I be without you?"

Giles turned to Gabriel. "You better not be fucking with me. There's a special section of Hell reserved for those who break their vows to dead people."

Gabriel's grin faded. "That's another thing you just don't understand. This isn't about good and evil. It's about opportunity. You should know that. You had something I wanted and I had the resources to get it. So I did. I win, and you lose. You think a mountain lion mourns for days over a deer it eats? Of course not. You were a predator. I was a bigger one. That's all there is to it."

He fired two shots at Giles' chest. Regina's tears resumed as she watched her employer fall to the ground, close to his lover. Mary cast a short glance at her brother before returning her gaze to her pill bottle.

She reached for Giles' wine glass, the only one untouched by all the commotion. She took a handful of pills out of the bottle and took them with the wine, washing it all down with the last of the gin. She let the pill bottle fall to the floor. Empty.

"Trying to kill yourself before I can," Gabriel said. "Clever girl."

Mary looked up at him. "No, I'm just trying to be happy. The world's a shitty place. Sometimes you need a little pick-me-up." Her head hit the table as she passed out.

The three intruders gathered around Regina, who

clutched the edges of her seat. They stood still, allowing her to cry for a few minutes.

As the sobs grew further apart, Gabriel spoke. "Comprender Ingles?" he asked. She nodded her head without looking up at him.

"Good. I was telling the truth to dear old Giles before. You will raise Jack and you'll do a fine job. Here's what's going to happen. You're going to go upstairs for the rest of the night. When you come down in the morning, Mary's body will be the only one left. We're going to take the other three and clean things up a bit. Suicida. The police will let you take Jack as his guardian. The lawyer, Chomsky, will see to that. Your papers are in order, right?"

Regina looked up, her eyes in a daze as she began to process what was happening. "Yes. I have a green card."

"Excellent. In fifteen days, one of my associates will drop off some money. Consider it restitution. When Jack is ready to graduate high school, we'll give you some more for his college tuition. After that, you'll never see us again. You have my word. But if you speak, you know what will happen?"

Regina nodded her head. She tried to muster up some courage, unsure where she might find any. "Good. Now, go upstairs. Get some sleep, if you can. I'm sorry for ruining your evening. Just business. Happy Easter."

She stood up slowly, afraid that her legs wouldn't be able to support her weight. She took one final look at the carnage and Mary's vegetated body, instantly regretting the decision.

She took a sleeping Jack into her bedroom. She locked the door, aware of the irrelevance of the action.

She paused, staring blankly ahead, unsure of what would come next. Sleep was out of the question. She tried to re-member what she was thinking about before the noise. An idea returned. Regina walked to her bathroom and turned on the water. Time for a bath.

Acknowledgements

Thank you to my editors, Elisha, Beverly, and Anna, for all your hard work.

I'd also like to thank my cover designer Robin Harper and my formatter Stacey Blake, who are always a treat to work with.

Both of my parents, Tom and Barbara, supplied substantial editorial feedback on this project. I am forever grateful to them for their continued support of my work as well as to the rest of my family, Colonel, Bibble, Jorge, and Nellie.

As always, I must express my gratitude to Amy Bartelloni for being the Harper Lee to my Truman Capote. Your friendship keeps me (relatively) sane in the chaotic world of publishing.

Finally, I'd like to thank Wall Street. You may have screwed the country, but I had a lot of fun writing this book. Guess that counts for something!

Other Books

June: A Month in Characters

The Princess and the Clown

Courting Mrs. McCarthy

A Trip Down Reality Lane

The Dialogue Books
Five College Dialogues
Five More College Dialogues
Dead Batteries Tell No Tales
Five High School Dialogues